Red Snapper

By Samuel J Parker

To Jean

And four very special people: Sam, Lucy, Annabel and Pippa.

ACKNOWLEDGEMENTS

Red Snapper would have been harder to write without the help of many people. I am indebted to Terry Murray whose patience and technical skills helped enormously to bring this project to fruition. I am also indebted to my daughter Andrea for her considerable Jamaican and English language skills. Finally, like all else in my life, nothing could have been achieved without the rock solid support of my wife Jean.

PROLOGUE

'The Caribbean is rapidly becoming a Communist lake in what should be an American pond,

and the United States resembles a giant, afraid to move.' Ronald Reagan – Presidential Candidate 1979.

A three inch mortar shell exploded ripping open the fragile wooden sentry box guarding the army headquarters in a quiet tree-lined suburb of St George. The young sentry, who seconds before was mentally reliving his last night's drug fuelled revelries, was now a grotesque and bloodied corpse. A revolution had just kicked off. The CIA agent witnessed the carnage from across the road in the Cabinet Office in the Ministry of Foreign Affairs. There was nothing he or the mighty US could do about it. He had the meagre satisfaction of knowing he had predicted its' coming but his forecasting skills had not told him it would start today, two days before the Ides of March, 1979.

Grenada was a small but symbolically important island to the US - an island of barely 100,000 inhabitants. It was a plantation economy earning its foreign exchange from the export of nutmeg and mace. The island was of no military significance but it was still important to the US their view of the world was correctly aligned. That is why they were keen to keep Sir Eric Matthew Gairy's corrupt and dysfunctional United Labour Party government in power.

But here was another country straining to break free of the suffocating legacy of imperialism and the international corporations exploiting the country's resources under the banner of free market capitalism. Here was a country ready for the march towards socialism and Moscow.

The CIA agent also forecast who would be behind the revolution – a young English trained lawyer by the name of Maurice Bishop, leader of the Marxist New JEWEL Movement [NJM] and his People's Revolutionary Army. He had closely followed and monitored the progress of the Marxist since his election to the Grenadian House of Representatives and noted with alarm his growing popularity with the working classes.

He had been in Grenada just two days, one of his quarterly visits to gather intelligence and 'oil the wheels' of the corrupt regime. Uncertain about his own physical security, should he be captured by the revolutionary army, he struggled to find the words to reassure the young Grenadian – the man who provided much of the intelligence that formed the backbone of his reports for the CIA. 'Just what have you to fear? They want Gairy and his gang of crooked ministers. What can they pin on you? Our dealings have been all about helping your country with our money. Just look at the potential new markets you are building. Just look at the good things we have done together.' The CIA agent was used to lying – had been trained in it – but sensed his words had a hollow ring to them.

Uriah Jagan, eyes wide with fear, sweat rolling down and across his furrowed forehead, his broad strong hands were gripping his chair as if trying to find refuge by anchoring himself to it. 'You don't understand – how can you? Gairy and my father were friends from the early days and I owe everything to Gairy – everything I have ever done with my life. He gave me this job. He paid for my mother to have a tumour removed from her jaw in England.' It was as if Uriah, by unburdening himself of his privileges, was seeking redemption.

 The CIA agent had reassured men before but what could he say to someone who had ruthlessly exploited his connections, benefited hugely from the granting of favours and undoubtedly had blood on his hands? Uriah had good reason to fear Maurice Bishop.

The signs had been visible for months; the rampant corruption, the cronyism and the growing social and economic disparities. Sensing he was losing his grip on power Gairy had also unleashed his private army, the brutal Mongoose Gang, to try to frighten off his political opponents.

There was a simple and unchallengeable morality behind Bishop's new JEWEL movement. A morality that sought fairness and a movement strengthened by the support from the charismatic leaders of the region and beyond. They were all anti-imperialists and in the game of creating a new model government. They were all using the poor, the plantation and agricultural workers, the unions, the unemployed and the elderly to legitimise their movements.

The CIA agent had monitored and reported on the situation and Washington had responded with its well organised propaganda machine designed to strengthen Gairy and discredit Bishop. Money had flowed to the corrupt regime from US controlled international financial institutions. The CIA had also provided the Mongoose Gang with its firepower and trained some of the gang members in urban warfare. But it had now spectacularly backfired on them. Grenada was now slipping away to forge a new future for its people and a collision course with the established order.

'You must get out now – while there is still time. You can hear the gunshots at the barracks at True Blue – they will come here next. Gairy left the country two days ago to address the United Nations. I drove him to the airport myself. They will be looking for his associates Bogo DeSouze and Cosmos Raymond to stop them from organising any resistance. They are the ones primed to take charge in Gairy's absence.' Uriah Jagan, a 42 year old civil servant in the Ministry of Foreign Affairs and recipient of generous US funding to help promote the export of nutmeg to the US and beyond was now pleading with his friend.

This generous funding propelled Uriah across the globe seeking new markets and a playboy lifestyle many of his countrymen resented and questioned. He also had a luxury house overlooking St George's picture postcard harbour that could not be justified on his modest civil service salary. Uriah feared the questioning would start soon and the presence of an American businessman would add greatly to their suspicions.

'I have a seat on a flight booked for later this morning. Hopefully I can get there before Bishop's men. When things have settled down I will be back – you never know we may still be working together.' These were meaningless and disingenuous words but they were the only ones that came to mind. This was not a new experience for the CIA agent – his back fully protected under the guise of foreign aid – he was used to abandoning people to their fate. He had made the decision Uriah was not worth protecting - he was now an embarrassing liability and one easily replaced.

'Go, please go. I need time to clear my desk – destroy some files.' Uriah had composed himself to some degree. His sweating and shaking had subsided. He returned to his expensive leather inlaid mahogany desk, the kind designed to make visitors feel uncomfortable, and turned on the radio just in time to hear the voice of Maurice Bishop broadcasting to the people. His sweating and shaking returned but with much greater severity than before. The voice of the triumphant Bishop here in the office with him was the final straw.

The CIA agent decided now was the time to escape and he ran to the waiting car. An immaculately maintained black 1965 P5 Rover coupe – originally imported for the use of the British Consular staff but now generously donated to the Government of Grenada for the personal use of senior ministers. The smartly liveried George Canter had remained steadfastly at his post awaiting his passenger.

George, the chauffer, came with the 1965 Rover. It was his pride and joy. He was attached to it in the same way as the Grenada pennant had been attached to the chromium plated radiator. George was in his late 40s but looked much older. He had been a plantation worker since he was 12 years old – a life of toil and drudgery had taken its toll. He progressed to chauffeuring when the British Embassy was looking to recruit a local driver. George talked his way into the job using his exaggerated tractor driving skills as the basis of his claim of relevant experience. He was perfect for the job and was popular from the Prime Minister down. A deeply lined face shrouded with white curly hair and gold rimmed spectacles suggested more a distinguished professor of social anthropology than a lowly government employee. Whatever the task and whatever the circumstances he had never let anyone down in his life. He opened the passenger door for the American businessman, saluted and set off at leisurely speed to Pearls Airport.

The crack of automatic gunfire and loud explosions could be heard coming from the army barracks. Black smoke from burning accommodation huts was billowing across the eastern part of St George. An early dawn attack was clearly designed to catch the local garrison off guard. They drove past police stations having already hoisted the white flag.

Outside the army barracks there appeared to be no organised opposition to the revolution. Local residents appeared to be going about their daily routine as usual – no sign of panic. Smartly dressed children in their starched blue uniforms, books tucked under their arms sauntering, presumably to school, without a care in the world. Ramshackle windowless green single floored buses shuddering to a halt picking up the elderly for their daily shopping errands.

'Any chance you could pick up speed George' enquired the passenger.

'Me goin' at 45 mph – this is as fas' as i-man kyan go.' A lifetime of subservient obedience had robbed George of the power to change the rules and he didn't recognise his passenger as someone with the appropriate authority to change them either.

At that moment a burst of machine gun fire raked the back of the Rover. The rear window shattered showering the passenger and driver with tiny glass fragments. These were familiar and unmistakable sounds to the passenger. George was about to stop to investigate the damage, and probably remonstrate with the culprit, when the passenger jabbed a pistol into the back of his head and shouted 'drive'. The passenger had much to hide. George had nothing to fear from the Revolution.

'I'm sorry George but I need to get to the airport in a hurry. I have a plane to catch. Tell them I forced you to drive on.' And on they drove still at the leisurely 45 mph but even at that pace it quickly put distance between them and the foot soldiers of the Revolution. The car was a symbol of the hated regime and their attackers had obviously associated the Rover with an escape – George would not be driving his car in this direction without a passenger.

Pearls Airport was 23 miles from St George and accessed by a narrow winding road over the mountains. At any time of day the road was normally busy but, with the exception of the odd horse and cart and grazing goat crossing in search of new pasture, there were no delaying road workings or slow agricultural traffic today. It took 53 minutes to travel the distance and the passenger was mightily relieved to see the faded white control tower overlooking the single narrow runway.

On the runway was a Leeward Islands Air Transport plane, a Rolls Royce Avro Turbo Prop, with room for 12 passengers. The LIAT initials were translated locally into 'Leaves Island Any Time' and the CIA agent was about to test the truthfulness of the strap line.

George was instructed to bypass the now deserted police security check point and wooden hut serving both arriving and departing passengers and drive directly to the one and only plane on the runway.

'I am sorry I had to do that George – here is $50 dollars.' The passenger got out the car and turned only to see George fling the money after him.

'Keep your filthy coil – i will no be bought. If dis be de Revolution then me don't need your dirty money.' George's friendly face was now transformed into one of hatred and anger – no longer the friendly looking academic of one hour earlier. Years of bottled-up resentment had just been freed.

On board the plane, the crew was struggling to understand what had happened – no one was manning the control tower – no one was giving out flight instructions – no engineering staff – no immigration staff. No one had bothered to tell the flight crew about the revolution.

The passenger walked to the front of the plane, lied to the pilot that all Americans and Europeans were being shot on sight and it would be in all their interests to leave post haste. The now frightened ex US Air Force pilot took no more persuading – he had his plane and crew to consider – it was now time to leave.

The CIA agent breathed a sigh of relief as he looked down on the small picturesque island. He traced the spreading cloud of black smoke back to the army base, the scene of serious violence. He had no way of knowing the outcome of the battle but he sensed the ordinary people of Grenada would not be resisting the Revolution.

'When we hear the news of the Revolution this morning, it was a joy, come out in the morning! Joy come out in the morning! As if I lifted up that morning! I lifted up above the sky that morning!

The Revolution make me young again. I young now as if I just in me teens! Me energy come through that happiness of the Revolution. Long live the Revolution! Long live Maurice Bishop and his party. And we praying for them day and night, because they not seeking for one and not the other, they seeking for all people, from baby to the old.'

[72 year old woman on the morning of the Revolution. Editor's Preface to 'In Nobody's Backyard – Maurice Bishop's Speeches, 1979-1983: A Memorial Volume.

CHAPTER 1

He was normally an outwardly calm man. Today he was not his normal self – a shade agitated and calm had given way to irritability. The casually dressed courtesy driver provided by his contact at the Ministry of Foreign Affairs shouted his oft repeated instruction 'windows up and doors locked.' They were on their way to Norman Manley Airport.

Urban folklore had it that unsuspecting white tourists who dangled their arms out of open windows had had their hands chopped off just above the wrist – apparently the quickest and most risk free way of acquiring a Rolex. There was no actual proof of any incident but no one took the chance when driving through Franklyn Town. This advice was faithfully relayed to every expat and tourist who ventured to Kingston in these troubled times. Fear was reinforced by the sight of a machete resting handily between the front seats of all Jamaican taxis.

Beyond this urban slum of brightly painted wooden shacks with their rusting corrugated iron roofs and barefoot inhabitants, the pot-holed Palisadoes Road running parallel with the clear grey blue Caribbean would surely qualify as the most beautiful airport approach road anywhere in the world – providing you were looking seaward! Looking landward and your eyes would be puzzled by the sight of rusting beached freighters and broken-backed ferries.

His demeanour was not helped by the timing of his Air Jamaica flight from Kingston, Jamaica. As he had come to expect it was delayed by another brilliantly inventive excuse which in essence boiled down to an admission of management incompetence. This time it was a lack of toiletries. He thought to himself, at times like this wasn't there some justification in lying – something much more inventive or imaginative than a lack of paper to wipe your ass. Sitting on plastic chairs positioned randomly and insecurely on a grimy tiled floor in a crowded and hot departure lounge for two hours longer than necessary could have been made that tiny bit more tolerable.

The reason for the mood swing was a series of agents' reports he had collected and intercepted on his travels around the Caribbean islands and Central America. Some reports were part of routine intelligence gathering from trusted agents, others obtained by threats of intimidation and blackmail and some from the innocent association with unsuspecting colleagues.

Based on similar intelligence he had predicted the violent revolution in Grenada and had monitored the role of the so called Cuban 'engineers' in supporting Bishop's New JEWEL Movement. He almost overplayed his cover and was fortunate to escape the island in the confusion at Pearls Airport on the last flight out before the revolutionaries took control.

Carlton Davies was now seriously pre-occupied with organising and prioritising his newly acquired information in such a way that might persuade a seemingly reluctant Washington to act. If his latest prediction was close to being correct then the region could expect to witness destabilisation on a much greater scale than occurred in tiny Grenada.

The plane was fully booked with a mixture of brightly and scantily dressed locals, red faced tourists with legs to match, smartly dressed businessmen and government officials and the inevitable 'bo-jangle', the medallion wearing Rastafarian drug dealer. A non-alcoholic fruit punch served by glamorous hostesses in orange figure hugging dresses, a short stop-over in Montego Bay to exchange a dozen passengers and a quick read of The Gleaner and Star helped fill the ninety minute flight time.

Any pick up in his mood was quickly dashed on his arrival in Miami. He failed in his attempt to bluff his way through the 'fast lane'. His credentials did not satisfy the sharp eyed and equally sharp tongued black immigration officer who was dangerously close to exploding out of her smartly pressed white uniform. She took her job seriously and Carlton meekly accepted the rejection and joined the queue of US nationals trying to re-enter their country.

Even for US citizen's, immigration clearance was always a frustratingly slow process. Whether it was because of his emotional state, today's delays seemed longer than normal. He even started to feel sorry for those visitors to the US – why, he thought, did they appear to entrust immigration control to singularly unpleasant, intrusive and obnoxious officials? He then remembered where he had just come from – one of the major illegal drug exporting countries in the region and couriers with ever more exotic cavities in which to disguise their cargo.

It was always a relief to see the back of Miami International, by his standards one of the most crowded and chaotic airports in the whole of the US. This was your main port of entry and 'mixing pot' for all those legal and otherwise travellers from South and Central America and the Caribbean. One minute you would be walking behind a square Bolivian bowler hatted flat-faced Indian carrying a boxed microwave, the next a bemused and gormless Brit just wondering where the hell in the world he was, and then by a stroke of good fortune bumping into what appeared to be Brazil's latest entrant to Miss World.

Miami Airport could also be your first introduction to biculturalism where Latinos clashed with Anglos and where all airport announcements were bilingual – English and rapido Cuban Spanish. The one and only advantage biculturalism appears to have bestowed on Miami Airport is the Cuban cafe, dressed up as beach bar, selling the best tasting coffee in the world.

Carlton was a regular to Miami International and quickly left the Arrivals Hall, fought his way through a 90 degree wall of oppressive humidity and located his car on the fifth floor of the characterless, grey multi-storey public parking lot. He paid his seven day parking fee to an attendant who was clearly occupied with more important issues – the baseball game showing on his antiquated TV monitor.

His white, 3 litre Ford Thunderbird with the black wheel arches trimmed with chrome, twin exhausts and black leather upholstery was one of his few luxuries in life. Purchased with the proceeds of some minor money laundering deals in Kingston, exaggerated expense claims and unspent per diems, it helped him escape the tensions and fears accumulated from his regular field trips. Here he was in a total control. Here he felt relatively safe – a world away from some of the double-dealing and dangerous individuals he was working with. Here was a rare opportunity to make sense of what was going on and to forecast how future events might unfold for him.

He checked into a Holiday Inn motel and noted the armed guard on each floor. He was aware Dade County had become the murder centre of the US but things must have got pretty bad a shotgun holding security guard was posted on each floor of what looked to all appearances a family friendly hotel.

 He recalled the daily updated murder scoreboard located on the highway as he entered Dade County and recoiled in disgust at what America was becoming. Just too easy to blame the waves of Cuban immigrants – there was something more fundamental happening to the social fabric of the country. But no one was denying Cubans had taken control of downtown Miami. The Columbians, Jamaicans and Italian Mafia were starting to feel marginalised that control of the lucrative drugs trade, protection rackets and prostitution were being taken from them. Increasingly bitter and violent gang wars, with a rapidly escalating body count, were erupting throughout Dade County and sometimes beyond.

'It's too late for the restaurant but I can arrange room service should you want a snack?' enquired the enthusiastic young desk clerk.

Obviously new to the job thought Carlton and responded positively. 'Can you arrange to deliver a Quattro Staggionni and mixed salad in about twenty minutes?'

He threw his battered leather studded briefcase and equally travelled leather holdall onto one of the twin beds. The room was standard and predictably inoffensive Holiday Inn with en-suite – just what he needed. He unzipped the side pocket of his holdall and extracted a bottle of Appleton's Golden Jamaican Rum and a bottle of Ting [sparkling grapefruit]. One third rum and two thirds Ting cooled down by ice was his favourite night time, in fact anytime, relaxant. After two of these his world took on an altogether more appealing and less threatening dimension. He was starting to appreciate this new and enticing world more and more.

He also unpacked his Berretta 92S semi-automatic CIA optional issue handgun. The gun was taped discreetly to the side of his bedside cabinet – he had once made the mistake of leaving his gun out of reach whilst in a hotel bedroom and nearly paid the price. A room delivery of pizza and another rum and Ting was enough to close down Carlton's mind for the night. Door locked and chair lodged under the handle were a primitive but necessary final safeguard in his line of business.

CHAPTER 2

At seven o'clock sharp next morning Carlton's military training had him on his feet, shaved and showered within six minutes precisely. Dressed in a pair of Brook's Brothers sports slacks with co-ordinated t-shirt, expensive blue leather deck shoes he sat down to a breakfast of fresh orange juice, two eggs over-easy and an Americano.

He was starting to prepare for his day ahead and his meeting with his boss Wynton McKenna. A man, who Carlton liked, got on with but at times resented because at every stage in his life there had been someone there to give him a hand up.

Twice a year they agreed to meet at the Bay Hills Golf Club and this was to be their fourth meeting since Carlton's secondment to the CIA in 1976. Bay Hills was chosen because Wynton held a country membership and it was also close to his parents' home in Winter Haven. This gave him the legitimate excuse to be away from Virginia but, more importantly, it was less than five hours from Miami International. Here he could get the latest information from Carlton about events in Central America and the Caribbean before his formal report was circulated [and before any other interested party, friend or otherwise, could get to him]. These advance insights were invaluable giving him the opportunity, when necessary, to distort, exaggerate or hide information prejudicial to his own game plan.

Carlton Davies had been a first class special operations soldier. Six feet tall, sharp angular features, muscular build and a shaven head that almost gave away his profession. A pair of Foster Grant's added one more dimension to his unmistakable military pedigree. He could easily have qualified as a Robert Mitchum stand-in. It would be hard to visualise him behind the desk in the local bank or managing a supermarket operation. Customers might just think twice about lodging a complaint or arguing the terms of a delinquent loan repayment schedule.

An interrupted education leaving him without qualifications had meant he had to seek recognition through other and more unconventional means. A broken home was the cause of his disadvantaged educational background – moving from state to state with his mother trying to build a new life with a drunken, violent and seriously disturbed husband. His route out of this was the army. Starting with a junior Ranger's unit and following a thorough evaluation of his mental and physical attributes, selection by a special operations unit.

His father had also been a soldier, a sergeant in an infantry regiment, when he had been involved in the bloody battles north of Saigon around the area of the Cui Chi tunnels – the underground network of tunnels connecting hospitals, command posts, cooking stations and living quarters of the Viet Cong. His platoon had got caught in an ambush by the Viet Cong and he was seriously wounded by one of their spiked bamboo booby traps leaving his body lacerated and punctured. Whilst physically recovered, his mind was seriously affected leaving him incapable of holding down a regular job. Drink, tobacco and drugs were his preferred escape route from the horrors invading his mind about that fateful day.

Carlton stayed loyal to his mother and father – a bond that grew stronger as he better appreciated the horrors of war and the courage of his mother in attempting the impossible of trying to provide some stable refuge for his father. Regular payments wired home, the occasional phone calls when he was in the US and, on average, one trip home each year never stopped the nagging guilt he could and should do more.

To the outside world Carlton was now a forty four year old respectable business man. His cover provided by the US Department of Commerce, operating out of the Miami Chamber of Commerce. His role was to work with the export development agencies of the national governments in the region sympathetic or sufficiently cynical or corrupt, to accept US help in opening up potential export routes into the vast and expanding US market. The job was sufficiently 'strategic' in nature that avoided him getting involved [or exposed] in the detail of negotiating or circumnavigating US import regulations. This role gave him the legitimacy to travel freely and also the opportunity to meet high ranking politicians and civil servants as well as maintain and develop his network of locally based agents.

By 8:30 am Carlton was heading north on Highway 27, after swinging west around Lake Okeechobee, he continued north through Sebring and Lake Wales. Bored with the unremittingly repetitive scenery and because he knew lunch was not part of Wynton's invitation, he pulled over at a roadside shopping mall for some refreshment. He was feeling more relaxed than yesterday but this was an important meeting, perhaps the most important meeting he had had with Wynton. It was important he didn't exaggerate the threat but equally important he conveyed the seriousness and urgency of it. He often reflected on whether his prediction about the revolution in Grenada had been accurately communicated – if he could see it coming why didn't Washington?

 Important as the meeting was Carlton was looking forward to the golf. The feel of a three wood in his hands almost acted like a low level mental tranquiliser. It enabled him to blank out all other distractions because Carlton was a competitive individual – he didn't like to get beat. Golf was a leveller – a level playing field where no amount of privilege or cronyism could produce an advantage. Here was an opportunity to put McKenna in his place.

At 12:30 p.m. he pulled into the car park at Bay Hills – a monument to wealth and the privilege it can buy and a community where cronyism ran riot. He screeched to a stop just as Wynton was unloading his top of the range Nikes and strapping them onto the buggy. The squeal of tyres had members muttering under their breath and shaking their heads in wonderment as to how his name had not been blackballed.

There was something about Bay Hills that disturbed Carlton. Maybe it was their need for a set of 'commandments' way beyond the ten Moses delivered for the benefit of all mankind. Any breach was likely to be dealt with by a punishment way beyond the usual fire and damnation. He wondered just what kind of people did they admit to this golf club?

'Hi Wynton, it's good to see you. As a matter of interest what does it cost you to be a member? I bet I'd struggle on my trade reps salary.' Carlton speculated casually – but also trying to make the point those sticking their neck out got paid a lot less than those sitting on their ass.

'Good to see you safe and sound old chap. How was your journey from Kingston?' replied Wynton. Wynton was aware Carlton was uncomfortable with the private golf club culture and the jumped-up minions revelling in the power of petty rule enforcement. His driving skills did not breach any existing rule but it would now be on the agenda for the next AGM. That was just Carlton's way of threatening authority.

'It's never a good journey. Had the misfortune to sit next to a fat higgler and she never shut up about her hero Michael Manley. On and on she went about what he'd done for the poor of Jamaica. It was totally lost on her she had to spend hard earned savings on a flight to Miami to buy cheap clothing to take back to sell to make a living. I didn't have the courage to argue – she was so fat she had me pinned to the back of my seat.'

'We tee off at 1300 hours and for God's sake please don't change in the car park. I got a letter of complaint about you last time from the Club Secretary. As my most privileged guest you are afforded all the facilities including the changing rooms. One more such breach and I will be summoned before the House Committee.' In sharp contrast to Carlton, Wynton was at home with people with money and influence. His ambitions extended beyond his career with the CIA. Politics was his ultimate goal.

'You are too young to die' muttered Carlton.

Carlton got his gear out of the boot. He was hoping and praying it looked respectable since it had been there since their last game. Whilst Carlton was a keen golfer he never bothered to carry his equipment and clothes with him when abroad – he borrowed, stole or hired what he needed when travelling.

The 'starter' got the game under way dead on time. You couldn't be trusted to keep your own timetable. Two buggies set off down the first on a parallel course before swerving left and right until they were 50 yards apart. That set the pattern for the day – the only time they came together was on tee and green.

 Wynton used these opportunities to catch up on Carlton's love life and his latest conquests. Carlton didn't regard these as state secrets and was quite happy to share these experiences with Wynton. Carlton also used the opportunities to update Wynton on the continuing fall-out from the revolution in Grenada and the vocal support it was receiving throughout the region. He also tested Wynton's knowledge about latest reports on Cuban covert activity.

By the time they got to the eighteenth tee they were all square. The real purpose of the day was beginning to creep up on Carlton and his mind was not as focused as it should be. He had stopped appreciating the landscape; the manicured greens, the close cropped 'patchwork' fairways, the azaleas and the polite consideration from fellow golfers. This was pure background now.

By comparison Wynton appeared totally at ease. His ability to stay calm and focused was clearly one of the crucial selection criteria fast-tracking him to a position of authority and influence within the organisation. He also knew by keeping quiet it would unsettle his opponent even more. The ten dollar side bet was the only thing that mattered.

Wynton's drive to the eighteenth was length and position perfect leaving him a 140 yard eight iron into the small two tiered green. Carlton tried to hide his anxiety and had the grace to comment with a muttered 'great shot'. Carlton hooked his drive leaving him with a recovery shot and miraculous chip to at least par the hole. It didn't happen – his concentration had slipped and with it the match.

'Well played.' Carlton was quick to congratulate his younger opponent and extended his hand in a genuine show of appreciation for what had been a closely fought match. He quickly handed over the $10 to show he had been beaten fair and square. Carlton could get over a defeat by the time they walked off the 18th with no excuses proffered.

'Thanks for the game old chap. Let's grab a shower and order some food and then we can get down to business. I reckon you must have a pretty good reason to fast forward our scheduled match.'

After showering and some light hearted banter the two retired to a quiet part of the Bay Hills members lounge. Conventions required a jacket and tie and Carlton, as usual, had to borrow one from Wynton's locker. The sheer ambience of the place, the waist-coated waiter, an eight page menu and wine list and the enormous trophy cupboard did make Carlton stop and think. Maybe sometime in the not too distant future he could start to enjoy a different life.

'Ok – let's have it straight. What's happening on your patch?'

'You know where I stand with regard to Fidel, Wynton. Every report I've given you, verbal or written, has documented in boring detail his growing network of agents and their interfering activities. I hate the bastard and all he stands for. But no one seems to be taking any notice.'

Wynton said nothing. This is how Carlton's reports always started and he reckoned it was necessary for him to have this opportunity to vent his frustration. Wynton learned things from this spontaneous outpouring.

He was fully aware of his record and how he had witnessed the ruthless cruelty of his army and supporters. He recollected the story of how Carlton had been sent to aid the military forces of the government of Anastasio Somoza against the Sandinista National Liberation Front in Nicaragua. Out on patrol with eight members of government forces they came under attack from the Cuban backed guerrillas. After a 30 minute shoot out three members of his patrol were dead, two injured and three took flight. Carlton had been shot in both the hand and leg – one bullet ricocheting off his rifle and lodged under his chin. The force of the bullet had knocked him out and when he came round dripping blood all had fled leaving only the three dead soldiers. Later he discovered two further members of his patrol suspended from a tree by their ankles with their throats cut. There were clear signs both had been brutally beaten and eyes gouged out before their deaths. This experience had strengthened his hatred of the Castro regime.

Carlton was a fierce defender of the American way of life. His politics were simple – anyone who opposed that way of life was an enemy of the US. He had no trouble categorising Fidel Castro as an ally of Moscow and therefore an enemy to be crushed. The subtleties of international politics were lost on Carlton – his world was black and white. Just occasionally it occurred to him his actions were unjust and unwarranted – why, he thought at these rare moments, was he denying some of the world's most disadvantaged people the opportunities he was prepared to fight so hard to maintain.

Wynton was fully aware of Carlton's loyalty to his country and the CIA and he knew he could rely, and if necessary, exploit it. He had a full and detailed dossier on all the activities, assessments and mission outcomes Carlton had been involved in. He had spoken with field commanders with personal experience of his conduct under pressure. His intelligence reports were objective, analytical and generally accurate. Whenever he had made a presentation to his superiors based on Carlton's information he had never ever been found to exaggerate a threat and, as a result, his credibility was solid.

He was also aware he was an opportunist – if there was money to be made with some low level illegality then he would be in. Similarly he couldn't resist a beautiful woman and this was always going to be a potential Achilles heel. There was, in his opinion, a loose connection between his brain and his dick.

'Nixon had the right attitude towards Castro. I still remember his unguarded comments after that press briefing – there'll be no change towards that bastard while I'm President' so continued Carlton. 'Rumours are circulating Carter is trying to normalise relations with Cuba. Whilst this softly softly let's get to know you better is going on I am recording increased covert activity throughout the region. The two simply don't stack up. Carter is suppressing all anti-Cuban and anti-Castro activity and Castro is ramping up his subversive activities all across the region. It is so damned obvious what is going on. Am I the only agent recording this?' Carlton paused to give Wynton the chance to reply.

Wynton sensed the anger and frustration in Carlton's tirade and tried to put the issues into a broader perspective. 'Carter is a different person to Nixon. To start with he is a Christian. He has kept the pressure on our friend over Human Rights and unlike Nixon there have been no threats, just a respectful dialogue. You've also got to remember Carter was elected because the people were fed up with Vietnam. They didn't have the stomach for more military action and more body bags. Carter seems to think he is making some progress.'

Wynton paused and summoned the waiter to order a bottle of the house Burgundy to go with the meal before continuing 'this puts Castro on the defensive so he is prepared to keep talking. He obviously sees some potential advantage in dialogue and maybe a different future relationship between the two countries. Carter clearly doesn't see it the same way as you.'

'OK I take your point. But clearly Carter is not getting copies of my reports and tell me what tangible result has this produced?' queried Carlton. He tried hard to control his emotions in the face of Wynton's defence of Carter.

'Some minor political prisoners have been released and some travel restrictions lifted but he is not going to give up on the Marxist bullshit - you recall the rhetoric - the right to work, education and health care' Wynton patiently responded.

Both knew reality and rhetoric were opposite ends of the Cuban spectrum. Their economy was barely functioning. Agricultural productivity was at a low because there was no money for fertilisers and pesticides but they also knew the CIA had funded a whole series of destabilising activities to help depress food production. These days many Cubans would rather risk their lives on the dangerous sea crossing to Key West rather live with the fear and deprivations of life in Castro's Cuba.

Wynton was more aware of the activities of Fidel Castro and his destabilisation tactics than he was prepared to let on to Carlton. He was closely aligned with Carlton's assessment and he was slowly putting together a comprehensive report he hoped would shake Washington out of its' complacency. He could see no future in Carters' policy – there was no end game in sight. The timing of his report was critical and with an election and change of government not far off urgency was not his immediate priority.

He was one of the first of a new class of appointees to the National Foreign Assessment Centre following the reorganisation of the CIA in 1977 and controlled a number of agents across the region. He reported to a director of counter insurgency for the region but frequently presented to a broader group monitoring known subversive groups across the world. People that mattered were taking notice of Wynton Mckenna.

Carlton, by contrast, had only one superior and one official channel of largely one way communication. There was no other route by which he could express his concerns and frustrations – the organisation was deliberately structured that way.

Carlton continued 'I hear what you say but it doesn't appear that way on the ground .I think we are facing a momentous political shift in the Caribbean and Central America. Fidel is trying to influence a growing number of these countries and since Carter poked his conciliatory nose in, we can do nothing openly about it. I am of the firm opinion Castro is buying time with this dialogue with Carter. He couldn't give a shit about normalising relations – Cuba and the US are light years apart.'

Wynton was becoming a little irritated by Carlton's repetitive grudge against Castro. He knew there was much more to come and was anxious to move on. 'What prompted you to call forward our meeting?

'Let me start with this prison in Cuba called "Combinad del Este" which they started building in 1972. It's located about 15 miles from Havana and currently holds about 1200 prisoners, half of whom are political opponents of Castro. Have you heard of it?'

'Yes I'm aware of it. It's one of a number that have started operations recently. I have been asked to compile a report and therefore anything you've got on this would be useful' Wynton responded encouragingly.

'This term 'political prisoner' is used to remove anyone who is suspected of opposing the regime. Criticising Castro, playing western music, reading banned literature, worshiping the Lord is all the evidence they need. It's exactly as I imagined it to be in Nazi Germany late 30's or Stalin's post Second World War Russia. Apparently the inmates have named it "El Valle de los Caidos" [The Valley of the Fallen]' Carlton paused to check on Wynton's level of interest.

'The prison is a four storey edifice - probably best described as a windowless office block. There isn't one in the whole place. According to this transcript the political prisoners are kept in virtual isolation in windowless rooms where the only ventilation is a 'hole' where the shit, blood and vomit accumulate. That gets washed away twice a week. In summer it gets so hot prisoners virtually bake but in winter they literally freeze to death. They don't get any medical treatment, medicines are denied and it appears they get beaten up by the guards on a regular basis for no other reason than being there. Fractured skulls, broken arms, ribs and so on go untreated.'

Carlton paused again but for his own benefit. He was genuinely sickened by what was going on inside. 'They are conducting experiments on the most determined prisoners and these experiments are being designed and monitored by Czech, Russian and Cuban doctors. Shows you just how involved Cuba is with the communists. I'll give you just one example but there are many. One experiment is to deny them any salt but after a few months of this they overload what meagre food they get with salt. Apparently the food is so salty they struggle to swallow it. After years of this kind of treatment these prisoners are no longer men – skin and bone, covered in sores, all kinds of horrific nervous and digestive disorders, parts of the body invaded by fungus – it is inhuman beyond belief.'

'How sure are you about this testimony?' queried Wynton.

'I am as sure as I can be. I have not met any of the inmates personally but I have met guards and friends of their families. Some, I believe, are now in Miami. The only people who might distort events are likely to be our own agents out to make a name for themselves. But this information came from totally independent sources.' exclaimed Carlton sarcastically.

'There are a number of other interviews and intercepts repeating the same and even worse experiences and will in time surface in an OAS report on Human Rights. It will take years for it to surface and just who the hell is going to do anything about it?' continued Carlton.

'Yes, rumours have been circulating but nothing as specific in terms of the actual conditions in these prisons. But OK Carlton where is this taking us.' Wynton's irritation had not subsided as he knew there was more to come. Life in Castro's prisons was not exactly the basis for a major political shift in the region.

'I am mentioning this because it adds a bit more to what we know about the man. This type of treatment will follow whichever country he gains influence over. Political opponents will disappear and there will be very little we can do without armed intervention. As you rightly point out Carter will not take the country down that route. What concerns me is just how close Castro is to Moscow. I can understand military and economic experts but to send over qualified doctors to oversee and take part in the barbaric torture of ordinary people just tells you all you need to know what a bunch of low level scum these socialists are.'

Wynton summoned the waiter and ordered another bottle of the house Burgundy. He needed to calm down – getting irritated with Carlton was not going to help.

'OK let's get to the meat of the issue. I'll start with Grenada. Clearly I'm not welcome there at the moment but one of my agents has reported Fidel's men are over there and has offered a wide range of support for Bishop's New JEWEL Movement. One agent is claiming there are 5,000 Cuban soldiers on the ground and Castro has offered to send a team of engineers to plan and build a new airstrip with the entire supporting infrastructure. I imagine this will put the total shits up Washington – another landing strip for military traffic and another missile crisis on the way if this information is even half correct.' Carlton took a moment out to see if any of this was registering with Wynton.

Wynton was aware of the situation in Grenada. Pressure was being put on Washington to respond but Carter was blocking any military response.

'The main reason I wanted this meeting is to do with Jamaica. I might be giving you old news but you know the next major conference of the Non Aligned Movement is scheduled for Havana next month. Now what might be news to you is a number of delegates to this supposedly non-aligned bean feast are going to propose old Fidel as the next Chairman. How a Marxist can even get his name on the ballot sheet defies belief and whilst alarm bells are going off strong and loud in those countries like India the word in the ghetto is Castro is a shoe-in.'

Wynton stared hard at his colleague. Wynton's mind was racing to interpret the potential damage this could do to America's interests in the region. This platform of benign neutrality was a serious threat in the hands of a wily old manipulator. A movement supposedly neutral as its name suggests, neither committed to either of the two great ideologies –free market capitalism and communism – now under the influence of someone who was a great deal closer to Moscow than he was to Washington. Wynton was fully aware Castro was giving support to those political leaders in the region who were trying to forge an independent path – the optimistically termed 'third way'.

'Now you are beginning to interest me. What else is there on this topic?' Wynton ignored the wine – this information was new.

'I thought it would be news to you. You may recall in one of my previous reports, I mentioned Fidel had stopped off en-route to some African conference to meet secretly with Michael Manley and Forbes Burnham in Guyana. I never discovered the purpose of the meeting but it is no secret both are prominent in this non-aligned movement and one might speculate, together with Maurice Bishop, are behind Castro's nomination.'

'What I have also discovered from one of my contacts in the Ministry of Foreign Affairs in Kingston, Manley has received an informal request from Castro to address this conference. The timing of this is significant. Jamaica will go to the polls next year and Manley's PNP is not doing too well.'

Carlton took some time out before continuing. He tried to second guess how Wynton might react to the news. He found Wynton difficult to read but he did expect some acknowledgement his intelligence was significant.

Wynton said nothing but was latching on quick. In fact he was struggling to understand the potential ramifications. The challenges of containing Castro had just got a whole lot more serious and unpredictable.

Carlton gave up waiting for a reply 'Well just to finish the evening off let me give you this final bit of information. Members of Cuba's Educational and Cultural Delegation have just set up shop in Kingston. This is a front organisation for some Cuban Insurrectionist Movement – a band of rather undesirables set on something as yet unknown. What they are not there for is art appreciation, dance and musical composition. These guys are in addition to the growing list of Cubans occupying key posts throughout the country – the hospital doctors, the engineers in Kingston docks and power stations, the so-called consultants in broadcasting media etc.etc. There you have it. When you add these together with my own personal knowledge of an increasing network of agents and subversives I worry very seriously about the future of Jamaica.'

CHAPTER 3

Before returning to his parents' home Wynton downed two sobering cups of black coffee. He sat for a few moments trying to digest Carlton's report and consider what his next actions should be. He never doubted for a moment the authenticity of the information but he struggled to decide whether now was the time to request a high level briefing meeting. His other option was to renew an old acquaintance.

Wynton was a calculating individual. He never entered into a relationship with anyone without considering the potential drawbacks or benefits such a relationship might have on his personal and professional life. He had been blessed with many advantages in life, a stable and affluent family life, intelligence, athleticism and looks. His mother's genes had endowed him with a full head of black hair whilst his father's Scottish ancestry had given him the rugged qualities of a highland warrior. Wynton was also an ambitious individual – his immediate sights set on a very senior position within the organisation and at thirty six years of age well placed to fulfil his wish.

His parents lived just over an hour away from Bay Hills Golf Club on the edge of a mid-sized town of about 30,000 residents named Winter Haven. The town was pretty unexceptional, a few expensive gated retirement communities, a number of modest shopping malls, full range of fast-food diners, rundown motels, way off Florida's tourist routes but it had served his parents well over the years. He was desperately hoping they would be in bed when he returned – he had enough to occupy his mind.

Joe and Maria McKenna were third generation Scottish and Italian immigrants. They had built a highly successful and profitable swimming pool construction and maintenance business serving the hotel, condominium and wealthy private housing market on the west coast of Florida. The business had echoed the economic fortunes of Florida but now they were approaching retirement they were converting their business model into a franchise. They hoped the rental income would provide a comfortable lifestyle in retirement. Both were members of the local leisure and golf club, Joe,Chair of the local Chamber of Commerce and regarded by most 'Havians' as a couple who had achieved their American dream.

 About 15 years ago this business funded their son through Florida State University where he graduated with a First Class Honours degree in Economics. They encouraged him to continue his studies and made no demands on him to join the business - they just wanted him to make the best of his substantial talents. He applied and was successfully awarded a fee paying scholarship at Yale University to study International Relations which, in time, led to him being awarded his Doctorate. Over eight years of fulltime study Wynton had never needed to work to supplement his income – his parents made sure of that. They had serious ambitions for their son – he was to be another visible sign of their own success.

Next morning he shared a breakfast of cinnamon bagels and black coffee with his parents and tried his best to reassure them 'yes mother I am keeping fit and well, the job is going fine and I am out and about meeting different people for most of the time'.

He knew off by heart the focus of the next question and anticipated it 'and I'm sorry to say I have not yet found the girl of my dreams.' They all appreciated the predictability of the conversation that helped maintain the bond and understanding between them.

After another twenty minutes of idle catch-up chatter Wynton said his goodbyes, hugging his mother firmly and genuinely, promising to return for a longer break sometime soon. This was perhaps Wynton's only disingenuous comment as he had absolutely no idea when that would be.

Carlton's report had set his alarm bells ringing. Questions had been asked by Washington about the level of intelligence and reporting on Grenada – everyone was looking to park blame for being caught wrong footed. This time around with another 'domino' set to fall he was determined the intelligence would be both comprehensive and timely.

Wynton had been targeted at Yale University by the CIA. Unknown to him, his professor had recommended him because of his academic excellence and his special interest in Cuban affairs. His Masters dissertation had been about the role of United Fruits in Cuba. This was a critique of the activities of the company and investigated whether it actually served the interests of the US or did more to fuel the revolutionary zeal of people like Ernesto Guevara and Fidel Castro.

His doctoral thesis was a brilliant exposé of the failings of the Bay of Pigs invasion and was based on interviews with commanders and soldiers who took part. To get this information he had spent over six weeks living amongst them in Miami and listening intently to their criticisms of Kennedy, the failure of the US to fully back the invasion, the lack of intelligence on Cuban defence capabilities and how they now planned to dispose of Castro.

The first hint Wynton knew someone was taking an interest in him was when he was approached by a member of the faculty – someone whom he recognised but knew very little about.

'My name is George T Draper. I'm doing some post doctoral research and was wondering if I might buy you a coffee?' George was about 5'6", thin, hair receding and running riot at the same time, rimless spectacles adding a coldness to his look, very casually dressed in Chino's and T-shirt and wearing open sandals. This was not a profile you would immediately associate with the CIA – more someone who has been shunted into a backwater to be kept out of sight and only wheeled into sunlight when the faculty was being assessed for research funding.

What followed was a number of meetings in which they shared their knowledge about Cuba and their feelings towards the likes of Castro and Guevara. After about 10 weeks Draper surprised Wynton with an invitation to join a special society at the university known as the Skull and Bones Society. Wynton had heard the rumours and also the story that George Bush's father, Prescott Snr., had been a prominent member. Bush's link with the society had been uncovered when he infuriated the Indian community by stealing Geronimo's skull from the sacred Indian grave in Fort Sill, Oklahoma.

The more he knew about the society the more enthusiastic he became. Patriotism, US first before others, God given right to exploit all and sundry and the defeat of communism were the objectives Wynton enthusiastically signed up to. He willingly participated in the initiation ceremonies including sitting in the middle of a circle of blindfolded members and revealing all his previous sexual activities and preferences. He could see how this bizarre ritual would bind its' members for evermore. Knowledge of a person's sexual deviances and fetishes could be a powerful controlling factor at some future date! It is said Bonesmen have few secrets from each other, but the rest of the world is for lying to.

Members of the Skull and Bones Society were either current employees of the CIA or being lined up for fast-tracked employment. After six months, the minimum probationary period, Wynton was offered an internship. It would be several years before Wynton fully understood the extent of the CIA's influence over US universities.

His first appointment was political and economic advisor to the Central America and Caribbean operations directorate. He was sent on basic low-level field missions throughout Central and South America looking at communication protocols between field agents and their controllers but the missions had a more serious objective. They were for the benefit of his superiors and used as a way of assessing his potential. He performed beyond expectation and after seven years was now controlling his own agents operating in Cuba and throughout the Caribbean.

After leaving his parents pretentious home with the extensive lawns, the curving drive way lined with alabaster Greco Roman statues and luxurious swimming pool, he set off north towards Orlando Airport. But he had no intention of returning directly to the 'pickle factory' [CIA headquarters, Langley, Virginia] instead he turned south down Highway 17 and stopped off in Fort Meade. He was not yet ready to brief his colleagues – he needed more information and he knew where to get it.

He located a quiet shopping mall, parked his hired Ford Fairmont outside of the Publix supermarket, found the public phone booth and dialled a Miami number – a number firmly lodged in his brain for the last 3 years. The phone at the other end went straight into recorded message mode and he spoke the one word coded message 'ganja'. He calmly replaced the receiver and started actively but mindlessly looking through the stacked directories. After about ten minutes the phone rang 3 times and stopped. Wynton returned to his car and continued south. The phone routine was a simple untraceable messaging system setting off a sequence of events culminating in a meeting precisely 24 hours after the time of the recorded message. It had been set up for just this purpose. It also confirmed a predetermined pick-up point. He was now operating on his own – outside his terms of reference – outside the ring of protection he could call on in an emergency.

CHAPTER 4

Carlton left Bay Hills Golf Club along with Wynton, agreed the time and place of their next briefing and drove towards Haines City where he booked into another less than salubrious motel. He worked on the assumption these down at heel motels were never fully booked. Completed registration, picked up his keys for his ground floor bedroom, parked his car several parking lots away from his room and, once inside, repeated the same basic security measures.

It occurred to him he was starting to live like a fugitive in his own country and for the first time since returning from Kingston started to think seriously about another life outside of the organisation. Having passed his information and responsibility to Wynton he decided it was time for him to catch up with his personal life. He had four days vacation and he decided it was time for a change of direction.

After an energy sapping day he had no problem sleeping an undisturbed eight hours. He was keen to get underway so he skipped breakfast, checked out, settled in cash and headed south. He avoided main highways and expressways, sticking with secondary roads running parallel to Highway 27. This was the easiest way of spotting 'tails' and the quickest way of losing them or even confronting them. Again it occurred to him how paranoid he was becoming but the last thing he wanted was anyone making a connection between himself and his next destination.

He travelled through a series of deserted ramshackle towns that served Florida's orange growing industry. It always intrigued him why so many residential properties had discarded agricultural machinery, some with potentially mysterious and secret rural applications, decorating their front lawns.

30 miles from the outskirts of Miami he rejoined Highway 27 and then onto the 821 through Hialeah. From here he headed east through a maze of back streets to South River Drive overlooking Miami River. He checked the address because the roads looked the same and he took some final basic precautions to make sure he wasn't being followed.

He wasn't sure who might be following – pro Castro Cuban agents living in Miami, CIA sponsored anti Castro Cubans or even CIA minders keeping tabs but he was determined he would not be followed. He turned left at the decaying wooden building that was the Catholic Mission, and his one unforgettable landmark, and pulled into the open underground parking lot in SW 4th Avenue.

He was now in an unmistakable Cuban area. You could smell it, feel it and hear it. Cuban radio stations blasted salsa, mambo and merengue rhythms interspersed with anti-Castro slogans from every car and open window. Gun shops, jewellery shops, shops selling cigars, bakery shops, cafe bars with their rich and heady smells of Cuban coffee, restaurants, metal bashing automobile workshops, gas stations, wedding dress boutiques, billboards in Spanish, all crowded in on each other and home from home for the thousands of exiles. Hookers, pimps, drug dealers, petty thieves and racketeers were no doubt seamlessly integrated into this seething cauldron of Cubanistas.

Poverty rubbed shoulders with wealth. Crime rubbed shoulders with profit. Profit rubbed shoulders with law enforcement. Criminals got along with law enforcement. An area that was both dangerous and exhilarating.

Carlton got out of his car, extracted his briefcase and holdall, avoided the lift and bounded up three flights, jogged along the open river facing corridor, rattled the front door of number 34 to announce his arrival, pulled back the fly screen and entered.

'Took your time getting here' barked a stunningly beautiful, light olive-skinned woman, long brown hair brushing her slender waist, just under 5' 8" with striking features belying her 34 years. Toys littered the room but there was no sign of children. 'Kids are at school so you have just less than two hours to explain in every way possible what kept you'.

'I got here as fast as I could but it is going to take me 72 hours to give you that kind of detailed explanation – it can't be done any quicker' replied Carlton.

That was the end of the formal welcome: they laughed at the banality of it, collapsed into each other's arms and disappeared with an ungraceful urgency into the bedroom. Clothes discarded as if they had suddenly caught fire.

Naty Rojas was just ten years old when she was hurriedly bundled on to a plane at Varadero Airport to escape Havana after the 1959 revolution. Both her parents were doctors and clearly targeted as intellectuals and enemies of the revolution. They left their magnificent detached mansion in Miramar with nothing but fear and uncertainty of what lay ahead of them as exiles in the US. They were angry they had been forced out of their home leaving behind everything they had worked for plus elderly parents who were too frail to travel. They had no strong political views, were not activists in any way just two professionals dedicated to helping the sick but now Castro had changed all that.

Naty grew up in what was becoming known as Little Havana. On arrival in Miami they were lodged with five other Cuban families sharing a square flat roofed converted warehouse just off West Flagler Street. Temporary and flimsy screens were hastily constructed to afford minimal privacy. The accommodation was a very long way from the standards of their Moorish style mansion and their army of servants, nannies and gardeners.

With both her parents doctors it was not long before they had set up a medical centre offering Cubans health care continuity with consultations conducted in Spanish. It was generously funded from Government Medicare and it was not long before profits were funding both an apartment attached to the medical centre and the refurbishment of a George Merrick designed mansion in Coral Gables. It never occurred to Naty to question how her parents had achieved so much in such a relatively short time.

Naty appeared not to have any of her parents' hang-ups about their beloved Cuba. She grew up in a fast changing, noisy, friendly, crowded neighbourhood. Neighbours looked out for each other and also exercised a kind of unspoken discipline on wild teenagers only occurring in close knit communities.

Educated at a Catholic and predominantly Cuban populated school five blocks away from her home she eventually went on to study Cuban culture and music at Miami University. Her ambition was to teach. But that's where it all ended. A love affair with a member of the local Mafia, an unhappy marriage her parents opposed, two beautiful children and then isolation as they went into hiding.

Her husband was a wanted man – overstepped the mark with his Mafia boss. Thought he might control part of the operation himself and keep the proceeds of a small scale protection racket. The Mafia court offered him one of two options - flee Miami for good or face retribution of losing one member of his family. He had the decency to flee but not before he was given a bullet through his knee to remind him what would happen if he ever showed his face again.

Rumours circulated he had fled to New York to continue his life of crime. Naty realised her marriage to Carlos had been an impulsive mistake and she took the decision she would be better off remaining close to her friends and family. There was never any thought of following him to New York – as far as she was concerned her love for Carlos had died along with his disappearance.

Naty took a job as a trade representative at Miami Chamber of Commerce to support herself and her children. The arrival of the Cubans in Miami had awakened in the Americans the commercial possibilities in South America. Her Cuban background and fluency in both Spanish and English meant she was in the right place at the right time. Her role was to help exporters by organising trade missions to South America. This is how and where the two met.

To maintain his cover Carlton was required to attend different training courses run by a variety of Chambers of Commerce. He was being trained as a superficial expert in the jargon of export documentation, import regulations and financial instruments of international trade. He could now talk for approximately 30 seconds on an extensive range of export related topics – enough for him to sound credible and to get him through 90% of conversations with his overseas connections. For the other 10% bullshit was insufficient and he knew when it was time for him to make an excuse and leave or at worst start offending his guest.

Bored out of his mind at one of these training sessions he first noticed and then fancied this brown haired, attractive employee of the Chamber with a great deal to say. No one was offended by her constant chatting and bossing because it was said with charm and humour. At the morning break he made light conversation and by the time the course ended later that day they had agreed a dinner date at a local restaurant. Over the next two years the relationship developed and was now seriously beginning to impact on Carlton's longer term plans.

 'I'm thinking of getting out of this travel business. I've had enough.' Carlton interjected suddenly. 'There is more to the job than I've told you – it's not just about squandering Uncle Sam's money on trying to set up trade deals. The job is going nowhere.'

'You do surprise me' Naty replied sarcastically. 'Trade representatives don't usually carry firearms, disappear for weeks at a time, attend courses if you were tested about it 30 minutes later would fail miserably and a body with more scars than a bull walrus.'

'Well I have one final project on and after it is completed I am getting out - moving on to pastures new. I was hoping we could settle down. I know we can't marry until you know what has happened to Carlos but at least I'll be around permanently.'

'Are you going to tell me what this job is?'

'No – and please don't push because I don't precisely know myself and that's the truth.' Carlton was keen not to upset Naty because he had felt the force of her Latin temperament on more than one occasion. He was trying to say how much he loved her but he had noticed the warning signs – the slight distancing, the sharpness of her voice.

'So I have to hang around here not knowing if you are dead or alive, wondering when you are going to show up – you trying living with that uncertainty. And if you don't know what the job is how do you know it's going to take just months.' Naty had felt at first an exhilaration she had not felt for a long time and then a cataclysmic let down as she realised it may never happen. Her background, her history told her that promises made just months ahead were not something to be relied upon in this climate of fear. She lived for the day.

'I know – I shouldn't have said anything. I do want to get out, it has been creeping up on me and the main reason is you, I want to be with you. But I just can't walk away from the firm – too many people depend on me. I know it is months because I will walk away from the job one day after the election in Jamaica which we think will be called early next year' Carlton felt he owed her that certainty.

Naty was not prepared to let him off the hook. 'I do want to get away from here and I'm not sure I can wait another 12 months. Do you know how many shootings and killings there have been? Last week two local small time gangsters were found dead in their car just two blocks away from here. I walk past the spot with Carlos and Dalia every day on the way to and from school. Most of the time its gang members killing rivals and nobody cares – good riddance, but now and then innocent people trying to make an honest living get caught up in it.'

'Where will you go?'

'Where can I go – I was hoping we could go north to Orlando, Fort Lauderdale or Tampa – just anywhere as long as I get away.'

Carlton noted the 'we' and tried to inject some optimism into the conversation, 'I will be back – I will be home often as I can but I cannot desert my colleagues at this time – please try and understand'.

An uncomfortable silence descended broken only when Naty calmly announced, 'I want you to meet my parents. They are calling in on their way back home. They have been to a medical conference somewhere and land in Miami in an hour – they should be with us in a couple of hours.'

This is the last thing Carlton needed but felt he had to go along with it. If he really meant what he said then he had better start behaving like a man who was going to take his family responsibilities seriously.

Carlton was still in two minds – to make an excuse and leave or do the decent thing – when the decision was made for him. The bell rang and in walked Roberto and Maria Santos. They were clearly delighted to see their daughter but enquired immediately 'where are my beautiful grandchildren. We travel all this way and they are not here?'

Maria was a slightly smaller, slightly plumper mirror image of Naty which Carlton took as a positive. Sparkling eyes enhanced by 'crows-feet' around the eyes, carefully applied make-up, close fitting two-piece suit over a shapely full figure and strings of gold chain necklaces created a lasting impression of one beautiful mature lady.

Naty sensed Carlton's awkwardness at being excluded from this very private reunion and to neutralise any doubt in her parent's minds quickly said 'this is Carlton, my boyfriend. He has been staying for a few days.'

Both Roberto and Maria moved towards Carlton in a gesture of polite but warm acceptance. Naty had spoken many times about him to her parents and therefore the encounter was not a complete surprise. With introductions over, the atmosphere more relaxed, Naty suggested 'Mother, why don't you walk with me to pick up Carlos and Dalia from school. They finish in twenty minutes and I do like to be at the school entrance to meet them. It will give daddy a chance to get to know Carlton' giving Carlton a wink as she breezed out the flat.

As soon as the women had departed the awkwardness descended as both men struggled to find the opening ice-breaker. Roberto won. 'And what line of business are you in? Naty tells us you spend a lot of your time out of the country.'

A relieved Carlton launched into a full and detailed description of his role as a trade ambassador with the US Chamber of Commerce. Each time he recounted his job description its' importance and scope was inflated a notch and he was also beginning to believe in his own commercial importance. He innocently described his recent travels to Grenada, Trinidad and Jamaica and his brush with the revolutionaries in St George.

Carlton did not sense any hostility from Roberto towards his relationship with Naty and decided to be totally upfront – man to man so to speak.

'I am very fond of Naty – in fact I would put it much stronger than that – I am hoping we can make a go of things together. We've been seeing each other for over two years now and I want to pack this job in. I need something more stable but I am contracted to complete one final assignment.'

Roberto listened intently - this was his daughter they were discussing. Carlton may not have been his ideal choice but he was reassured the guy seemed genuine. 'I guess you have found out the hard way how strong willed Naty is. There is nothing we can say, or would say, to interfere. Just please take good care of her' Roberto responded.

Carlton was taken aback by the weight of compassion in his voice. A father looking for the security Castro's Cuba or the Mafia had failed to provide. His comment stirred in Carlton a feeling of guilt about whether he was such a man. It also awakened a determination in him to honour his promise to Naty. This was his opportunity to find the emotional bedrock that was missing in his childhood and positively unattainable whilst working for the CIA.

CHAPTER 5

Wynton arrived in Miami mid afternoon. He took a chance and drove direct to Ocean Drive and parked close to The Tides Hotel – the hotel designed to represent a luxury liner – a supposedly iconic masterpiece of the 1930's Art Deco style. He reckoned he would be as anonymous here as in any small back street flea-pit hotel. It also had the perceived advantage of being safer.

Crime in Miami had driven away many of the European tourists but The Tides was still a bustling, noisy Mecca for businessmen, gangsters and pimps and for the no-bodies who wanted to look like businessmen or gangsters. Gangster's molls and hookers from brilliant white to midnight black and every shade in between paraded their wares within calling distance. The hotel was also miles away from CIA safe houses which helped minimise potentially embarrassing chance encounters.

Wynton liked returning to Florida and Little Havana in particular. It was the only part of town that had any reality. The Cuban's had created a place of substance. They had their own newspapers, radio stations, statues were appearing honouring Cuban heroes, street names providing constant reminders of Cuba and virtually everyone speaking staccato Cuban Spanish. It was a place where he could practice his modest vocabulary. Little Havana had both the substance and appearance of a foreign city.

There was no other historical legacy to either Florida or Miami. Miami's history had and is still being imposed upon by exiles, immigrants and visitors. A land of make believe or make it what you want - an escape from Cuban tyranny, an escape from the cold of the New York and Canadian winter, an escape from the poverty of Caribbean Islands or an escape from reality. Disney World, Epcot, Busch Gardens and Universal Studios just some examples of the places people went for their mindless escapism. It was also home to his Cuban contact.

There were plenty of rooms available at the hotel and after completing registration with a false name and cash payment, no questions asked, he was shown to a room with a splendid panoramic view. Pity the furnishings didn't match. The room was 'tired' and in need of refurbishment. Wall paper peeling at the seam, cracked tiles in the shower with black mould creeping along crumbling plaster, a chipped and marked TV sitting incongruously on a black lacquered Japanese style cabinet, two faded and torn upholstered chairs round a small mahogany veneered table helped feed the impression Miami needed to find a new reality.

Wynton now had approximately 15 hours to prepare himself for his rendezvous with his informal, 'off the books' and non approved contact. He was still digesting Carlton's report and still uncertain whether he was right to risk his credibility, and potentially his job, in invoking this emergency protocol. He quickly dismissed these thoughts as he realised he now had no option.

Three years ago it would have been a simple matter of meeting his contact in a local coffee bar but since Carter's new policy towards Cuba such meetings were impossible. According to official policy he was now dealing with a terrorist organisation and as such should be pursued and brought to justice for a series of mainland atrocities against Cuban officials on legitimate business at the UN.

At 11:00 am precisely the next day and on the corner of Domino Park, given its name for the simple reason this is where Cubans play dominoes, located at the junction of SW 14th Avenue and SW 9th Street, a white taxi pulled up.

'You the guy selling ganja?' enquired the Latino.

Wynton didn't reply and just got in the back seat and lay down. No point in raising any suspicions – no matter how small the risk there was always the chance of the unexpected. They drove for 20 minutes and then entered a private courtyard after which an 8 foot black metal door was slid into place and locked. He reckoned he was still in Little Havana but could not describe precisely where – the Cubans surrogate homeland since they first started fleeing Cuba in the 1960's. Cuban exiles, and particularly the terrorist genre, would not risk straying far from Calle Ocho!

'Wait here' commanded the Latino.

This was the first time Wynton had used his contact in the last three years. He looked around a totally dilapidated court yard with broken furniture, threadbare tyres, and weeds sprouting from every area not covered by badly laid concrete. The place looked as if it had been abandoned. He was beginning to sweat. Unarmed and not quite as fit as he used to be, he started to look for potential escape routes should things not work out as he originally imagined. Had he set himself up?

Twenty minutes later another two swarthy Latinos, probably Cuban emerged from the same door used by the taxi driver.

'You armed?'

'No'

'Get out the car slowly and put your arms on the roof.'

Wynton was quickly and expertly frisked – they were obviously used to the task and not prepared to accept the innocent denial. They were looking for armaments and recording or transmitting devices – they trusted no one but didn't find anything.

Instructed to follow them, Wynton entered what could be described as a small two storey apartment block with central corridor and staircase with doors leading off presumably into private rooms. A stale smell hung over the place and walls that had never been decorated for years. He was shown into a ground floor room.

'Welcome my friend, or am I presuming too much?'

Sitting at the head of an old oblong wooden table was a man mid to late 50's, dressed in a light blue cotton open necked Guayabera shirt that had seen better days. A hefty paunch put the shirt under strain. A wild unkempt head of hair matched by an equally uncared for beard out of which poked a cigar. Smoke filled the room which like the rest of the building was cheaply and tastelessly furnished and decorated. A coffee pot and two cups on a side table being the only evidence of domestic activity. He stared directly at Wynton anticipating his response.

'It is good to see you Manuel Franqui. You haven't changed a bit' replied Wynton, anxious to get the meeting off to a positive start. 'I have no reason to come other than a friend. You or some of your friends are still pissing off some of the politician's big time' smiled Wynton 'but my colleagues are not too upset by your activities. Official policy may have changed but hearts and minds haven't. We do our best to keep the FBI off the scent.'

'Well be careful my friend we believe we are under surveillance. Since Kennedy betrayed us and Carter classifying all exile groups as terrorists, life has certainly got tougher for us in Miami – no funding, no support – nothing. Friends get arrested on false charges and are in and out of prison. Perhaps I should stop there but I can tell you we continue to plan for the day when we can rid our country of that socialist puppet.'

'As long as Carter is President we can't openly help you on that score - in fact the opposite. We are supposed to contain and discourage open opposition groups like your OMEGA 7 but, for what it's worth, most in the department are reluctant to go along with this appeasement policy' Wynton replied, again anxious to keep his host on side.

'You have taken a big risk seeking me out so it must be important. By the way did you finish your research or whatever it was you were studying for?'

'I was very grateful to you for organising those interviews for me. Those six weeks we spent together were very happy days and I don't know of anyone else who has got close to providing your side of the story. It got me my doctorate which in turn got me into the intelligence service. And I am sure the summary found its way into the power structure. So I do owe you an awful lot' replied Wynton genuinely. 'If I'm ever in a position to help you directly or indirectly I will, but I'm afraid I'm here again seeking your help.'

Wynton had rehearsed this moment several times in his head. The last thing he wanted was for Manuel and his merry warriors to misinterpret or misunderstand the implications of what he was about to reveal. It could potentially be an opportunity for OMEGA 7 to strike a blow against Castro but it would merely be a small and inconsequential victory in a much broader and more significant war. He was also sufficiently experienced not to trust or accept as truth every word Manuel spoke. This was a dirty business and genuine loyalties existed, if at all, only between those who had been through much together to achieve shared aims.

Wynton started 'I have evidence to suggest Fidel is about to absorb Jamaica into his socialist empire. Paradoxical isn't it – on one hand railing against the American and British imperialists but on the other trying to extend his influence way beyond the usual economic and political links. I don't know how far Michael Manley would be prepared to go down the Cuban route but these two are close buddies. If Manley could see a way of holding on to power permanently then I'm sure he would be tempted. This would not be in America's interest – whilst Jamaica is not in the same league as Cuba strategically it could be a similar scenario to South East Asia. Once one country goes down that route others might follow. You must know what is happening in Grenada, Guyana could very quickly follow and then potentially Trinidad. We have to try to put a stop to it now. I have unsubstantiated reports Castro has offered Maurice Bishop economic help and also engineers to construct a new airport in Grenada. This is going to give Carter nightmares. How soon will it be before the Russians are tying up their destroyers at some expanded dockyard?'

'I presume your intelligence is good' enquired Manuel fully aware Wynton would not be divulging all the details or his source.

'It hasn't been verified but I am as certain as I can be at this stage. We have more work to do but I can't afford not to do the groundwork.'

'I am here seeking information', continued Wynton. 'As you probably know Jamaica will be forced to go to the polls next year. Manley's Peoples National Party [PNP] has to be in trouble. The economy is declining rapidly, unemployment is growing, he has taken control of the tourist hotels on the north coast and is offering 50% discounts to the locals so international tourism has bombed. Western capital, or what's left of it, repatriated. Hard currency is in short supply and his 'Third Way' import substitution model is having the perverse effect of making Jamaican exports prohibitively expensive. All the educated middle class and entrepreneurs are queuing up for their Green Card with thousands already on their way to a new life in Canada or here. He is going to be forced to call an early election'

'Cuba all over again – you, I mean the CIA, failed to stop it so why should Jamaica be different? Manuel enquired. This description reminded him of what had happened to his beloved Cuba and how he had done everything in his power to resist Castro. He never supported the corrupt Batista regime but he hated the communists infinitely more. He had lost many friends both in the disastrous Bay of Pigs invasion, some of who still languish in jail, and other ill fated US backed assassination attempts.

'Well by my reckoning in a 'free' election the PNP will lose heavily. However I don't think Castro will allow that to happen – the election will be rigged, voters intimidated or worse, key players bought, the country will be destabilised and the blame heaped on the US and so on. You know the score. Fidel and Michael are too close for comfort and if Castro helps the PNP to win he will forever be under his influence. A new Cuban styled socialist state will have been born. The democratic preferences of the people will have been crushed.'

'Doesn't Carter see this' replied Manuel somewhat incredulously. 'Or is it a case he doesn't want to see it. It would expose him as being a weak politician – Reagan will use this ruthlessly in his election campaign. He could put a credible spin on the view Carter is being used by Castro to get him to curtail CIA activity in Cuba and dissident exile groups in Miami and New York. Mind you my friend, just reflecting on this, it could work in our favour.'

'I haven't briefed anyone yet. As far as I am aware I'm the only one with an opinion on the subject. I need more evidence and I also need to be able to understand how Castro is planning to help the PNP. I want to know how to rig an election' replied Wynton.

'I think you mean, how you stop an election from being rigged?' prompted Manuel. 'What I do know is the local Mafia have been eyeing up the north coast of Jamaica as the new location for their casino operations. They have been looking for a new base for their 'slots' since they were kicked out of Cuba. A PNP victory will not go down well with them. Could be their intelligence is different to yours. They are not expecting a PNP victory' so commented Manuel.

Wynton tried his best not to look surprised.

'Well my friend you have raised a number of interesting questions and possibilities. I presume you want me to enquire further – am I right?'

'You are right.'

'And what do we get in return? Life is difficult for us at the moment' moaned Manuel.

'If you can provide me with any insights into what Castro is planning and who is talking to whom, we will willingly pay for it. We will make it cash through the usual drop system' replied Wynton who was not prepared to offer a blank cheque. 'We have our own agents but I am sure you are reaching the parts denied us. I promise you a decent return on your investment, Manuel.'

Enough had been said; both understood the score and the same contact routine confirmed with a 'no response' from Miami conveying a lack of progress.

As he drove back to Orlando Airport Wynton reflected on his meeting with Manuel. He would be kidding himself if he believed his friendship with his Cuban contact would protect him should a betrayal prove advantageous. He started to worry about what Manuel had said about it working to his advantage. He operated in a world of parallel dimensions where it was occasionally necessary to cross boundaries. Wynton had done just that and now sought anxiously to defend and justify his actions. Had it been really that important and just what had been accomplished? His mind moved to a sort of balanced state where he rejected the most negative of consequences and focused on the fact he had reopened a dialogue with someone with the potential to provide confirmation of Carlton's prognosis.

Manuel had given very little away but the Mafia comment was totally unexpected. Neither of them mentioned the Havana NAM conference or the cultural delegation so there had been no corroboration of Carlton's report. Wynton was now painfully aware Manuel would be considering very seriously how he could exploit the situation for his own and OMEGA 7's advantage.

CHAPTER 6

Sitting round the highly polished mahogany table, in a windowless secure room at CIA headquarters, Langley, were Dexter Broadbent, Director of CIA Operations Cuba Station, George T Rosenberg, Deputy Director Covert Operations in Central America and Caribbean, Joaquin Roselli, Cuban-born CIA head of Operation 50 [top-secret group formed to eliminate Cuban leftists living in the US], Mitch Randall, CIA Covert Operations – Special Assignments and Wynton McKenna.

George T Rosenberg, Wynton's direct line manager, was sufficiently alarmed by his subordinate's report he immediately short-circuited standard communication protocols and invited Dexter to join him for an impromptu briefing. The outcome was an urgent, drop all else, request for key personnel to attend a formal briefing and strategy meeting –now code named Red Snapper.

Dexter Broadbent was in the Chair. Everything about Dexter was excessive - his voice, his size, his facial hair, his drinking habits, his language, his knowledge of anti-Cuban operations and his extensive list of contacts that owed him favours. He thanked Wynton for his presentation.

Dexter, like many that had gone before him in this position, was a consummate liar. He would stonewall, defy authority, distort the truth and go to any length to preserve his anti-Cuban operations because like many of his colleagues he had an intense hatred of Castro. He paid lip service to President Carter's conciliatory approaches and would interfere to destroy any attempt to bring Cuban exiles to justice for assassination attempts on Castro or Cuban officials. He would do this even when such attempts were on American soil – something that was explicitly forbidden in the CIA charter and mandate. But Dexter would go to extraordinary lengths to protect his own – a true Bonesman.

'What I want to know is why we have to concern ourselves at all with Jamaica? If the PNP is heading for a major defeat why do anything?' queried Joaquin Roselli. 'Why put our agents at risk – half of Jamaica is an ungovernable shithole.'

Joaquin Roselli was a commander in the failed Bay of Pigs operation. He led a group of saboteurs who had infiltrated Cuba prior to the landing to clear away beach obstacles, booby traps etc. Whilst succeeding in his primary objective the invasion delays meant his team had to spend many hours longer than planned avoiding Cuban defence forces. This delay forced them in land and away from the landing areas and not in the right position to destroy Cuban artillery protecting the beach. He could not be blamed for the fiasco but he felt a deep bitterness towards Kennedy for not giving the invasion force the air and sea support it so desperately needed. Joaquin avoided capture and made his way back to Key West along with two of his comrades in a stolen speedboat. He vowed he would continue the struggle to rid Cuba of Castro by any means possible. His actions came to the notice of CIA agents and he was recruited into the organisation under the direct control of Dexter.

'To start with we cannot assume with any certainty the PNP is heading for defeat. The election is probably just over 12 months off and the only real evidence we have is some research done by the University of the West Indies suggesting opinion is moving away from Manley and towards the Jamaican Labour Party. We can't trust this research – we don't know who commissioned it and just how the hell do you conduct an opinion poll when you don't know how many people are eligible to vote, how many are too scared to vote and how many will still be alive on voting day? And what idiot is going to risk his life in Spanish Town and Trench Town knocking on tin shacks asking the questions?' interjected Wynton, not happy Joaquin was questioning his prediction.

'The issue to me is can we take the risk of doing nothing?' George T Rosenberg entered the debate in support of his subordinate. 'We know for a fact Fidel has sent over this cultural delegation and we know some of their team. Culture is not on their agenda. Assassins, explosive experts, urban warfare experts are part of the delegation and these make up about 10 percent. These are agents we know about but there are about 40 in total? Furthermore we don't have anyone on the inside and so have no way of monitoring what these others are up to. The nearest we have on the ground is one of Wynton's men and he is not even Cuban, doesn't speak good Spanish and looks like the all American boy. Not exactly what we need right now.'

Dexter sensed the potential for the meeting to drift away from what he hoped would be a unanimous endorsement for covert action to undermine the actions of the cultural delegation and monitor what other support Castro would be lending Manley. 'Thinking aloud here, Castro will have been provided with a more detailed analysis of the situation on the ground by Manley's supporters than we have accumulated. Let's speculate they are reaching the same conclusion as us – the PNP is going to lose out. Castro will do everything in his power, pull every dirty trick in the book, and remember they have a dossier 20 feet high of our own tricks he can turn against us if he so wishes. They will be most certainly out to change the minds of voters or rig a number of key constituencies or in a worst case scenario put the military in charge'

'My initial reaction is to question why I have been invited to this meeting' Joaquin said. His body language was starting to exude indifference. 'We all know my role and it certainly doesn't extend to fighting Cubans in Jamaica. You are not paying me enough for that.'

'You will fucking well do what you are told' Dexter exploded. 'Let me remind you, you are still a guest of Uncle Sam. You are tolerated because you annoy our friend Fidel. Once you cease doing that you present us with a dilemma – we are not going to keep apologising for the 'Pigs' fiasco. Do I make my point?' There was clearly a history between these two.

'Not really. I assassinate people. What is it now – three to be precise - three prominent pro-Castro side-kicks with well documented connections. Who the hell do you want me to assassinate in Jamaica – I don't know the country – by your own admission there is no network on the ground. Where's the intelligence coming from?'

'Have you been half a fucking sleep or what? Who mentioned assassinations – you have either jumped twenty steps ahead or do you just enjoy killing? We have just been presented with a scenario where Jamaica is turned into a Cuban satellite state – the beginnings of Fidel's empire. We are still assessing, evaluating, predicting and the last thing we have asked is for you to barge in there shooting every fucking Cuban or his associate. Your plan lacks a certain amount of sophistication.' Dexter snapped back sarcastically. Clearly Dexter did not appreciate this kind of negativity and his colour was beginning to match his language.

Wynton was beginning to make an uncomfortable connection between Joaquin and Manuel Franqui. Bay of Pigs was the common denominator. Wynton had never met or heard of Joaquin Roselli or Operation 50. There was no reason for him to be brought into the loop because up to now Joaquin was operating solely on US territory. It is inconceivable Joaquin and Manuel did not know each other. Bay of Pigs was a small operation and survivors living in Miami, officially or otherwise, were bound to know each other – the issue is how much intelligence and gossip have they shared? Had Manuel informed Joaquin of Wynton's approach? Was Joaquin better prepared for the meeting than he was letting on? Or was Joaquin's status such he had to maintain his anonymity? Did either of them have links with the Mafia?

'The whole point of this meeting is to work out a plan, a strategy, a way of making sure Manley's PNP loses the election. That is our sole and only objective. How we do it is the difficult part. The point of inviting you here to this meeting Joaquin is to explore what role Operation 50 can or cannot play. So I would be very grateful if you would hear me out.' Dexter thought it better to be a bit more accommodating – he may just need Joaquin.

Dexter continued 'Gentlemen, we have on our hands one almighty conundrum. Do we instigate our own destabilisation strategy and blame Castro, or do we stop Castro from destabilising Jamaica and come over as the good guys or do we discredit Manley or do we blow his fucking head off? Do we go the other way round and promise aid, get the World Bank, the IMF, the Commonwealth Secretariat and the European Commission on our side, get our business consultants in and exaggerate the potential of Jamaica in order to boost potential jobs and incomes to help Seaga's image? Do we ignore Carter's appeasement policy towards Castro which he then uses to go about his business unhindered or do we discredit Carter and force him to drop his support for Castro? This is not your simple us and them or black and white campaign it's all the fucking colours of the rainbow campaign.' Dexter sat back in his chair, mopped his brow and poured himself a glass of his favourite Scotch having created an air of expectation everyone clearly understood. He was waiting for a reaction.

Mitch Randall was first to puncture the growing tension. 'You have given us about seven different options. With respect to Wynton, he has given us unverified reports and speculation about the role of this cultural delegation and what Castro and Manley might get up to at this conference. This is hardly the basis for planning full scale operations. We need more intelligence.'

Mitch was one of the most experienced covert ops men in the CIA. With three years to go before enforced retirement he was still as enthusiastic about his job as he had ever been. He had seen it all – had worked with the Mafia to bypass customs on illegal drug imports to fund unofficial operations, had shielded Mafia gangsters involved in various CIA misdeeds from prosecution, had been involved in a wide range of covert ops in Cuba to destroy agricultural processing plants, had set up counterfeit money operations to destabilise economies of unfriendly governments – by any stretch of the imagination a highly experienced and thoroughly evil man. But in this company he commanded respect. His experience had given him the confidence to make his contributions count. He spoke when he had something to say and people listened.

George concurred 'Mitch is right. You have set out all these possible routes we can go down but we have no basis for accepting or rejecting any one. We need more knowledge. I am inclined to accept Wynton's take on it but we could be operating without full government support, it's going take a substantial amount of money to fund and if we cock up our necks could be on the block.'

Dexter was sufficiently sensitive to the mood. He knew they were right – he was just so anxious to have another go at Castro his judgement had been partly obscured. But Dexter was quick of mind and brought the meeting to an end. 'You guys are right. I want more information about what the hell is going on at this conference in Havana next month. I want more details about this cultural delegation and we need someone on the inside. I want to find out more about what Manley is up to. I want our agents in Cuba to monitor shipments to Jamaica. I want to know which Jamaicans are flying in and out of Cuba. I want to know who our friends are in the media in Jamaica. We convene in eight weeks on 26th September – three weeks after the Havana jaunt is over. The venue will not be here – George will fix up a safe house in Miami.

CHAPTER 7

Carlton Davies had been briefed by Wynton McKenna on the outcome of the Virginia meeting and details for the scheduled follow-up meeting for the 26th September. Carlton was given two clear objectives – the first was to identify key news reporters for all the main media in Jamaica who could be relied upon to get a story published and secondly to identify someone, an inconspicuous and innocent insider, to provide information on the Havana conference. It was also suggested he should look for every opportunity to create the stories which might weaken the PNP and strengthen the JLP in the minds of voters. Truth should not be an obstacle.

He also knew from the nature of these tasks his role had been down-graded and he was now very much a bit-player in the operation. However he had the satisfaction of knowing Wynton had taken him seriously and convinced the powers that be action was needed.

What surprised him more than anything was his inner reaction to the knowledge he was not being included or trusted with an operational overview. In fact he was relieved. It confirmed his conviction that he was tired of this way of life. Instead of destroying life he now wanted to make a new life and he had been right to make the promise he did to Naty.

He landed in Kingston at 4 pm – approximately two hours late. He now carried what he needed with him because on three previous occasions he had 'lost' the odd item or suitcase. The complaints and lost luggage procedures were deliberate examples of mindless officialdom that discouraged such actions and did much to undermine one's sanity. He carried his gun hidden in a side pocket of a toilet bag – just enough to avoid the most cursory of inspections. Gun laws were pretty severe in Jamaica, instant and prolonged jail sentences for those found in possession, but he continued to rely on luck to avoid detection and diplomatic connections if he was caught.

Passport control was cursory and customs too busy bossing European tourists to take much interest in a lone businessman. The Arrivals Hall was manic with all kind of colourful vendors offering anything from refreshments to accommodation, tour guides marshalling their latest conscripts, relatives embracing returning loved ones, police in their smart blue and red striped trousers, soldiers in full battledress with automatic weapons and public transport drivers.

Carlton knew who to trust and made his way to the registered taxi rank of aging Cadillacs and instructed the driver to get him to the Mayfair Hotel. The driver, like many Jamaicans, wanted to talk but not necessarily listen. He was clearly upset about what was happening to Jamaica - the lawlessness, the drug dealing, the corruption, the deserted street kids who had never felt the love of a mother, and above all, a deep concern about what another PNP victory would mean for people like him.

He told Carlton how he had fortified his home – had built a wall inside the hall of his home approximately 10 feet from the front door. If anyone came to the front door he could hide behind the wall shouting for the visitors to identify themselves and at the same time protect himself and his family from automatic gun fire being sprayed through the wooden front door. This would at least give him the chance to return fire. Carlton had heard similar tales before – there was an escalating brutality in the tactics used by the JLP and PNP to frighten off the political opposition.

Carlton settled the 15 Jamaican dollar taxi fare together with 2 US dollar tip. US dollars were very welcome in Jamaica at this time.

'Good to see you Carlton. How long are you with us this time?' enquired Jim, assistant manager of the Mayfair Hotel.

'Five days this time – that OK with you? Then I'm off on my trips to Trinidad and Guyana, probably have to avoid Grenada until things settle down. Not in the mood to take in a revolution just at the moment' Carlton always took the opportunity to openly declare his official business – he felt, rightly or not, it strengthened his cover.

'You want dinner this evening?'

'Ok plus a rum and Ting now if you don't mind – I could murder a drink.'

Carlton had gotten to know Jim over the months. He liked the Mayfair – clean, value for money – slightly out of the way – responsive staff – often sharing your bedroom with squadrons of giant cockroaches and willing chamber maids.

He also liked Jim's wife – a native born wife of mixed parentage with a keen business mind. He would take tea with Marion whenever he was resident and present at 4 pm. Any later and he wouldn't be invited. He enjoyed this quaint English ritual with the Wedgewood tea service and black bun. It always intrigued him how these colonial traditions had been maintained when other aspects of imperialism had been so vigorously dismantled. Though he did recall how his taxi driver still harked back to the days of law and order that existed before Independence. He boasted his taxi, an open topped light green Cadillac, was the one used by Queen Elizabeth on that great day in 1962. A day supposed to herald a bright new dawn of freedom and prosperity!

Jim was very much second in command at the Mayfair. Carlton suspected his wife was the source of wealth and was determined to do her best to preserve it. Jim was also a deserter. Nobody knew quite what service or regiment he had left and why but he originated from a place called Crosby, near Liverpool. He couldn't return to England and had made a comfortable life for himself in Kingston. His main tasks were to make a mess of simple DIY repairs around the place, manage some of the outside staff and manage the bar.

This is where Jim was in control and together with his faithful assistant Reid offered the best and most potent collection of cocktails in Kingston. The Rum Punch made to a secret recipe but known to contain 3 different types of rum, was what first hooked a diverse but regular clientele. The bar was about 50 yards from the main hotel building with its own private car park. Secluded by dense jungle growth interspersed with Ackee, Tamarind and Breadfruit trees, the place was idyllic in daylight but given the security situation was quite sinister and frightening in darkness.

It was the favourite drinking hole of the Kingston expat community and the other odd deserter. Every night, without fail, at least a dozen expats from Australia, England, Scotland, USA, Canada and Israel would gather to talk, joke and share tales about Jamaica friends back home would not believe.

Uninvited, Jim joined Carlton at his dining table. 'Things are getting pretty bad here. We can't get cooking oil, we haven't been able to get butter for two weeks, fresh meat, other than chicken, is expensive and there are petrol shortages. Guests with the hard stuff are rare – just the odd businessman like you.'

'Sounds tough – anything I can do?'

'Just keep coming and tell your friends. I shudder to think what will happen to Jamaica if the PNP get back in. We won't last another year' sighed Jim.

'Am I your only guest?' enquired Carlton just wondering if this conversation was leading somewhere.

'I have a party in from Barbados for the cricket and I have a young guy booked in for a couple of days. Nice bloke – from Thailand but he doesn't drink. Quite rare that. Says he is on his way to Cuba to some conference. Your colleague from the Ministry dropped him off yesterday. I don't think he knew what to make of him - chalk and cheese. First guest I have ever had from the Far East for a very long time. I think he is scared stiff.'

Carlton feigned disinterest. 'What's he to be scared of in this beautiful oasis of calm?'

'Very funny – we had a shoot out here last week. Police helicopter searchlight picked him out and one on the ground shot him. God knows who he was. Probably a robber – they shoot to kill these days. They expect every criminal to be armed' replied Jim.

'Are you joining us tonight at the bar – some of your mates will be there?'

'No, or not yet at least, I have some work to do to prepare for this conference tomorrow at the Pegasus. Bloody waste of time but we have a few thousand dollars to spray around to encourage some manufacturers to sell their products to the US and also trying to set up a deal to supply fruit to Guantanamo. Incidentally where is your Thai guest?'

'He is booked in for dinner at 7pm. Oh by the way, thanks for wiring that money over to England. My mother sends her thanks and apparently celebrated with a gang of her mates down at the Legion – she keeps telling me she can't manage on her pension. Here is $3,000 Jamaican dollars – should cover your expenses.' Jim discreetly handed over a bulging envelope of cash.

 This was just one of Carlton's many money laundering deals. He would wire US dollars to a UK bank account from the US, receive a 50% margin over and above the US/Jamaican official exchange rate from Jamaican residents, settle his bills with Jamaican dollars and bank his expenses back home. Everyone a winner apart from the Government of Jamaica.

Carlton took his time over dinner. He had met Vietnamese, Chinese and Cambodians but not Thais. They were a particularly rare breed out West and positively unique in Jamaica and he pondered if they just might have a shared interest.

At 7:30 pm his fellow guest finally appeared. He smiled at Carlton and put his hands together in eastern fashion and bowed. Carlton got out of his chair and held out his hand. The Thai took his hand very gently, bowed and, without a word, walked to his table and sat down with his back towards him. No opportunity there for a conversation.

As there were only the two of them in the dining room Carlton decided to try a different approach – he had nothing to lose. He walked over to his table and stood directly in front of him and enquired 'I believe you know my friend Duncan Palmerson from the Ministry – Jim told me he dropped you off here earlier.' Carlton spoke slowly not knowing whether his fellow guest had command of the English language.

'Good evening. Please have a seat. My name is Toungtong Suphanochakul but Westerners call me Toffy. Everyone outside of Thailand has difficulty with my name.'

Carlton could just about understand his response and fully grasped why he liked to be called Toffy.

'Yes I do know Mr Duncan, he has kindly agreed to introduce me to some local farming cooperatives before I go to Cuba. I am an agricultural economist by training and always looking to see what we can learn.'

'Very pleased to meet you Toffy, my name is Carlton Davies and I am with the US Chamber of Commerce. I am here trying to get the Jamaicans and other Caribbean countries to export to the US.'

The two of them continued chatting for a few minutes before agreeing to take coffee on the wooden colonial style veranda. They sat by side on comfortable rattan armchairs overlooking the dimly lit swimming pool. The sound of the tree frogs and cicadas was deafening interrupted only with the occasional sound of gunshots. That was typical Kingston. You could sit outside in the cool evening air staring at a still, jet black sky dotted with brilliant white stars that appeared millions of miles closer than anywhere else on earth. You lived with the sound of gunfire – it only registered when it appeared to be getting closer and then you calmly retired inside and locked the door. There was no point in panicking or calling the police.

Carlton, unlike most Americans, was brilliant at encouraging people to talk. He knew how to use a silence to make the other say more than he intended and he was at it again. Toffy also liked the opportunity to test his English. Over the next hour Carlton learned quite a lot about his Thai friend. He also learned about the reason behind his trip to Cuba.

By the time Toffy had made his excuse to leave, Carlton had extracted a promise they would meet up again after the conference. Kingston was on his return route home as there were no direct flights from Cuba to the US and therefore nothing suspicious if their paths crossed again. Carlton had casually asked if he could obtain a copy of the speeches of Castro and Manley and any other prominent Caribbean politicians. He openly explained to Toffy the US was not welcome at the conference but the US was very keen to bolster trade ties to help these countries escape poverty. Lying was second nature to Carlton. He also promised Toffy he would provide the names of potentially useful contacts which might further his interests. The lies simply rolled off his tongue like the waters from Dunns River flowing into the Caribbean.

CHAPTER 8

Toffy checked out of the Mayfair early next morning. The manager of the Trewlany Banana Growers Cooperative, Wayne Richards, whisked him off in a battered open backed Land Rover on a tour of some of the more progressive farming communities in Trewlany and St Ann Parishes.

The strong patois vocabulary of his host made conversation and understanding difficult but there was no misunderstanding the warmth of the hospitality being extended to him. However two days of intense political arguments between Wayne and anyone prepared to listen interspersed with similarly intense family ructions was getting too much for Toffy. He was a much relieved individual when Wayne dropped him off at the airport for his Air Jamaica flight to Havana.

In just under two weeks Toffy had travelled Thai Airways from Bangkok to London, spent three days sightseeing in London before catching a British Airways flight to Kingston and now he was en route to Cuba. Not only had his journey spanned half the world but reinforced his convictions about the inequitable disparities existing between the Western developed world and the poverty that engulfed most of his home country and, if his observations were representative, Jamaica also.

Toffy had been chosen as an observer by the Thai government to attend the Havana conference of the Non Aligned Movement, part as a reward for his diligence in his job at the Ministry of Foreign Affairs and part because they needed as much information as they could about how to improve their agrarian economy. Rapid population growth and export development were critical issues and this conference provided a huge opportunity to meet with others from the developing world facing similar challenges.

Toffy was just 5' 4", weighing just under 8 stone and with a thick head of black straight hair. At first glance his face gave the impression of a rather glum individual who had just been given disappointing news about the inadequacy of his penis. He could, however, normally rely on his smile to disarm the sternest of officials – but not today. Clearly nobody had told the staff of Varadero Airport that the country was hosting delegates from over 100 countries. Arriving passengers were viewed with suspicion, kept under close surveillance by members of the army and bossed around as if they were about to stage a coup. No welcoming desk, no signage and obviously expected to make their own onward travel arrangements. Don Mueang Airport was no palace but it was light years ahead in terms of decor and customer care.

There was a great deal more to Toffy than his slight and inconspicuous frame might suggest. Born into a poor rural family in Chiang Rai, Northern Thailand he was driven to break free of the bondage that ensnared many of his male friends. He rebelled against the powerful traditions that bound families together and from an early age had decided he could not follow his mother and father into the back breaking work of the salt fields. Scraping together the sun baked salt deposits and bagging them for shipment for less than 50 baht a day was not for him.

He wanted a life and he was prepared to challenge the Buddhist teachings and expectations that had governed his life since childhood. Aged 18 he enrolled at Ramkhamhaeng University, Bangkok - the university established specifically to help the urban and rural poor of Thailand. Working nights and weekends as a street vendor to fund his course in agricultural economics he passed all the challenges presented to him. Respectful acceptance of what was taught and faithful reproduction without question was the way to succeed.

One day this cosy academic relationship was shattered with the arrival of a visiting Cuban American professor. He started to challenge widely held assumptions about authority, power and ownership in an agricultural economy. He made Toffy question why his parents had to labour six days a week, live a subsistence level life, see his elder sister depart for life as a sex worker in Bangkok whilst those making the profits live a life of luxury and privilege. These same people are those with the money to 'bend' the politicians to their cause. Corruption is a freely available option for those with money in Thailand.

This encounter changed Toffy but he was not a revolutionary – he was an entrepreneur. Respect for authority was so ingrained he never thought to challenge it but to exploit it. He wanted the life that money could buy. Revolution in Thailand could wait.

With no money Toffy took the first available well paid job opportunity that came his way. He was in the right place and time to be offered a job as an agricultural economist with the local government of Songkla Province. Due respect to superiors and exemplary diligence earned him a secondment to the Ministry of Agriculture. His role was to explore agricultural reform in countries that were fully signed-up members of the Non-Aligned Movement. This was the natural association for Thailand – keen to steer a neutral path away from Moscow and Washington. Cuba, Guyana, Jamaica, Trinidad, Belize, Honduras were just some of those countries he had been tasked with investigating. The Havana conference provided him with the opportunity to make his contacts.

He also planned to provide his new found friend with the information he requested. Toffy sensed that Carlton might just be worth a lot more for his personal ambitions than all his Havana contacts put together.

After waiting patiently in line for about 20 minutes a large black taxi saloon pulled up. Rather than communicate directly he showed the driver the printed hotel reservation provided by his travel agency. The driver seemed to understand, muttered something into his beard and roared off. Smoke billowed from a broken exhaust, horse hair [or something similar] poked out of multiple holes in the bench seat, floor littered with rubbish, with one window cracked and taped together all combined to put Toffy into a state of extreme anxiety. He hadn't expected this.

The journey from Varadero to Havana was about 80 miles most of which was on a dual carriageway incongruously called Via Blanca. There was little traffic, including the horse and carts, and what motorised transport there was seemed to belong to a different era. There were unflatteringly similarities to Thailand – piles of discarded rubbish along the sides of the road, wooden shacks housing barely dressed locals, dangerously uneven pavements and unfettered cattle wondering close to and sometimes onto the road. At regular intervals huge posters had been erected displaying flattering portraits of Fidel Castro and his revolutionary mantra 'Socialism or Death'. Again just like Thailand but there it was large posters of the King without the mantra. Sugar plantations next door to oil derricks and nodding donkeys gave a surreal impression of total unplanned chaos.

Two hours later, feeling nauseous and physically drained, he arrived in Havana. Nothing had prepared him for what lay before him. Large black gas-guzzling dust covered American automobiles dotted the ramshackle streets, the likes of which had never made it to Thailand. Overcrowded buses, with people toe-holding every protuberance and tractors pulling people laden trailers created an unforgettable scene.

Queues of people were outside every shop and at every bus stop – mid afternoon and people were clearly trying to buy something to eat before setting off home. The once magnificent buildings were either crumbling out of existence or boarded up – presumably having finally crumbled. This was not the image Toffy expected. Surely not the image of a country saved by the charismatic revolutionaries!

Nervous and unsteady on his feet, Toffy paid off his taxi driver in US dollars and stared up at Hotel Sevilla – his home for the next two weeks. Not as dilapidated as the surrounding mansions but sadly in need of urgent maintenance. Inside he has welcomed by friendly staff and shown to reception. His luggage was whisked away from him with the bell boy clearly hoping for a tip.

Having registered, he quickly walked up the staircase to the fifth floor, tipped the bell boy, slammed the door shut and fell on to his bed. It immediately slid off the two building bricks and clattered to the floor. Somehow he wasn't surprised – it was fully in-keeping with his fast diminishing expectations.

Each time he left the hotel his confidence grew. Havana was safe. Constantly propositioned by cigar and sugar cane street vendors, cafe owners and prostitutes by the dozen he never felt threatened. He drew a further parallel with Thailand – poverty and crime didn't have to go together – or was there something more sinister that kept them apart? The one thing that did unnerve Toffy was wherever he went he noticed the same man walking about 20 yards behind. He even followed him back to his hotel and always headed for the bar in the open-air courtyard. This man was casually dressed, never made any attempt to communicate and Toffy finally concluded he must be part of a government protection scheme.

On the morning of the 3rd September Toffy walked the mile to the Palace De Convention for the opening address of the Sixth Conference of the Non Aligned Movement given by its prospective new Chairman - Fidel Castro. The sky was clear blue, the air fragrant fresh from camellia bushes and the streets quiet. But the hookers were already at work. Toffy had learned Fidel now tolerated student hookers as being gainfully employed for the legitimate purpose of generating hard currency. The hookers had roughly seven or eight days left to maximise their earnings before the dictators, princes, prime ministers, ambassadors, observers, reporters, hangers-on returned to their home countries. They expected business to reach a climax towards the end of the week as delegates grew tired and bored with the posturing, lecturing and hand-wringing of those invited to speak.

The Palace De Convention was purposefully constructed to host this most prestigious of world conferences. 94 countries were expected to attend and Castro was keen to showcase a successful symbol of his Cuban economic model. Unfortunately no one seemed to have told the construction team. The timescale for completion was approximately eight weeks too optimistic. Piles of rubble, scaffolding still in place and dumper trucks running wild were only partly obscured by the massive posters portraying a smiling and reassuring Fidel.

The concrete and glass edifice was impressive in its size and originality but the socialist mania for functionality over style meant it was unlikely to be shortlisted for any architectural award. Inside the foyer the scene was one of orderly chaos. The more important representatives were targeted and chaperoned into the media visible seats. The atmosphere was without doubt welcoming and no delegate was left on his own to ponder his fate. Cuban hospitality was prominent, genuine and efficient. Toffy was targeted, interrogated and shown to the part of the auditorium reserved for those classified as observers – one level below a delegate.

He felt a sense of anticipation. This was a rare opportunity for those not closely aligned with Washington or Moscow to come together under the media spotlight. Television crews were preparing live broadcasts and film crews were on hand to record those whose views coincided with their country's own. At 2pm precisely a loudspeaker announced the arrival of Fidel Castro, First Secretary of the Communist Party, President of the Council of Ministers and of the State and Commander in Chief of the Armed Forces – wherever he went he always insisted on his full title. He timed his entry to coincide with the final stanza of his introduction walking the full length of the auditorium, dressed in military fatigues and smoking his trade mark cigar as if this was just part of his daily routine. The audience rose as one applauding enthusiastically. He climbed the stairs to the stage, stood before the light oak wood lectern draped in Cuban colours, milked the applause for a full three minutes then raised his hand for silence. A relieved audience stopped and immediately sat down. It was dramatic for here was a man that had already earned his place in history. Few would forget Fidel Castro.

The NAM conference was focused on two main themes. One was the vitriolic denouncement of the imperialists by many of the Caribbean, Central American and African representatives. They had been emboldened by Castro and Bishop's revolutionary rhetoric and newly found prominence in the movement. The other theme was Kampuchea. Kampuchea bordered Thailand and border tensions were running high throughout South East Asia. Many delegates from across the world condemned the Khmer Rouge but Toffy was not listening.

Toffy chose to attend all the main conference speeches and break-out meetings that were given or hosted by Caribbean governments. His personal ambitions were uppermost and he was determined to impress his American friend. He had started to dream of establishing his own import/export business with contacts supplied through VIP introductions. He had never met a more important businessman than Carlton Davies.

And all through the conference his minder kept a watchful eye over him.

CHAPTER 9

Carlton left his meeting with Toffy believing he had achieved his first objective. All he had to do was time his return to Kingston to coincide with Toffy's stop-over on his journey home. It was now time for him to focus on his second task.

Carlton had met a number of media executives and reporters at various embassy functions and Chamber of Commerce conferences but none he had ever considered as 'agent' material. Some were too idealistically opposed to the US, some were as bent as a Jamaican banana and others, he considered, could be 'turned' for the price of a meal. Given his new task he reckoned he might have to reassess his original opinions.

The ambitiously titled export symposium at the Pegasus Hotel attracted only a handful of potential exporters but was well covered by a bunch of free-loading journalists. There was clearly a dearth of other news worthy events planned for Kingston today for so many to be in attendance. The Pegasus could always be relied upon to put on a first class lunch whatever the deprivations.

There was a film crew from the Jamaican Television Company, a reporter with tape recorder from Jamaican Broadcasting Corporation, Muriel Sharma – Business Editor of The Gleaner and seven other representatives from assorted specialist press, business organisations and trade journals.

The delegates, speakers and media representatives took their seats in a conference suite designed to host two hundred. This was the nearest the hotel had to an international conference in nearly two months and they were not going to miss the opportunity. The speakers table was decorated with massive displays of Bird of Paradise and palm leaves, numerous bottles of cordial, stacked delegate packs and a sole microphone. To the TV viewer and newspaper reader the setting projected a conference of substantial significance.

Suddenly Carlton emerged from the foliage to announce 'good morning ladies and gentlemen. Welcome to the US Department of Commerce's sponsored export symposium. My task today is to persuade you Jamaican exporters enormous opportunities exist within the US market for your products. You may have products with specific appeal to your fellow countrymen such as your ethnic cosmetics or are part of your cultural traditions such as canned Ackees. There are growing African-Caribbean communities in Chicago, New York, Philadelphia, Miami and the opportunities are big. We can help you connect with distributors, we can help you with promoting your products and we have money to help you' so started Carlton. He was now on the knowledge equivalent of thin ice and quickly introduced his audience to the three specialists who had flown in this morning from Miami to speak about specific sector opportunities. Questions from the floor were now their concern. He felt he had done enough to maintain his cover and was anxious to renew his relationship with Muriel Sharma.

Carlton had met Muriel in her home country, Belize. Muriel had been a senior executive in the Tia Maria drinks company and a frequent traveller around some of the countries that were on Carlton's schedule. The relationship had started out purely commercial but soon developed into something more personal. They regularly slept together but this ended abruptly when Muriel became pregnant to her Jamaican boyfriend.

Muriel was forced to resign from her job and relocated to Jamaica to be near the father. As is the norm in Jamaica the father quickly moved on to new conquests leaving Muriel to bring up her daughter on her own – no family support and few friends. She had made a number of good contacts on her travels and this helped with her application for the post of Business Editor of the Gleaner. It also explained her presence at the symposium.

At the first available opportunity Carlton was over to greet Muriel.

'It's great to see you – you look fantastic' Carlton simply couldn't stop himself. All thought of the symposium had disappeared.

'It's good to see you – I've missed you. Come and tell me what you have been up to.' Muriel responded warmly.

They retired to the pool-side bar. Both of them were oblivious to how this might look to the other delegates. There was no shortage of conversation topics but mainly focused on the personal - Muriel anxious to test whether any feelings were reawakened by their chance meeting and Carlton on the possibility of getting her into bed.

The conversation, as every other conversation in Jamaica does, eventually switched to politics.

'I am seriously thinking of getting out of Jamaica. The Pegasus is the best hotel in Kingston but you walk 200 yards on to Half Way Tree Road you take your life in your hands. It doesn't matter who you are – you can get robbed at any moment day or night. I've got to be real careful working for the Gleaner.'

'What's your take on Manley and the PNP? Will they get back in?'

Muriel took a bite of her BLT sandwich, stared at the young white kids playing in the pool as she reflected on Carlton's question.

'In a free, open and regulated election the PNP would get blown away. Go into any supermarket in Kingston and see what's on the shelves – an extensive range of fly and cockroach killers and mosquito coils! But people need food. People need food they can afford to buy. If you are in the know you get advance warning when butter or cheese might appear. Unemployment is high and growing – nobody knows what the statistics are because nobody seems to be counting. Businesses are not investing – why? Because the central bank won't release the US dollars to pay for imported technology, fertilisers, pesticides and anyone with money is looking to change into the greenback or sterling to get it out of the country by any means possible.'

'So what you are saying is it won't be a free, open and regulated election'

'Come off it Carlton – you are not that stupid. Since when was the last time Jamaica held a free, open and regulated election. I'll tell you what is making it worse this time – Cuba is destabilising parts of the administrative structure of the country – helping it descend into chaos - picking on those parts of the civil service critical for social stability – the judiciary for one. They are also providing the PNP activists with Kalashnikov's – they can out-shoot the military. Manley is not sure about the loyalty of his army and police force and I am convinced Cuba is building up some kind of para-military force on the island. Do you know, an acquaintance of mine had two visitors over from Canada and they were taking a drive to see the sunset from the Blue Mountains. They stupidly got out of their car and were promptly kidnapped by this gang of young thugs. They took what they had, threatened to rape the woman but eventually freed them. My friends went straight to a police station and the police forced them into a jeep to help them go and look for them. Nothing wrong in that but the police had no bullets in their rifles – there wasn't any available. What use are they in an emergency?'

Carlton was both reassured and alarmed by Muriel's comments. He was reassured his original assessment was right but alarmed events were moving faster than he anticipated. He was also considering at what level he could, or should, maintain his relationship with Muriel. Getting her into bed might complicate things and his conscience was beginning to bite. He remembered his promise to Naty. He sensed an opportunity but didn't quite know how to proceed. He quickly rejected emotional involvement and decided his best bet was to secure her cooperation in some other way.

'Where will you go if you leave Jamaica?' Carlton enquired innocently.

'Back to Belize because it's the only place I can go. Not ideal but I can't get into the US. It could take a year for the US embassy to process my application. I probably would have to return to Belize just to do that. Have you seen the queue outside your embassy here? Everyday people are queuing up for hours just to register their application for a Green Card.'

'Are you under any political pressure in your job?' Carlton continued.

'We are still trying to maintain some objectivity and truth – however you want to define it. We get press releases from all the different Ministries and we are expected to publish in full but we don't. We try to verify and if we suspect it is propaganda we relegate it to a brief footnote. So I would say we are no longer a free press – two of our reporters were attacked last week by unknown assailants. They were reporting on crime and drugs and probably getting too close to some PNP sponsored misdeeds. It's an open secret the PNP are active in the drugs business.'

'How will you report today's proceedings?'

'We will put a positive spin on it. How the caring US is trying to help Jamaican business grow and increase employment. How the wonderful Mr Carlton Davies is devoting his time and energy to helping the developing world.' They both laughed at the thought.

Muriel suddenly turned angry 'Some of those other press guys will be reporting today's event very differently. They will be interpreting it as US interference and undermining Manley's attempt to break the shackles of imperialism. The story line will be the duplicitous Mr Carlton Davies from US is trying to stop Jamaica from developing true independence. That the money you are offering is a bribe to maintain the US's influence over some of the key players. There is growing confidence amongst this group because of what Maurice Bishop has done in Grenada.'

Carlton mused inwardly they weren't too far off the mark.

'What do we do – let Jamaica go down this socialist route or try to keep it on the path of democracy and under our influence? Can I ask you something personal Muriel – just between the two us? Not waiting for an answer Carlton continued, 'where do you stand on all of this?'

'I love this country. It is a beautiful island – the north coast is stunning. I did feel comfortable here. But it is not a developing country – that's a fancy term intended to convey optimism about the future. It is actually regressing. The best educated are fleeing and that's what I have to do too. Read today's Gleaner – 8,416 immigrant visas granted by US to Jamaican nationals in last seven months. I'm a free spirit and I want to live where I am free to do what I want and what is best for Faith.' Muriel felt comfortable with Carlton and had no difficulty pouring her heart out.

A silence descended. Carlton reckoned this was his opportunity.

'It's important not just for me but for the US to keep getting the right messages across. We have to do what we can to kick Manley out of power and restore some sanity and the media can help'

'Why does it matter that much to you? Surely a man in your position simply moves on to another island. If you've got dollars to give away you'd be welcome any where' queried Muriel.

'There's more to it than that. It's important we keep Jamaica allied with our view of the world. If we don't we reckon Castro is ready to move in. You see what Bishop has done in Grenada – we took our eye off the ball and guess who is moving in with his engineers. Any US president other than Carter would not have allowed it to happen.'

'Am I being a bit dim here – but do I get the impression you are suggesting I modify my journalistic principles?'

'Just a bit and yes my job is to encourage trade but I do have to do what I can to make sure we get the right government in place. It would help me enormously if I had someone who could get me access to the local media and correct some of this socialist bullshit that is being communicated.'

Muriel was taken aback by what Carlton had just said. She interpreted his comments as a request to manipulate the stories being printed in the Gleaner and possibly beyond.

'I don't like what you are suggesting here. We meet up after 2 years and you are asking me to betray both my own principles and those of my employer. You certainly have changed. Normally the talk would be centred on the removal of my knickers.'

'Yes I'm sorry – got carried away. Can we focus then on your knickers?'

Both laughed. At this very moment both realised their emotional attachment had faded to friendship.

'Can I leave you with this thought – if you can help Uncle Sam, and not put yourself at risk, I will guarantee you your Green Card the day after the election result is announced.'

Muriel was left to ponder Carlton's offer – a guaranteed Green Card was an insurance policy that thousands of Jamaicans would give their right arm for. She started to question whether her journalistic principles were worth preserving when weighed against a new beginning in the US for Faith and herself.

The only people left at the conference were the three US consultants flown in specifically for the event. 'What a frigging waste of time. Those guys in the audience were rent-a-crowd – a bunch of consultants who had been asked to attend and represent the interests of different sectors. One of them, the guy representing the Reggae music and floriculture sector, said they couldn't persuade anyone to attend. They were finding life so difficult to make a living the last thing on their mind was looking for new markets.'

'OK – we did our best – we got our press release out and hopefully the Gleaner will publish pictures just to reassure the locals the US is still their friend and keen to help.'

Carlton thanked his colleagues from Miami and apologised for the turnout. 'It may have looked a disaster but it goes down in the records. In six months time no one will remember the turnout just the fact that we sponsored the event.'

To provide a little in the way of compensation Carlton added 'I have arranged for the driver from the Ministry to take you back to the airport.'

As Carlton was leaving the Pegasus, Muriel slipped him her business card, kissed him on the cheek and whispered 'keep in touch'.

CHAPTER 10

Carlton still had much work to do. There were 'wheels to oil' and agents to 'work'.

Sunday morning in Kingston meant one thing – golf at Caymanas Golf Club. A group of expats had formed a golf society open to all. New comers to Kingston were always made welcome. Handicaps were dished out on the day, usually based on last week's performance and whether Stableford or Medal the prize was always new golf balls. Very much appreciated by all and usually provided by the last person to return from the US or UK.

Carlton arrived at 9 a.m. and made up a fourball with Sham Zaidi, currently on secondment from the Indian Civil Service to the Ministry of Foreign Affairs, Felix Curtis, commercial attaché at the British High Commission and John White, furniture manufacturing consultant sponsored by the European Union and black market currency dealer. All the expats were either using their Jamaican posting as a means to enhance their career or escape some personal or economic disaster back home. Divorce, bankruptcy, unemployment, love affair gone wrong or mid-life crisis was the usual motivation. Whatever it was they made up a friendly, interesting and entertaining bunch.

Caymanas Golf Club was the preserve of the Jamaican rich and the expat community. Isolated from the tensions of Kingston it boasted some of the most challenging and picturesque holes on the island. The setting was almost fairly tale with lakes and dense jungle combining to create magnificent green locations.

All the expats had stories to tell about Caymanas. Carlton never forgot the first day he played the course. A guest of Sham Zaidi, they first had to negotiate their way through Spanish Town. This was normally one of your major trouble spots – frequent gun fights between gangs. The cause may have been drugs related or political or even something very minor, like adultery, but the consequences were the same – a steady flow of murder victims.

Spanish Town used to be the capital of Jamaica and boasts the oldest Spanish Cathedral in the West Indies. The outskirts is now basically a shanty town made of up of hundreds of wooden houses with flat corrugated roofs. Dogs roam in packs. Roads are hard dirt that turns to mud in the wet. Few houses appear to have running water or electricity. But on this Sunday hundreds of people were dressed to kill – men in their dark suits, collar and tie and bowler hats, ladies in bright floral dresses with hats to match and all clutching their bibles. They were on their way to their local Pentecostal Church for their weekly Sunday morning service. Carlton admired the resilience and pride of people who had so little.

Having successfully negotiated their way through Spanish Town, they headed in land through sugar cane fields. At this point Carlton started to appreciate the beauty of Jamaica. After about 4 miles they pulled into the club's car park. Suddenly about 20 young black men appeared from nowhere and surrounded the car. Sham didn't seem bothered but Carlton recalled being scared witless. Somewhat tentatively he got out the car and followed Sham round to the boot. One of the young guys got Sham's clubs and shoes out and stood back. There was a rush and one of the guys emerged with Carlton's clubs and disappeared. Carlton had just witnessed a Jamaican tradition – who ever touched your golf bag first was your caddy for life. Carlton had just acquired the services of golf caddy Errol.

Today Errol was in his usual resting place hoping one of his regulars would show. At the site of Carlton's borrowed jeep he was on his bare feet ready to grab the clubs and disappear to the first tee. Carlton learned later that the caddies would now be laying bets on who would win.

'Good morning big bout yah. How are the i?' Errol was somewhere in his mid twenties, beaming smile, or it could have been if all his teeth were still present, about 5'6", skinny as a rake and dressed in shorts and t-shirt. He lived in Spanish Town with his mother and younger brothers and was the family breadwinner.

'Good morning Errol, I'm in good nick thanks and you?' A predictable conversational start to the day but the two had an easy relationship. Unknown to Errol he was actually one of Carlton's agents. Carlton worked him in a most casual way to find out what was happening on the ground in Jamaica and you couldn't get closer to the ground than Spanish Town.

He used his time on the golf course to find out how locals got and paid for their guns, about the level of violence and what the local MP was doing for his community. He paid for this information by providing shoes and t-shirts for his younger brothers, packs of new golf balls he could sell, the odd packet of cigarettes but nothing too excessive. He made sure he paid the standard rate for his services plus generous tip – the last thing he wanted was for the other caddies to have any suspicions about their relationship.

Carlton sliced his drive to the tenth into dense undergrowth – he thought to himself no chance of finding that.

'Its over yahso big bout yah' called out Errol.

Carlton followed Errol's path and there was his ball sitting up on recently flattened vegetation and with a clear shot to the green. This happened often and no questions asked. Errol could manipulate the ball between his toes – he clearly had backed Carlton to win.

At the very next hole Carlton again sliced his drive but this time on to the adjacent fairway. As Carlton approached his ball a group of about 15 men were marching towards him. They were locals, all carried machetes, knives or clubs and looked to all the world they were up to serious mischief. This presented Carlton with a dilemma – he looked around, Errol had disappeared, and his playing partners were about 150 yards ahead by the green and clearly and deliberately ignoring him. Should he run, land the first blow or what. Without a word they formed a semi-circle round him as he took his stance. His seven iron shot soared over the fairway trees and with a touch of back-spin ended up 6 feet from the hole. The menacing looking gang politely applauded, commented on his skill and quietly moved on – they were clearly returning home from morning service! Carlton graciously and enthusiastically thanked them and moved off as fast as possible without portraying panic. This was Jamaica at its most unpredictable, exhilarating and unforgettable. Another day he could have been knocked senseless or worse and robbed. He would not have been the first to have been robbed at Caymanas.

During the round, without any prompting, Errol volunteered 'Thin's are gettin' bad around yahso i-dren. You know dere is an election next year and it's started now man. Last week a box of Kalashnikov rifles was found just over dere. Police came and took them away but I knows they didn't get fe no Babylon station man. No one is playing golf yahso anymore man. De people is just too scared.'

'What happened to the guns?' Carlton asked trying to feign genuine disinterest.

'Who knows man but dem have disappeared somewhere in Spanish Town.'

'Why are the people scared?' queried Carlton.

'You ever lived drough an election man?' Errol screeched incredulously. 'If dey dink the i are gonna vote JLP the i gets attacked. Used fe be di acid or machete man, now it's di automatic – its gonna get a bans heap worser. I just hopes you keeps comin back.'

No need for anymore probing. Carlton had learned all he could from Errol.

'Whatever happens Errol I'll keep coming back. I have a job to do. You look after yourself.'

Errol dumped Carlton's clubs in the back of the jeep and resumed his resting place hoping he might get a second bag. Carlton joined the gang of expats in the clubhouse, shared a Red Stripe and sandwich and listened to the latest gossip.

Over the next 30 minutes the grouped swelled to three four-ball's - all expats - civil servants on secondment, embassy diplomatic and operational staff and an eclectic bunch of management consultants.

There was no need for Carlton to prompt or direct the conversation. There was enough spontaneous content to satisfy his curiosity. All had implemented additional security measures in response to a deteriorating situation. Four of the golfers related stories of disturbing incidents – someone had his car bonnet sprayed with automatic gunfire transporting his young children to a party, one reported an attack on his local secretarial staff, another described a failed kidnap attempt and one was actually robbed at knifepoint. There was some disagreement about the cause of the upsurge. The diplomatic people interpreted it as a deliberate attempt at destabilising the country whilst the remainder tended to the view it was due to a demoralised and underfunded police force. Whatever the cause the PNP was implicated and deeply unpopular.

By mid afternoon the conversation had run its' course and they all returned in convoy to the outskirts of Kingston before dispersing to their hotels or guarded compounds.

Carlton was slipping a few hundred US dollars to one of the UK's embassy staff to provide him with a diplomatic insight into how overseas governments were interpreting local events. How they might react locally in the event of a PNP victory. These opinions were expressed during the course of lunch, intertwined with the general flow with no one but Carlton aware of their significance.

Carlton was dropped off at the Mayfair where he planned to hang around just long enough to catch up with Toffy on his return home to Bangkok.

CHAPTER 11

Cordoba Mansion in Coral Gables lived up to its billing. Located on an avenue shaded by giant banyans and oaks backing onto a canal, this George Merrick designed property was the home of Drs Roberto and Maria Santos.

Roberto and Maria had furnished their mansion in a style that reflected both the reality of their life in Miami and their hopes and aspirations for the future. A George Merrick mansion in Coral Gables was by any American standard a symbol of success, a sign of substantial money flows and the fragile basis of respect from others. The entrance foyer was massive, marble columns and flooring dotted with art deco furniture, lamps and ornaments designed to give the visitor the impression of a family in tune with the fashionable values of modern day Miami. Decorating the walls of the foyer, staircase and beyond were a unique and priceless collection of prints and paintings by the famous Cuban impressionist artist Carlos Gomez. As soon as the money started to flow, Roberto and Maria had set about collecting his work. This was their secret, their way of keeping alive their dream of returning to Miramar. The pictures, inspired by popular myths and realities of Cuba beyond the capital Havana, and before the destruction wreaked by Castro, provided the reminder and motivation they needed to keep their hopes alive.

Today they were hosting a party, or what looked to be a party to anyone watching. A dozen or so lively, laughing children diving and jumping into a lagoon shaped swimming pool and a quartet of mothers being served cocktails by waist-coated butlers was the innocent looking backdrop to a more sinister activity taking place indoors.

A meeting had been convened by Roberto Santos at the suggestion of Manuel Franqui. Also in attendance were Joaquin Roselli and Marcello Mancini. All four exuded money. All four leading double, and occasionally, triple lives. Expensively but casually dressed, adorned with gold watches and rings they gave a good impression of what success looked like in Miami.

Dr Roberto Santos, owner of the Miramar Medical Centre and father to Naty Rojas, pulled himself forward on the black leather sofa suggesting to the others it was time to get down to business.

'It is good to see you all again. I have asked you to come round today at the request of Manuel. It appears events happening in the region might just present us with some interesting opportunities. Over to you Manuel.'

'Thanks Roberto. I had an unofficial visit from this guy from the CIA. He was looking for information about what Fidel is up to in Jamaica. Appears he has gathered intelligence suggesting Fidel is up to his old tricks but with a more serious twist. He thinks this information points to him trying to take control of the country either through his manipulation of the PNP or failing that by military might. The motive is to exploit Carter's weakness, strengthen his influence in the region and attract more financial and military support from Moscow. Do you want to add to this Joaquin?'

'I was called to a meeting at the Pickle Factory and met the guy Manuel referred to. Appears his report has put the shits up the CIA and they are starting to take it seriously. They are totally screwed up by Carter's relationship with Fidel and firmly believe Castro is playing a double game. My take on it is the CIA needs us. The question for us is how do we react?'

'What do we want out of this – let's be clear with one another' interjected Roberto. Roberto, in addition to being a first class doctor, had still not given up hope of returning to Cuba. Now just turned 60, his hair still full and black with no sign of greying and had maintained the body of a 40 year old through daily exercise and swimming. Devoted to his wife Maria, frustrated with his relationship with Naty, adoring of his grandchildren Carlos and Dalia but he could never shake off the feeling he had betrayed his country. Running away, though it didn't seem so at the time, had left him with the burden of guilt. A guilt that could only be lessened by words and deeds directed against the Castro regime. It was his loyalty to Cuba he used to justify his relationship with the CIA. He took massive CIA authorised payments through Medicare based on fraudulent non-audited invoices. Some of this money was used to fund unauthorised CIA activity against Castro the rest to support a lavish lifestyle.

Marcello was the first to respond. 'We need to move our operations to Jamaica so we don't want either the PNP or Fidel controlling things. Montego Bay and Ocho Rios are just the perfect locations for our casinos. Cruise liners can dock there and together with the loaded Europeans we sense an opportunity. Once we have the legitimate face of business we have a platform for a whole range of other activities.'

Marcello Mancini was a Miami Mafia boss. Fat, sweaty, hairless, unpleasant, ruthless – you name it, every negative characteristic you could nail on a villain. When he was born his parents must have taken one look and immediately put his name down for the Mafia. He was the perfect stereotype. But he was also a brilliant businessman. He didn't get where he was by not understanding the numbers, making things happen and knowing how to handle people. He had built a solid working relationship with Roberto, Manuel and Joaquin. He could supply the guns, the boats, the explosives, the extortionists, the torturers, the plane drops, the guerrilla training facilities and other destabilising paraphernalia through legitimate front businesses.

He also was in the pocket of the CIA. He frequently acted as the 'front' that protected the CIA's ass. He was in the business of providing much the same set of services as he did for the anti-Castro's. Just how much Roberto knew of this went unsaid.

Marcello was the first of the Mafia bosses to decide it would be better to work with the Cuban immigrants than try and fight them. He held a deep seated hatred of them as wave after wave of middle class exiles had quickly adapted to life in Miami and turned it into their Habana. They first took the jobs of the local blacks, next they took ownership of the small businesses and employed their own, they relentlessly moved up the food chain to take in real estate, legal and medical businesses and then they branched into the illegitimate. All the time pushing out and marginalising the other ethnic groupings. Finally they started to take control politically. Marcello didn't have the fire power to repel them. Marcello was quite happy to witness and encourage the growing hostility and violence between Miami blacks and Cubans. But Marcello's strength was his relationships – not even the Cubans could match his network – networks took time to build. Symbiosis was Marcello's mantra.

'Jamaica is just the most heavenly place on earth for me to do business. I have got the resources to do what you require - I just don't have a strategy' concluded Marcello somewhat mockingly.

'Thanks Marcello – you have left us in no doubt where you stand.' Roberto also recognised the necessity of the relationship with the repulsive looking Mafia boss. Roberto could not achieve his ambitions without Marcello.

'My objectives are clear and which I am sure you understand. I will do anything that hurts, marginalises and undermines that worm that occupies our country. Jamaica holds no special appeal to me except as a potential new battleground - if we can take money off the CIA in the process so much the better.' Manuel seemed to sum up the feelings of the triumvirate of Cubans and they all smiled in unison at the pure simplicity of it.

'You all know that I have the capacity to fund, let's say, a certain level of covert activity but the plans are drawn up by others. I implement or fund what is asked for and don't have the control. If it goes well I get richly compensated if it doesn't I am reminded of just how precarious my position could become. They run a brutal business.' Roberto didn't have to spell out everything in detail but equally all knew the limits of their right to inquire further. Sometimes, in this world of espionage and subversion, it was better to remain in the dark. If there was trust there was no need to know.

Roberto, after a moment's reflection, added 'the fact both Manual and Joaquin have been contacted clearly suggests we are going to be involved in what they have code named this Red Snapper operation. We need to be in a position to judge if what they ask for helps us achieve what we want. If not we have to think up ways of adjusting their plans.'

After his initial contribution Joaquin had listened intently to the views and reactions of his fellow countrymen. He mentally dismissed Marcello as a dangerous thug whose only interest was making money. He was becoming concerned at the speed and willingness the Red Snapper operation was being endorsed by Roberto and Manuel. 'Let's hold back a moment and think through why we might become pivotal to this operation. I accept that the CIA, and the Republican right wing will not tolerate another country in Uncle Sam's backyard turning into a satellite of Moscow but it's the Democrats that are in power. They have turned us into a terrorist organisation to be hunted down - just why the hell are we bending over backwards to help. If this operation goes the same way as the Bay of Pigs, guess who will be made the scapegoats?'

'It's the price we have to pay. We all live comfortably here in Miami. We do the dirty work in return for financial support and protection from FBI investigations. Being selective is not an option. Start picking and choosing, the funding dries up and FBI investigations start. Do not think for a moment the CIA has not covered its ass in the event of failure. Nothing will be traced back to Langley. We are the expendables. That's why we have to make sure the operation suits our purpose, we only agree to those things we can achieve and we are handsomely rewarded.' This was Roberto's way of trying to say the meeting was closed.

However Joaquin was not finished. 'Sorry Roberto but we haven't exactly firmed up on what WE want from Red Snapper. I want to get back to Cuba. I'm sick of living this life of having to do what we are told but at same time being persecuted if we make one false move. I want to assassinate Castro, I want to get rid of his regime, I want to do everything in my power to discredit Carter and I need money. Isn't that what we all really want? Do you really care what happens to Jamaica? In my humble opinion if you achieve these objectives you can stop worrying about Jamaica.'

Roberto regarded Joaquin as his closest confidant. Joaquin had been involved in three assassination attempts on Castro – two had to be aborted because Castro changed his schedule at the last minute and once when he had Castro in his sights when the lights went out. Castro, like Hitler, seemed to live a charmed life when it came to thwarting assassination attempts. Having driven his economy to the brink of collapse the power generators responded by saving his life. As a consequence of these failures Joaquin was on borrowed time with the CIA and he knew it.

'As usual you talk sense Joaquin. However let's not close our minds as to how this Red Snapper operation might help us achieve your objectives. It is becoming so much more difficult to strike at Castro in Cuba so a new theatre of activity might just throw up some new possibilities. We have our own man in Kingston as part of this cultural delegation which puts us one step ahead of the CIA and furthermore we will not be sharing 'Almeria' with them.'

Roberto genuinely appreciated Joaquin's contribution but also recognised he was impatient. This impatience was being brought about by the pressure he felt he was under from the CIA to chalk up something of significance. This made him a potential liability to the group. Roberto knew when it was time to exercise his leadership skills and now was the time to be decisive. 'Right gentlemen this is what we will do. Joaquin has reminded us of our task and it is critical we are not sidetracked by what we will be asked to do. We will continue with our intelligence gathering both with 'Almeria' and our friends in Havana. We have no option but to wait until the CIA decides to involve us and we have a clearer idea of what is expected.'

'I want to know how to handle McKenna when he next makes contact. There is an obvious connection between the two of you and if he makes contact with Roberto he will expect Joaquin to be in on any conversation. But no one has admitted to a link with me. How do you suggest we handle this Roberto?' This was the kind of issue Manuel expected Roberto to resolve.

'Volunteer nothing. If he asks then admit to knowing us – it would be stretching his credibility to expect that we had not at least heard of each other. He is expecting you to provide some information about what the Cubans are up to, in particular this Cuban delegation in Kingston and we need to think very carefully what you tell him. Putting some distance between us might be a good move.'

'Is that agreed?' enquired Roberto as he surveyed the faces of his three compatriots for any sign of dissent or doubt.

Roberto, Joaquin and Manuel knew each other. All professional people from well established families, they arrived in Miami during the exodus of 1959. Roberto had become the unofficial leader of the trio – there had been no formal vote just a creeping acceptance he had the characteristics of a born leader. He listened, he reassured, he helped, he funded and was decisive. The impatience of Joaquin and the laziness of Manuel had forced Roberto into his leadership role. Manuel had also been closely connected to the criminal world of the Cuban Mafia using his professional connections to move profits from gambling to off-shore accounts in Panama, Cayman Islands and Switzerland. There was always a lingering doubt about Manuel Franqui.

Marcello, on the other hand, was the outsider. Marcello knew it and didn't care. He provided the services they needed and got well paid for it. They each could testify to have each other jailed for life and it was this, and only this, that sustained the relationship.

CHAPTER 12

Wynton and his boss had taken a flight down to Miami together and separate taxis from the airport. The agreement was to meet at Miami Docks – travel independently – dress for a day's fishing and arrive between 10:30 and 11:30 a.m. The rendezvous was the pleasure cruiser 'Lucy Jane' moored at pier 47. Dexter Broadbent and Mitch Randall were on board having sailed the cruiser down from Fort Lauderdale. This was George's latest creative interpretation of a safe house.

The cruiser was hired out to them by Atlantic Cruisers – a tourist operation and front organisation for CIA covert activities. Its history included clandestine runs to the north coast of Cuba to land and lift agents involved in attacks on sugar processing plants. Even with the latest radar and other electronic surveillance gear the boat had been involved in running gun battles with Cuban coastal patrol boats. Identification markings and gun mountings came and went as needed.

The boat had been swept for listening devices but the biggest danger was the four of them being seen together. Assumptions and conspiracy theories would follow any such sighting. All kept out of sight until the boat was half a mile off shore.

Weather conditions were perfect, clear blue sky, a gentle ocean swell and four fishing rods angled to convey the innocent impression of four tourists enjoying a day's excursion. The captain kept his distance – a contract employee of the CIA and knew the rules. His job was to keep his eyes open, ears closed and provide the refreshments when asked for.

Four Budweisers were passed around and Dexter opened proceedings 'whose fucking idea was this?'

'Mine, sit down and get on with the business. I thought it was a brilliant idea.' George responded with a big grin on his face. There was a mutual respect between the two that extended beyond the hierarchical. The reposte had them all laughing and helped relax the atmosphere.

'Make it the last. I can't stand water. If I was meant to be on water I would have grown fins and attended church more regularly.'

'OK guys – let's recap. Our primary and only objective is to stop Manley and his PNP from forming the next Jamaican government - any questions?' Dexter looked at each of his colleagues in turn searching for any signs of concern or doubt. 'Good – let's hear the intelligence.'

Without waiting for an invitation, Wynton decided his information provided a crucial but disturbing back-cloth to proceedings. 'I was asked to investigate proceedings at the NAM conference in Havana. We 'hooked' a Thai national to provide us with copies or summaries of keynote speeches by representatives of Caribbean governments. What we heard was disturbing. A detailed analysis of the content of speeches given by Castro, Manley, Burnham and Bishop left you in no doubt whatsoever this gang of four were very closely aligned with Moscow and their socialist ambitions. Manley was a fervent admirer of Castro and his ideas for the Cuban economy. He saw this as the way forward for Jamaica. Throughout their speeches there was fierce criticism of the imperialists and constant interference in their affairs. I'll just read you what Carlton reported about Manley's speech – Manley strongly pressed for the development of what was called a mutual alliance between NAM and the Soviet Union to battle imperialism and then there was this verbatim "all anti-imperialists know that the balance of forces shifted irrevocably in 1917 when there was a movement and a man in the October revolution and Lenin was the man". Based on these comments alone it strongly appears to me Manley fully intends to take Jamaica and turn it into a Cuban satellite. Talk about kissing Castro's arse. It is obvious to me Manley concocted this speech in collusion with Fidel – a mutual appreciation society.'

'I thought the whole point of this conference was about finding a third way – sounds like it was a Soviet style boys club' Mitch reacted somewhat incredulously.

'Some of the big players, India and the like were outraged apparently – they saw Castro using his position to set the agenda and didn't go down well, as you might imagine. Maurice Bishop and his overthrow of a corrupt western leaning government made him into a hero and, according to our source, every time his name was mentioned half of the delegates were on their feet. Seemed to appeal to many of the African dictators and despots. Bishop must have been horrified that his efforts were recognised by that gang of crooks - a bunch of political chameleons seamlessly blending their views with anything or one if they sniff money – one minute condemning the imperialists whilst at the same time filching what they can from international aid.'

Dexter, keen to move on, interjected 'and what's your conclusion – are we right to go after the PNP?'

'Quite simply Manley is so far up Castro's ass he will be extremely difficult to prise loose– admires his political and economic model and, in our opinion, will accept all the help he can get to stay in power. Manley firmly believes this is the way forward. So my conclusion is Carlton's fears were justified.'

'Just so we know, who is this Thai gentleman?'

'According to Carlton, he met him on route to Havana. Stopped off in Kingston to investigate some agricultural schemes and stayed at the same hotel – Carlton promised him a few favours in return for relevant papers and a take on the mood of the conference. Totally innocent and neutral with no axe to grind and couldn't possibly have understood or recognised the motive behind Carlton's request.'

Wynton paused for a moment to make sure he had their undivided attention, 'two hours after he had met with Carlton on his return home via Kingston and after handing over his information, he was found dead – murdered – decapitated.'

'Who knew about his link with Carlton?' questioned Dexter in a most matter of fact way.

'As far as we know, no one. Maybe he talked too much when he was in Cuba – maybe he boasted about his relationship with an American businessman – we'll never know. There was absolutely no communication with him whilst he was in Cuba. None of our agents were aware of him. Our joint opinion is it's a coincidence – small guy, easy prey for robbers – the murder rate in Kingston averages 10/15 a day. It would have been a good bet he was carrying something of value and therefore worth the risk.'

'What are the chances there was a connection?' queried Dexter.

'We explored two other scenarios and dismissed them. The first is he was tailed on his arrival back in Kingston and once he was seen meeting with Carlton handing over documents he was killed. Carlton would have been exposed and the possible motive could have been revenge but then why didn't they kidnap him after the contact and find out what information was passed and, more importantly, why did they assume he was up to no good in the first place?'

'And the second?' queried Mitch.

'He had exposed his contact and therefore was of no further use and killed as a warning. Carlton would now be the marked man. The police report suggests robbery because nothing of value was found on him. One presumes he was wearing a watch and carrying a wallet and the weapon appears to have been a machete'

George entered the debate 'I agree with Wynton the most likely scenario is an opportunist robbery – it's difficult to work out whether the murder rate is politically motivated or just reflects a growing lawlessness. We do know visitors to the NAM conference were shadowed by some security personnel but that is just normal. Tracing a link back to Carlton in Kingston is, in our opinion, a low probability.

'OK let's leave him to get on with his tasks – presumably he is now on heightened alert and anymore such coincidences he is pulled. Have you anything else to report?'

'PNP activists are threatening and in some cases attacking journalists suspected of supporting the JLP and/or working for the Gleaner – propaganda machinery is in full swing with all sorts of bogus stories emanating from all ministries. There is clear evidence of arm shipments to townships linked to police complicity. There are also rumours of paramilitary activity which we are connecting to our friends in the cultural delegation. Increasing number of Cubans are being put into positions of influence and no doubt supported by inside informers. Economy is in deep shit, severe food shortages but hard to work out if this is deliberate or just one more manifestation of clueless politicians. Agricultural productivity, particularly the sugar crop, dropping like a stone – and that's before we get to work.'

Wynton's last comments caused amusement as all four had either planned or participated in clandestine activities in Cuba that were designed to achieve the same result.

'Thanks Wynton – you clearly have been busy.' It was not often Dexter Broadbent complimented anyone. It was not his style. He liked to think he worked with professionals but more than ready to savage subordinate or superior alike if they fouled up.

'OK Mitch – what do you want to add about this festering dung heap?'

'Our agents have logged arms shipments of AK47's, RPG's and small arms going in by light aircraft and supped-up pleasure cruisers. We have also detected military clothing – which is a worrying sign. Drugs are coming out the same way – presumably in part payment. We also understand there is a group of senior PNP activists who travel regularly between Kingston and Varadero.''

Dexter felt he had heard enough. His mind had been made up. 'OK guys take a break. Check your rods or whatever else you do on these crafts. Reflect on what you have heard – when we come back it's decision time.

Complex political problems required creative solutions – particularly when the solution involved covert action. Dexter fully understood this need and always allowed break-out time for new and innovative ideas to be formulated. No point repeating past successes – opponents very quickly wised up. He also anticipated George and Mitch would have reached the same conclusion and would have their own ideas.

After a lunch of mixed salads and seafood with a couple more beers the group reconvened. Again Dexter opened proceedings 'please correct me if you think I'm misinterpreting or over-exaggerating something but it looks to me Jamaica is a goner unless we step in.' Again he looked them each in the eye and all nodded their agreement. 'OK where do we go from here?'

Dexter took up his own invitation 'it is not going to happen. Cuba, Grenada and now Jamaica is unacceptable – who the fuck do they think they are. Our backyard and it's beginning to look like Eastern Europe – don't they realise we control things down here. So let me reiterate my original comment – the PNP will not form the next government and you guys are the ones who are going to stop that happening.'

Mitch, George and Wynton expected nothing less from Dexter. They were in total agreement – a new and exciting challenge is how they saw it.

'Now for the easy bit – just how in the world do we do it?' Dexter sat back and waited for a response.

Mitch was first in trying to clarify some of the issues. 'I reckon military action is out of the question. Carter will not sanction it – am I right Dexter?'

'Correct. I should have briefed you on that. I spoke to the President's military adviser and they are not going to put that option to the President. They have given a green light to covert operations because they do not want this socialist revolution gaining any more traction. Some in Washington are hopping mad nothing was done about Grenada. Grenada has focused opinion on the need to do something. So apart from an invasion all options are open.'

Again Mitch sought clarification 'do we presume our links with the anti-Cuban terrorist groups remain a secret?'

'Correct. If we use them on Red Snapper then it must remain so. I think we need their manpower – they'll be happy to have a go but we need to keep full control. You know my big fear with that gang is they use our operation to settle old scores and then the operation is compromised. We have to keep control whatever we decide. We also need them to cover our ass as they say.'

Mitch, the most experienced of the quartet, was rising to the challenge with growing enthusiasm 'who are you putting in charge of Red Snapper?'

'Wynton', replied Dexter. ' I have discussed it with George and it's time he was given the responsibility. This is his operational area – he has the network but he will need our full and total support. Is everyone OK with that?'

Mitch nodded his agreement. 'I am in total agreement – providing he finds me an active role. I would like to sail off into retirement with one more notch on the belt.'

Wynton had been given advance notice of the proposed appointment and therefore was keen to express his appreciation 'thanks Mitch. I will be delighted if I can use your experience – whether just to bounce an idea off or to lead some mission.'

As Wynton's supervisor, George was keen to make sure a clearly defined action-plan and timetable was agreed. That all four were singing from the same hymn sheet as it were. 'Based on what we know as fact I have four suggestions. The first is we need to understand the supply chain for the weapons flowing into Jamaica, where they are originating from, who is transporting them, what is happening to them once they are landed in Jamaica and then we set about destroying the set up including the paymaster and recovering the guns.'

George waited for a response but none was forthcoming.

'The second is to ramp up the propaganda war. We need to discredit Manley and the PNP. I hear what you say they are doing a good job in discrediting themselves but they are managing to deflect blame onto outside interference. We need to hit them closer to home to make sure that the blame sticks to them. We need to expose them for the useless bastards they are even if we have to help them make an even bigger mess of their economy. As Nixon once said let's make their economy scream.'

George paused again both to let the idea sink in and give an opportunity for comment.

Dexter responded 'this propaganda, or should I say news stories, have got to find their way into the international press. It's got to make those in positions of influence at the IMF and World Bank think twice about extending loans to Jamaica. The terms of any new loans have got to be renegotiated. We have got to give our friends the ammunition to put the boot in.'

'Good point' said George. 'The next thing we need to do is to nullify this cultural delegation. Our interpretation of events so far is this group will recruit and train a paramilitary force in the event the election doesn't go their way. If they continue to underfund the army and police force the way they are doing, forcing them to stay off the streets and remain in the barracks, it will only take a group of a few hundred trained men to take control of key establishments. They need to be taken out. We also reckon that this group will be active in the townships changing the minds of voters so we need to get in there and change their minds back again'

'And your fourth point George?' asked Mitch.

'We need to get Carter to lift this ban on anti-Castro groups operating out of Miami. We are going to need them on this operation and they are going to question why they should stick their necks out for us. We will remind them of course but they are going to be a damned sight more enthusiastic if we could get Carter off their backs. Somehow we have got to blow this Castro/Carter relationship wide open and expose it for what it is. We need to keep our ears to the ground and eyes wide open for every opportunity.'

The off-shore wind was beginning to increase in intensity and the captain popped his head round the cabin door suggesting they should start their return journey.

Dexter was only too pleased to call a halt. 'Thank you for a most productive meeting. Planning and implementation of Red Snapper has now passed to Wynton. We meet as and when with George, despite my better judgement, still in charge of venues. Monitoring, procurement and funding the operation are with George based on Wynton's requisitions. I will brief Washington on what we want them to know.'

CHAPTER 13

Wynton had achieved his ambition - operational control of a major assignment - one to roll back socialist expansion in the Caribbean. A demonstration to the rest of the region Castro's influence stops here and now.

 Wynton needed time to think. Time to plan and select his team. He needed time to erect firewalls to protect his back and where to position blame if things went wrong. But time was not on his side. Dismantling a well established arms supply route, raising the stakes in the propaganda war, changing [or protecting] the hearts and minds of Jamaican voters and all the time looking for the opportunity to discredit Carter were non-trivial challenges. His appointment was a massive vote of confidence in him by Dexter Broadbent and George T Rosenberg. It was his biggest opportunity to date and one that would surely put him one step closer to the directorship he so strongly coveted. Failure would result in career stagnation or worse.

 He shared his plans and details of his operational team with his boss George T Rosenberg. George was regarded by the organisation as a 'safe pair of hands'. There was nothing flamboyant or unpredictable about him - his dress sense was smart conservative – his voice calm and reassuring. It was only when you got closer did you get a feel there might be something deeper. He wore a swept back wig of black hair and his piercing blue eyes were set in a face scarred by severe burns only partly hidden by a carefully groomed grey beard. George had been a USAF fighter pilot who came off second best with his Korean adversary. No one really knew what effect the experience had on George's personality.

They agreed to sign off the operational plans of Red Snapper with a meal at a local upmarket steak bar. The private seating booths made it a favourite with spooks and adulterers.

'I think you have done a thorough job in interpreting the brief. There is nothing I want to add at this stage - you have gone through all the due processes. You perhaps jumped the gun a bit in sending Mitch to Jamaica but it was the right decision.' George was keen to endorse his junior's plans – he wanted to send him on his way knowing he was in full and total agreement. If things went wrong he would stand behind him – that's what Bonesmen did – they would find a way of shifting blame.

'I appreciate that George and thanks for sponsoring me for Red Snapper.' Wynton was genuinely grateful for his superior's support.

'May I give you a word of advice? You will be using the resources of Roberto Santos. Roberto is a medical doctor and runs the Miramar Medical Centre, came over to the US in 1959 and has been running a number of anti-Castro operations. He has a number of good men working for him – you've met Joaquin. Dexter keeps tight control over him and pays him generously. The thing to remember is we both have our own agendas – most of the time they overlap but just occasionally they become mutually exclusive. Just be on your guard when you are dealing with him.' George had experience of working with the Miami based anti-Castro brigade and had learned some valuable lessons about loyalty. In this business expanded relationships meant betrayal was but a matter of time.

'Roberto will fund all the activities that involve the Cuban's or any others operating outside the law through the Miramar Medical Centre. Dexter has sufficient firewalls in place to protect us so no need to worry on that score. You will need to draw up a list of your equipment needs and we will supply these through our locally based business operations – I will arrange all payments through appropriate bank accounts in the First Flagler National.' George concluded the meeting by wishing his protégé good luck and disappeared rather urgently into the waiting car parked outside the restaurant. He didn't like to keep his wife waiting.

This final meeting with George was the culmination of a series of briefing and brainstorming sessions with experts who had succeeded and failed in similar operations. The CIA regarded itself as a learning organisation and knew there was much to learn from failure as well as success. Where there was clarity and all alternatives evaluated and rejected, Wynton acted. He didn't wait for final approval – he took considered and calculated risks.

CHAPTER 14

Mitch Randall was now stationed at a CIA safe house in Devon Place, off Devon Road, Kingston – number 10 to be precise. Many apartments were rented out to expats by Jamaicans living in Miami or further afield with rents paid in dollars or sterling direct into overseas bank accounts. Expats came and went with regularity as few expats would risk renting a house in Kingston or the suburbs.

The only feature that distinguished number 10 from the other apartments was a 12 foot radio antennae extending above a rear facing bedroom window. Few, if any, would connect the comings and goings at number 10 with an ambitious plan to return Jamaica to a free-market liberal democracy!

Number 10 was one of a three-sided block of 12 apartments with a central swimming pool encased by poinsettia bushes, sweet almond trees, fig trees, bougainvillea and rambling hibiscus and would have been worth a small fortune if located on any other island. The apartments consisted of two bedrooms with en-suites separated by a large lounge opening through French windows onto a patio protected on three sides, floor to ceiling by iron railings. The latest must have – your own personal prison.

Wynton had decided to visit Jamaica to get a feel of the place, to understand the geography and the mood of the people. To see for himself the alleged deprivations – the queues for petrol, the empty supermarket shelves – the line of people outside the American embassy. There was no substitute for personal observation.

His plane was a mere 38 minutes late which excused the pilot from offering an apology. Thirty eight was well within the 'on-time' slot. His 'red plated' registered taxi dropped him in the open car park at the front of the apartment block. He paid off his driver in US dollars because he forgot to buy Jamaican dollars at the airport. The taxi driver didn't complain. US dollars went a lot further than a non-tradable currency.

He watched a pack of five wild dogs trot purposefully through the car park, cross the road and smell the bloated carcass of a dog that must have lain untouched for days. Lawlessness and unsolved crimes had clearly encroached on the canine world.

He nodded to the security guard lounging half asleep or half spaced out on the front steps, bounded up the carpeted steps to the first floor and knocked at number 10. He could have been Attilla the Hun accompanied by Coco the Clown and doubted whether the guard's reaction would have been any more inquiring. Though there was always the outside chance that's precisely who he saw approaching!

'Welcome to Kingston, Wynton. This your first trip here?'

'Hi Mitch, no just the odd business trip here and there, I have stayed at Montego Bay many years ago when I was a student. A few of us flew out for a golfing break but we didn't stray far from the north coast.'

Mitch got his guest a Red Stripe and they sauntered out on to the patio overlooking the swimming pool where a beautiful dark-haired English lady was watching her toddler playing with a tennis racquet. The racquet was the height of the toddler and he struggled gamely to bat jets of water ejected randomly from a garden sprinkler. Two minutes of this and a screaming tantrum developed stopped instantly by a swift change of scene – a three foot drop into the pool. Equilibrium and peace had been restored by the fast thinking mother.

Three years off enforced retirement at 60 made Mitch Randall 59 – he had consistently lied about his age. 5' 8", tanned, the physical shape of a professional sportsman suggested a man even at that age should not be messed with. Shorts and T-shirt promoting the Ganja University completed his informal appearance. Divorced twice and outside of active duty lived a lonely life. No children or close family to care about – a price many covert specialists had to pay for their life of secrecy, danger and extravagance. He was fearful of very little but very fearful of retirement – as he saw it a life without focus or reason – a dark abyss from which there was no escape except death. He responded as enthusiastically as ever when Wynton asked him to take control of the operation to stop the supply of arms to Jamaica.

'I'm here to get a feel for the place. Up to now I have had to rely on Carlton's reports. It's too risky for me to meet up with him here - I just have this doubt about what happened to the Thai. I do not doubt Carlton's version of events but maybe there is something he isn't telling us. OK Mitch – where are we up to?' enquired Wynton, keeping his eye on the lady below.

'I have hired two contract employees, ex Jamaican Defence Force. We have employed them before. Both are living in Miami legally, dual passports and extensive family connections in Negril and Spanish Town. They know the island like the back of their hand. Both appear to have an exemplary military record which means they have effectively avoided official reprimands for drug dealing and blackmail. They are experts in covert operations and excel in unarmed combat and wouldn't think twice about sticking a knife in a Cuban. Both families now live in Miami, one or two working illegally, so we can exert pressure if needed.'

'And their role?' queried Wynton.

'Intelligence from Cuba indicates two shipments of arms and equipment every three weeks - one by fast speed boat and one by light aircraft. They have identified a pattern – shipments by sea come in late on a Friday evening and by air very early on a Monday morning. Shipments are suspended for rain and wind – clearly not taking any risks – if a shipment is suspended it is reinstated seven days later and so on. They are obviously keen to minimise radio traffic. They know we are monitoring radio broadcasts from Cuba. Photographs show at least two different boats – a 44 foot Trojan cabin cruiser and 36 foot yacht – a Trojan tri-cabin job both with high powered auxiliary motors and three light aircraft – a Cessna 172 Sky Hawk with 160 hp engine, Cessna Hawk XP with 195 hp engine and a Piper Turbo –Twin Comanche – proof of high level complicity to run this kind of show. What we don't know is their landing sites. These aircraft have been specially selected because they can land and take off from a possum's arse. We are assuming several landing points to avoid anyone noticing a pattern.'

'Clever bastards – they've thought this operation through. Border controls and customs agencies are still very active trying to combat drug shipments from Columbia but if they come across an arms shipment it could seriously embarrass the PNP. The JLP would cry foul and possibly move to have the election postponed or the military steps in with a State of Emergency. So what are your next steps?' asked Wynton closely monitoring the lady downstairs.

'The two guys, Ebenezer and Christian, sound like a couple of travelling evangelicals, are mapping all possible landing sites. We then commission our friends at Miami University to position their Marine Biology Deep Water Research vessel mid way between Cuba and Jamaica and on a given signal start tracking suspect craft. We have been given four weeks use of the research vessel to track at least two consignments. They have the latest in radar and surveillance equipment and as soon as they have a flight path they can project this onto known landing sites and radio off the coordinates.

'Who's the lady downstairs?' asked Wynton nonchalantly.

'She and her husband moved in about four months ago. I met them at a drinks party at No. 6. He is over from the UK on secondment from some university. Apparently works in some export development capacity. They have two other kids – both go to Priory School just up the road. I need to keep track of who's moving into the block and a party is as good a way as any.'

'Anyone else we should know about?' enquired Wynton.

'Not really. Mainly expats on short term contracts with the exception of Wilson at No.2. Condemned to spend the rest of his life here as apparently he is a deserter – he cannot return to the UK. He offers all newcomers a pistol to keep under their pillow. He is quite a character but not a threat.' Mitch had spent a couple of interesting evenings with Wilson. 'He came home the other night with three bullet holes in the roof of his car. What intrigued me was the holes had been made by bullets fired from within – jagged edges of metal were sticking upwards. When I asked what had happened he told me there had been some kind of industrial dispute on the estate where he works. It started to get ugly and the strikers started climbing and jumping on the roof of his car so he calmly fired off three warning shots - worked a treat apparently.'

Wynton had stopped listening and was now staring vacantly at the scene below. He had fathered a child whilst at Yale on a Spring Breaker at Key West – a secret he had kept from his parents. It was not what he wanted from life but he didn't walk away – he secretly and generously provided for his son. The boy's mother went on to be an interpreter at the UN – she decided very early on in her pregnancy that she didn't want any involvement with the father. In one respect this suited Wynton – if it ever emerged some way down the line that he had an illegitimate son, political rivals would play havoc with his moral principles. But on the other hand he struggled with his conscience - he desperately wanted his son to know who is father was. For the time being personal ambition was just edging out his parental responsibility. The sight below was a sad reminder of how life might have been.

'And what are your plans after that?'

'We identify as many landing sites as we can. Once we know one is on its way we use predicted map coordinates from the ship to target possible places. We will have located the best hiding places on all possible sites and simply monitor the action. We will then pick one shipment and follow it – expecting it to go to Kingston. This is where Ebenezer and Christian come into play – hopefully they can pick up the routes once they hit the townships – they have contacts and will have money to open mouths and guns to close them if necessary.'

Wynton had confidence in Mitch and reckoned he could safely leave this part of the operation in his hands. 'And just where are you up to now?'

'Landing strips are the easy bit. We have three potentials. We reckon they will pick the shortest route and therefore we are looking at the north of the island. Flying round the island or over the mountains adds uncertainty and risk. We reckon they have been using the straight bit of road from Discovery Bay to Duncans. It is regularly used by drug smugglers and quite a few didn't make it - wrecked aircraft litter the fields. These are light drops – probably military uniforms, other clothing, tents etc. The plane doesn't stop – someone just heaves the stuff out. Heavy arms shipments will come by boat and they will need somewhere where they can get transport very close to the off loading point.'

 Mitch showed no resentment working for his comparatively inexperienced and younger boss – he'd had his opportunities but recognised years ago his preference was for hands on. He was happy to let others do the planning providing they let him get on with the job.

'What I do need guidance on is when do we act? The amount of weapons they are bringing suggests they are not all finding their way into the townships. What would be the point – frightening ordinary men and women doesn't need that kind of arsenal. The uniforms suggest they are building for something special – a possible military takeover if the election doesn't go the way they want.' Mitch was interested to see how his boss would react to this bit of scenario planning.

'You make a valid point. We do not want to show our hand too soon – we need to know what is happening to the weapons. If they are storing them we need to know where. About six to eight weeks before the election I expect they will increase the frequency of these shipments. This is when I want you to take out one of the transporters – make it look like an accident with no survivors. Make them think but give them nothing to point the finger at us.'

Mitch was warming to Wynton – his thoughts exactly. 'There will come a time when we need to put these weapons beyond use and take out the Cuban artists and musicians. What are your plans on that issue?'

'I don't have any plans worked out yet. The weapons will be your task. Eliminating the Cubans will require a bigger team. I am discussing options with George.' Wynton was not prepared to disclose the fact he hadn't found a solution to that problem.

Mitch was happy with his clear set of operational orders. He had been given the freedom to act as he saw fit and the tasks ahead were well within his comfort zone.

The balcony of number 10 both overlooked the swimming pool and a large block of expensive and well maintained apartments opposite. The apartments were home to senior foreign diplomats and leader of the opposition Jamaican Labour Party - a curious name for a right wing political party. The place was heavily guarded by armed police with attack dogs.

 Almost every night you could expect the still blackness to be shattered by the arrival of a Jamaican Defence Force helicopter with powerful searchlights seeking out something or someone. The balcony of number 10 provided a grandstand view to observe. You rarely found out what was happening unless there was a gunfight, a body and a brief news item in the Gleaner.

Most occupants of the apartments of Devon Place spent their evenings on their balconies – chatting, entertaining other residents, reading, playing cards or backgammon, and drinking, with privacy protected by the droning sound of air conditioning units. Marylyn and Martin, from number 4, were constantly on the lookout for new Bridge partners or those with the potential to be trained up. Smoke from mosquito coils drifted in the still evening air.

Mitch and Wynton shared a bottle of light rum together with half a crate of Red Stripe as they sat into the early hours talking through the different options and risk factors. It was hard to connect the peaceful tranquillity of the scene with the barbarity of the violence being perpetrated daily within the townships of Kingston.

Wynton's original plans included a quick walk about in downtown Kingston but Mitch talked him out of it. He suggested their time would be better spent surveying suspected landing sites on the north coast and for Wynton to spend a night at the Intercontinental Hotel at Ocho Rios. Mitch had work to do and didn't want to be burdened with his boss watching his every move. Wynton could take the hotels' courtesy airport shuttle to Montego Bay for his flight back to Miami.

Next morning, the sun casting long early shadows across the car park, the two set off in Mitch's hired white Honda Accord. Imported cars carried with them a 100% import duty and therefore new models were both rare and expensive. Owners of new cars fell into three categories – local politicians, diplomatic staff, which were expected to remove their duty free car when their tour of duty was over, and drug dealing or gun running criminals. There was a good chance the Honda Accord had been illegally sold on by a departing diplomat eager to capitalise on a market where demand was far in excess of supply.

'We'll start with our cultural friends. I have driven past a couple of times but there is little to see - just the name above a double shop front in a three storey block and a few window posters of Fidel Castro. It never seems to be open for any kind of business. There are a number of locked shipping containers at the back of the building which must belong to them.'

Coming out of Devon Road they turned left onto Waterloo Road. 'I presume that's where Carlton spends some of his time working on his export development strategy' said Mitch laughing as he pointed out the export department of the Ministry of Foreign Affairs. A delightful colonial style single storey white painted wooden building shaded by Lime and Avocado trees. An unoccupied gatehouse and raised security barrier suggested security was not an issue.

From Waterloo Road they carried on into Trafalgar Road and then a right down Old Hope Road. 'That's Bob Marley's house. Do you notice the smoke drifting over the wall? I picture half a dozen Rastafarians in black, yellow, green and red hats squatting in the garden, drifting off into a world of peace and tranquillity.'

'Maybe they should try exporting their religion instead of drugs' commented Wynton.

'I'm afraid they go together – you can't get to this world of peace and tranquillity without the ganja.'

As they entered downtown Kingston windows were checked and doors locked. It was not unknown for opportunists to open doors and snatch what they could when cars stopped at traffic lights. Windscreens were washed whether they needed it or not by the homeless kids looking to make a few cents whilst others used the opportunity to sell copies of The Star or Gleaner or packets of roasted peanuts. There was never a dull moment when you drove into downtown Kingston.

Close to the waterfront they turned right onto Marcus Garvey Drive and Mitch slowed down to point out the HQ of the Cuban Education and Cultural Delegation, the name blazoned above the shop front in the red, white and blue colours of the Cuban flag. There was no external activity but Mitch knew surveillance cameras would be in operation and any observers would be quickly noticed. Two white males would raise questions and further investigations would follow. Kingston was a small town. Even the kids at the traffic lights knew where you lived. Mitch didn't hang about.

They continued along Marcus Garvey Drive until they reached Spanish Town and then took the grandiosely named A1 road towards Ocho Rios. They passed through Bog Walk – a colourful and vibrant ramshackle country village. Heavily built women in their pink and white silk blouses and green cotton skirts carrying straw baskets laden with fruit on their heads and donkeys with bulging straw panniers crammed full with other merchandise suggested market day.

Wooden shops lined the centre of Bog Walk - Beverley's Record Den 'for the latest in local and foreign hits', next door a Rastafarian rum bar blasting out Reggae rhythms, painted in vertical red, green, yellow and black stripes trying to visually correct a 30 degree lean, next door to open wooden stalls selling straw hats and wooden carvings designed to appeal to passing tourists and finally next door to another rum bar proudly promoting 120 percent rum and Guinness. Each window or doorway had its own resting resident in place uniquely shaped and moulded to fit the opening whilst keeping a watchful eye on proceedings.

At the end of the village were enticing displays of fruits and vegetables: grapefruit, lemons, oranges, green and yellow bananas, small and large bananas, cho cho, callalu, paw paw, bread fruit and root vegetables. The colourful pageant was interrupted only by the burnt out rusting wrecks of wheel less vehicles. This was another example of Jamaica's contradictions and unforgettable landscapes.

From Bog Walk they drove to Ewarton where the gravel verge, road surface and embankments turned red from dusty spillage leaking out of the Alcan bauxite mining operation. Just beyond Ewarton they pulled in at a series of roadside food vendors.

'You must try this Wynton – corn on the cob cooked in Manish water.'

'And what's Manish water?

'Don't be put off but it contains goat's testicles. A local delicacy.'

'You serious?'

'Take my word for it. You will never ever taste sweet corn like this. Also try these small bananas – they don't grow them on the plantations just on a few small holdings – they taste wonderful. And then finish off with a handful of Ginnips – just for the experience.'

Unlike Kingston the locals were friendly – happy to make a sale – willing to stand and talk. But life was hard – Michael Manley and the international press had done a good job in reducing the number of European and American tourists.

They continued on their way driving around the tight corners of a road brutally carved out the side of the mountain. Overhanging fragile looking rock formations and unprotected precipitous drops cut conversation for a while before the road settled into the four miles of dried up river bed winding through Fern Gully. The sides of the gulley were covered in tall ferns, allegedly over 500 different varieties, and the overhanging trees blocking out much of the sunlight to create an eerie mid-day vista. Narrow shards of sunlight pierced the gloom creating the ideal cover for the occasional tourist car-jacking and robberies. A fallen tree across the road nonchalantly being observed by a small group of bystanders was the signal to put the car into reverse and get the hell out of it.

'Before I drive you to your hotel I want you to take a look at this area. It's a stretch of coast line between Rio Bueno and Discovery Bay. Apparently Columbus and I share the same opinion – this is an ideal place to land a boat. This is our number one candidate for an off-loading point for their speed boats. Natural harbours, hidden caves to hide a boat if the need arises, a fair number of pleasure craft so another boat wouldn't look out of place, beach hidden from the main road and paths that could handle pick-ups or similar vehicles.'

They parked their car at Columbus Park and took a casual stroll along the beach and when the beach disappeared climbed the cliffs to get a panoramic view of the bay.

'If it's like this all along this coast then there must be literally hundreds of different options' mused Wynton. 'You have to admit this place is stunning.' Wynton took time to embrace the magnificence of the scenery – the white sands, the limestone rocks, the palm trees and dense green vegetation all ringed by the gentle lapping waters of the Caribbean. Here was one idyllic illusion of paradise.

'We have mapped this area and identified our surveillance point. As soon as we are ready to start operations we will be stationed over this side of the island. A radio message will give us the predicted map coordinates and then we will take up our position to observe. Our main task is to tail the consignment – we are expecting a journey into a PNP controlled township or some secure storage depot – it may be as simple as the shipping containers on Marcus Garvey Drive. It doesn't matter whether it's a consignment by sea or air – as long as we can pinpoint the destination.' Mitch was keen to reassure his boss he had the operation under control so he could safely leave him to get on with it.

Wynton was indeed satisfied with Mitch's operational planning and had decided it was time to leave. 'OK Mitch – drop me at the Inter Continental. I will fly back to Miami tomorrow. I need to meet with our Cuban friend and others but I also need to make sense of what is happening in Cuba. '

Wynton had made the assessment this part of the operation was self contained. Providing Mitch put the armaments and whatever else was coming in beyond use then he would have done his job. His presence on the island was not secret but there was no reason to advertise the fact to any other operational arm. He would however serve as a useful back-up should other parts of the Red Snapper operation go belly-up. Wynton was happy Mitch was part of his team.

CHAPTER 15

'Come quickly' Maria shouted as she ran half dressed on to the sun deck beside their palm shaded swimming pool. 'Something bad is happening in Cuba.'

The sound and tone of her voice was sufficient to alarm Roberto and he quickly pulled himself on to the patio and ran to his wife. 'What has happened?'

'Manuel has just telephoned. He says people are rioting and hundreds have broken into the Peruvian Embassy. This is only a few hundred yards from our home in Miramar, Roberto. What can have happened?'

'I don't know. I find this hard to understand. Castro doesn't allow people to gather, even in small numbers and what have the Peruvians to do with anything?' Roberto was struggling to make sense of the information. His wife was not prone to exaggeration but she was clearly distraught – she still longed to return to her home and she still had friends and some distant relatives. Her parents died in 1975 and she struggled daily to suppress the thought of them dying isolated and alone. She bitterly resented both the American and Cuban politicians who wreaked so much anguish and hurt on the lives of ordinary people caught up in their ideological war. The news from Cuba raised her spirits that it just might lead to the chance of returning one more time to say her goodbyes.

'I told Manuel that you would be going to the medical centre and for him to meet you there if he has further news. He is in touch with his contacts in Havana but they don't know what is happening either. That is all he could tell me.'

Roberto tuned into the local Miami based Cuban radio stations Radio Mambi and Radio WQBA and found the airwaves full of the news. Small additional snippets of news were being added, such as the death of a Cuban soldier added to the growing tension. Roberto's mind was beginning to speculate – was Castro dead – was this the beginning of the end of his hated regime or was it merely the beginning of a more draconian crackdown on dissidents?

Both Maria and he were scheduled to be on duty at the medical centre and wasted no time in driving the 20 miles from their Coral Gables mansion. Traffic was no heavier than usual and no visible sign the news was disturbing the hectic normality of Little Havana.

On arrival they were met by their Cuban security guard, Luciano. He had been a loyal employee of the Miramar Medical Centre for over 15 years and always looked to Roberto for help. He was clearly agitated and yanked the driver's door open immediately the car had stopped. 'What is happening Doctor Roberto – tell me please?'

'Calm down Luciano please. All I know is the same you are hearing on your radio. I will call the staff together after the morning appointments. I am hoping to have more news by then. Until then can I please ask you to continue with your duties? They are important.' Roberto tried his best to reassure Luciano and the others who had just turned up for work and joined the conversation.

Roberto and Maria had made a decision to complete the morning appointments but to get the centre's medical secretary to try and cancel the afternoon list unless they were urgent. They would under no circumstance refuse help to anyone with a critical medical condition. The Miramar Medical Centre was more than a doctor's surgery – it was a focal point for the exiles. It was a place that provided moral and social support to vulnerable and isolated families. The Centre also provided the perfect cover for Roberto's clandestine anti-Castro activities.

At approximately 14:00 hours Wednesday 1st April Manuel and Joaquin visited the Miramar Medical Centre. Roberto was reassuring the mother of a small child her high temperature was due to an ear infection. He was gently guiding the mother through the reception area and into the street and promising her the prescription of an anti-biotic would solve the problem in a few days. The lady didn't have time to question Roberto as she found herself gently pushed on to the street with the door closed and bolted behind her.

'Let's meet in my office' he ushered Manuel and Joaquin in and summoned Maria to join them.

Joaquin wasted no time on preliminaries 'what we know is a mini bus was driven through the gates of the Peruvian Embassy yesterday morning at about 8:30 a.m. with 6 of our countrymen on board claiming political asylum. This is not the first time. The soldiers guarding the embassy opened fire and, please remember these facts have been passed from person to person, one soldier was killed. Who by, we don't know. Castro demanded the Peruvians hand over the 6 Cubans to stand trial for his murder but the ambassador, Ernesto Pinto- Bazurco, refused. Castro then threatened to remove his guards from the embassy entrance and it is our understanding he did so yesterday. This morning hundreds of Cubans are just walking into the grounds of the Peruvian Embassy and claiming diplomatic asylum.'

Manuel interjected 'Radio Mambi and Radio WQBA are broadcasting more or less the same story. We are getting our information direct from Cuba and so far the two seem fairly consistent. Nobody knows who shot the guard.'

At that moment the phone rang. It pierced the tension and Roberto snatched the phone off its cradle, dropping it in the process. 'Yes' he barked.

'Dexter Broadbent here, what the fuck is going on in Havana? Is Castro dead?'

Roberto would have dearly loved to tell Dexter where to go. He was not in the mood for Dexter Broadbent. The two spoke when necessary but it was Dexter who set up the whole financial scam with Medicare that gave Roberto his lifestyle, his legitimacy and his power. And it was Dexter that could bring the whole deck of cards crashing down around him. But the one positive characteristic Dexter was credited with was his directness – no messing about – straight to the point.

'Good morning Dexter. I take it you have heard the news?' trying to interject a professional calmness into the conversation.

'Of course I have heard the fucking news but I need you to tell me what is really going on.'

'We are fairly certain Castro is not dead – sadly. Hundreds of people are walking into the Peruvian Embassy this morning claiming diplomatic asylum. That is all I can tell you. I have people hammering at my door asking for news about friends and relatives' Roberto exaggerated as a way of convincing Dexter that he was telling the truth.

'I smell one fat fucking rat. Castro doesn't let people walk freely of their own mind into an alien embassy. We've been in touch with the Peruvian Ambassador in Washington and they are playing it by the book. Granting everyone who asks for it diplomatic asylum. The world has gone mad.' Dexter exclaimed in a rare conciliatory tone – suggesting he accepted Roberto's explanation.

Dexter continued 'Castro has got to respond to this and I am very unclear what his options are. CNN and BBC World News have picked up on it and he must understand the world spotlight is on him. You and Wynton need to be talking and be ready to act whichever way Castro responds. This might impact on Red Snapper and we need to be ready.' Dexter concluded the conversation by slamming the phone down.

'You heard the great man' Roberto sighed sarcastically. 'His tone suggests the CIA is not behind it for once. He must be awfully disappointed 6 ordinary Cubans have caused this much panic – much more than he has been able to do for some considerable time. There is nothing more we can do but listen and keep in very close contact. I need to speak to the staff now.'

The response of the staff was a mixture of heady excitement and fearful trepidation all fuelled by a great uncertainty. All were allowed home with the exception of Luciano – crime didn't sleep in Little Havana.

Roberto and Maria also returned home. They monitored Radio Mambi broadcasts throughout the night and continued with their nightly vigil until the 6th April – Easter Sunday. They continued to receive regular bulletins from Manuel and as the evening wore on the news became more alarming – the hundreds had grown to thousands. Word of such an event as this was obviously spreading across the country. The information was suggesting the embassy had become so crowded people were climbing trees within the grounds just so they could claim asylum.

'What must conditions be like in the embassy Roberto? The embassy was smaller than our house – remember we used to go there for cocktails. It's hard to imagine 500 let alone thousands.' Maria couldn't sleep because of the tension and the fear of how Castro might react.

Then a message came so unexpected and so unbelievable that Maria and Roberto just stared at each other. They asked Manuel to repeat it. As soon as the phone was replaced it rang again- it was Dexter Broadbent 'Just what the fuck is happening in Havana?'

'For Christ's sake Dexter I got to hear a rumour I can neither believe nor understand just sixty seconds a go. I don't know what to think. Can you believe Castro has said those who want to leave Cuba can do so? Well neither can I.' Obviously Dexter was just as incredulous.

'Well get on to it – get your friends on to the streets – find out how are they expected to leave – can we use this as cover to do some damage? I need answers Roberto.' This was Dexter's subtle way of saying it's time to earn your money. And again his subtlety was demonstrated by a crash as he replaced his receiver.

As soon as Roberto replaced his phone it rang again 'it's true Roberto. Castro has issued some edict telling people to get out of the country, Cuba doesn't want them. It's not just those seeking diplomatic asylum – it appears to be an open invitation for anyone who wants to leave. Anyone wishing to leave has to travel to the Port of Mariel providing there is someone there who can transport them to wherever they want to go. He is definitely not laying on the transport.' Roberto kept asking Manuel to repeat his message, asking him to explain how he got the information and asking him if he could trust his source.

Maria ran into the room 'Radio Mambi is broadcasting the same – people are free to go. Can you believe it?' Tears of joy were running down her face.

CHAPTER 16

Six weeks to the day after the bus crashed through the perimeter walls of the Peruvian Embassy Roberto convened a meeting with Joaquin and Manuel at his home in Coral Gables.

'Over 60,000 have left Cuba in the last six weeks. We have funded three round trips and helped 67 people escape. Our fat friend has charged us $10,000 dollars – not a bad return for 3 days work. I believe we have helped all of our friends and relatives who wanted to leave but there are still thousands turning up at Mariel. I am now of the opinion the time has come for us to call a halt.'

This shocked Joaquin and Manuel – they had felt a strong moral duty to do what they could to help their countrymen.

'Is it a question of money Roberto?'

'No. Let me give you the facts that have been relayed to me by Dexter. Castro was incensed so many of his supposedly loyal supporters wanted to leave his beloved Cuba. He has started to demonise them – he calls them scum, social deviants, parasites, counterrevolutionaries and criminals. His officials and party activists have started attacking the families and homes of those who have left or want to leave. Castro's official press have published detailed reports about the criminal elements behind the exodus and keeps referring to them as Marielitos [little people from Mariel]. He is setting out to create the impression anyone who wants to leave Cuba is a criminal, a prostitute or a homosexual. He wants to brand all Cuban exiles in this way.'

'So what if he calls them names. Who cares what Castro thinks? Nobody is going to believe that in Miami' responded Manuel.'

'Unfortunately that is precisely what is happening in Miami. It is the Cubans in Miami who have made a good life for themselves who are concerned the Marielitos are tarnishing their image. There is no doubt they are different to those of us who left at the time of the Revolution. They tend to be the unemployed or working class, most of them are black and it is absolutely proven beyond doubt Castro is loading the boats with hardened criminals and mental patients. Prostitutes and homosexuals are being actively encouraged to leave. The crime rate in down town Miami has started to soar.'

'Can you believe Dexter Broadbent?' queried Joaquin.

'Surprisingly on this occasion I do and the reason is Dexter is in a position to see the bigger picture. A few thousand of the unsponsored Marielitos were sent to Fort Chaffee in Arkansas for processing. They resented being temporarily locked up and decided to start a riot, injured a number of the prison guards and caused millions of dollars of damage. This was given nation-wide news coverage. The popularity of the Governor, the democrat Bill Clinton, plummeted and it is very doubtful that he will be re-elected as Governor of Arkansas. So it is having some very profound political effects' replied Roberto.

'I think I know where you are going with this. Going back to our last meeting one of our objectives was to do what we could to discredit Jimmy Carter and get him to drop his support for Castro' mused Joaquin.

'You have it in one. We have our very own moral dilemma – do we help our fellow countrymen to get out of Cuba or do we use the opportunity of the Mariel exodus to get Carter to drop his support for Castro and stop him interfering in our activities.'

Silence descended on the trio. It didn't take Joaquin too long to formulate an opinion. '60,000 and counting is going to create a whole host of problems here in Miami. Where are they going to live? What effect will it have on the labour market? The local blacks are not going to take too kindly to them, that's for sure. Hardened criminals are not going to change a lifetime of habits. I agree we stop funding any more rescue missions but what can we do about the hundreds of other boat owners making the trip?

'Nothing. They are going to keep on picking up anyone who wants to leave until the whole thing blows up. It's an embarrassment for Carter and Castro. But what it can do is help get rid of Carter in the next presidential election. This is our big opportunity to drop Carter in the shit. The electorate won't forgive him for this.'

Manuel was not convinced 'you are suggesting we betray our own? We walk away; we deny them the opportunity of a new life, an opportunity we have fully benefited from.'

'I've struggled long and hard with this too Manuel. We all have more to gain in the longer term if we can find a way of getting rid of Castro and I just think this is one of those situations that might help us achieve that.'

'OK, what does it mean if I go along with you?' asked Manuel, clearly angry and uncomfortable with what was emerging.

'Dexter is prepared to pay very handsomely for any negative stories that feed the impression the Marielitos are causing havoc in Miami. These stories will not be connected to us in any way but will find their way into the media. The aim is to discredit Carter. An election is coming up and we can help both ourselves and the Republicans.' Roberto didn't try to disguise the brutal reality of the proposition. He had been friends with Manuel too long to attempt to mislead him.

'So not only are we turning our backs on them we are now setting out to actually destroy them.' Manuel was getting very close to losing his temper with Roberto – the very first time he had felt this level of anger with Roberto.,

'That is unfair, we have done a lot to help our countrymen as you very well know' Roberto could only sympathise so far with Manuel's lofty ideals 'I am thinking about the future of Cuba and finding the best solution for all our people.'

'You have to admire the sheer audacity of the plan, the CIA funding a propaganda war against their government. I have to admit when you see it in those terms the scheme has merit. If we can continue to help those who have arrived to find homes and jobs than I'll go along with it. If we can use some of the money we get from Dexter to do this then I'll be happier still. If we can get Carter off our backs then what are waiting for?' Manuel was beginning to understand and understand fast the wider implications of the proposal.

Roberto added by way of a conciliatory note 'remember we can play this to our advantage. We don't have to report every criminal or subversive act – just the ones committed by the career criminals and mentally unbalanced. Our aim is to put the blame for the upsurge in crime and violence solely onto these people irrespective of who the perpetrators were. We feed the storyline there are two categories of Marielitos – those that should still be locked up in prison or mental institution and those immigrants who want to work hard and create a new life for themselves. We will have no trouble with the local Cuban press and if we stick to the story line we might just start to influence the likes of the Miami Herald. Maybe we can help protect the ordinary hardworking and honest Marielitos and deflect all the blame back on to Castro. Carter will be blamed for not vetting them more closely on arrival and for not sending back the criminals. When he made his promise to offer everyone fleeing from communism a home he certainly wasn't putting out the welcome mat for criminals, the mentally insane, hookers and homosexuals!'

Roberto and Joaquin could see the irony of it all and once again Roberto had used his natural persuasive and leadership talent to maintain the cohesiveness of the group. Manuel was almost back on an even keel. They all laughed at the potential discomfort this might cause Carter.

Roberto cautioned about getting carried away. 'It's one thing using these stories to discredit Carter but we do have to exercise some judgement otherwise we could be engineering a public backlash. We are still very much a minority group! We have just received this story which is quite horrendous. A gang of criminal Marielitos robbed a jewellery store and the whole thing was witnessed by this local white eleven year old boy. They shot him dead to stop him talking. I think this is one story we don't pass on – this is the type of news story we don't want any Cubans name attached to it.

CHAPTER 17

Four failed attempts to reconnect with Manuel almost pushed Wynton to the point of abandonment. Doubts were beginning to grow he had, perhaps, been unwise to resurrect the relationship. On what was going to be his last attempt he was taken totally by surprise when the public pay-phone anonymously announced the next meeting was on.

24 hours later, the same routine completed, Wynton was driven into the grounds of the same rundown apartment block and shown into the same building he had visited some weeks before. It did start to occur to him this building neither looked nor felt like home. He started to speculate if it was not a home then what precisely was its' function. He made a mental note to have it checked out but then recalled he had no idea where he was! He decided there and then to make it his business.

'Good to see you again my friend and apologies for not responding to your calls sooner. It took longer than expected to collect the information we needed. Cuba is crawling with informers – we have to be very careful who we deal with' Manuel explained as he ushered Wynton into the same ground floor room.

The two sat facing each other across the same wooden table. Nothing had changed – Manuel was even dressed in the same faded Guayabera shirt. It still struggled to contain his paunch and it was still showing the same frayed alforzas, missing button on the right patch pocket and a bright yellow stain on the left collar. This image registered and worried Wynton.

Manuel disturbed Wynton from his concentration 'Can I offer you a cup of coffee?' For a brief moment the rich aroma of the freshly poured coffee over powered the smell of neglect in the room.

Wynton used the Mariel boatlift as his conversation opener. Manuel replied expressing his concern as to what this might be doing to the local community – the same generalisations were being openly discussed in newspapers like the Miami Herald or broadcast on Cuban radio stations. Manuel was fully aware of the private deal that existed between Roberto and Dexter Broadbent about the flow of negative news stories and was very careful to restrict his conversation. The last thing he needed was to plant the idea in Wynton's mind that such an arrangement existed. He was however in no hurry to end the conversation – but eventually took the opportunity of a pause to move the agenda on.

'I have a number of items of information which I hope will either be new to you or provide independent corroboration of what your agents have told you. Before I start can I confirm you are still prepared to honour our agreement and make funds available in return for this information?' Manuel was not a charity – never did anything for nothing - he was a fund raiser and years before the CIA had been his biggest paymaster. It was also important for his credibility he struck his own deal with Wynton.

'Of course - we may have to negotiate based on the usefulness of the information but I would like to keep the arrangement on-going. The last thing I need right now is a dissatisfied spook.' Now Wynton was playing games, he was certain he would not want a continuing relationship. Too many doubts were cropping up about Manuel Franqui.

'Good. I'll take you at your word. Before we get down to the specifics I agree with your speculations about Jamaica. There were clear warning signs we missed. It's only when you raised the prospect did a number of other 'events' fall into place and we could begin to understand their significance.' It was now Manuel's turn to play games by inventing this imaginary background he hoped would add credence and value to his intelligence.

It was Manuel's intention to impress Wynton with his first disclosure. He was about to reveal something very few people could have known about. 'Does the name Toungtong Suphanochakul mean anything to you?

'I don't think so. It's not a name you could easily forget even if you could spell it.' Wynton struggled to connect this name with anything or anybody. 'Have you anything else to go on – is it male or female?'

'Male. From Thailand – mid thirties' replied Manuel.

This hit Wynton like a thunderbolt. He struggled both to hide his discomfort and decide how to react. This had to be Carlton's contact. 'Possibly - I say that because I have not heard the name but I am aware of a Thai national stopping over in Kingston before travelling on to Cuba for the NAM conference. Could it be they are one and the same person?'

'Very probably' responded Manuel who waited for Wynton to add further insight.

Wynton was caught off guard by this revelation. He very quickly decided he had little to lose by adding what he knew about the Thai. 'One of my men met a Thai in Kingston. He had stopped over in Kingston en route to Cuba. He saw this as a good opportunity to get information about what was going on at the conference and get copies of the speeches and discussions involving Caribbean leaders and their delegations. We needed some insights and quickly and this guy seemed to be on the inside and an ideal courier. We wanted to know what Manley was up to. He was definitely not CIA or on the books.' Wynton decided to stop there – no need to involve Carlton any more than necessary.

'Well it seems he went about his job diligently, if indeed he is the same man. As you well know all the delegates would have been shadowed - that is the nature of the regime. Let's call this man 'Toffy' to make things a bit easier for ourselves.' Manuel paused to check whether this brought any change to his guest's expression. Not detecting anything he continued, 'it seems Toffy developed an obsessive interest in all things Caribbean. He surprisingly lost all interest in the topic which one thought would have interested him the most – Kampuchea. The communists may very well invade his country at any time but all Toffy was interested in was Manley, Bishop and anyone Castro talked to.' Manuel could clearly tell his information had hit home and left his guest puzzled.

'His behaviour then became the subject of some discussion and closer attention. His minders became more and more intrusive – bedroom and personal items were searched and bugged – every conversational contact he made was scrutinised but, according to my informant, nothing out of the ordinary was found. But deep suspicions remained.' Again Manuel paused to see if the silence would draw Wynton into exposing anything.

'They alerted the Cuban delegation in Kingston and on his return to Jamaica he was tailed back to the Mayfair Hotel and that's where the story ends.' Manuel's body language clearly indicated he was not going to say anymore about the Thai at this stage of the conversation. He wanted to draw Wynton out on the topic.

'All I can add, if we are talking about the same man, he was found murdered in Kingston. The police have classified the murder as a robbery. He passed some low level intelligence on to our man in Kingston and two hours later that was it. We did our own investigation and reached the same conclusion as the police – the motive was robbery.'

'The Cuban secret police, which is twice the size of the uniformed police force, were working on a different theory – Thailand is the crossroads for major drug traffickers – much the same way Jamaica is a staging post for the movement of drugs from South America into America and Western Europe. I guess we will never find out the truth now he is dead' concluded Manuel.

Again Manuel's comment surprised him. He had never connected the crime with the drugs trade but it got Wynton thinking about Carlton and whether he had spotted an opportunity for a shady drugs deal on the side. It wouldn't have been the first.

There were now three possible reasons for Toungtong Suphanochakul's death – a straightforward robbery, poking his nose into an established drugs operation or suspicion of spying for the CIA

Manuel's disclosure whilst of little strategic value confirmed his Cuban spy network was well integrated into the political and security establishment. The quality of information about Toungtong Suphanochakul could only have been provided by someone of seniority with high level security clearance. Whoever it was, was taking a big risk. The disclosure also helped raise Manuel's credibility.

'Perhaps we will never know the truth but let us move on. In the scheme of things and with the exception of his family, Toffy's death is of little consequence to Red Snapper. This next item relates to the conference itself. We monitored the conference in exactly the same way as Toffy. Our representatives attended every session involving Castro or one of his close political allies – the likes of Manley and Bishop. Everything pointed to Manley and Castro dancing to the same rhythm. There is no need to go into detail but I can give you a full transcript of the main conference speeches as well as secretly taped discussions that took place in the break-out meetings. I am sure you have done your own analysis of the speeches but you could not reach any other conclusion than these two are working very closely together. Manley sees the Cuban model as the way to take Jamaica forward win or lose the election. This movement of theirs is gaining momentum – what Bishop did has given them a great deal of encouragement. Does that fit with your intelligence?' asked Manuel at the same time handing over a sheaf of papers and a box of cassettes.

'Very closely indeed' confirmed Wynton. He never doubted or questioned Carlton's report of the conference but there was something about Manuel's commentary disturbed him. Something was said that didn't quite fit the known facts. He recalled George's advice about different agendas but struggled to connect what Manuel had said with his suspicion. 'We have reached the very same conclusion. And the third item on your list?

The two stared at each other for a moment – there was an uncomfortable pause. Wynton wondering if Manuel realised he had let something slip, Manuel wondering why Wynton was looking so intently at him.

'This has the potential of making life more difficult for you. In addition to this cultural delegation operating out of Kingston they are now preparing to send over a team of experienced commanders. Our sources suggest a team of three. They are too old to be on active duty having been part of Fidel's inner sanctum since the start – they've seen action in Nicaragua, Ethiopia, Mozambique, Ecuador and probably a host of other countries as well. Our agent thinks this team will operate semi independently of the cultural delegation and their role is to train a locally recruited guerrilla army. We don't know the reason behind this deployment – you will have to do your own digging.' Manuel had cleverly used the first two reports to raise his credibility before revealing this new and alarming development. He was anxious for Wynton to take him seriously.

Wynton inwardly screamed at this latest development but did his best to take it in his stride 'this will make our task more difficult – it would be nice for once to be surprised on the upside. This looks like the PNP is facing up to defeat at the ballot box and getting ready for their revolution - Grenada all over again. Are you sure about this? Where did this information suddenly spring from?

'You know the rules of the game – I can't reveal a source. I will however add one more bit of information for you. There is a rumour, and that's all it is at this stage, a training camp is being prepared near May Pen in Clarendon Parish which is about 40 miles west of Kingston. Far enough out to be invisible to security forces but close enough should the need arise – whatever that need might be' added Manuel.

Wynton could not get his mind around this latest disclosure. If true it was a game changer. There was no way he had or could raise the manpower or firepower to defeat a guerrilla army. If true, Jamaica was going to go down the same route as Grenada and his name would be attached very clearly to it. Bonesman or not, his ass was going to grow too big to cover!

Manuel could clearly see his friend had been deeply unsettled by his report but was anxious to move on. He poured Wynton a coffee, got up from his chair, pulled out a cigar, half filled the room with smoke and continued 'and finally we come to this group operating from down town Kingston. I suspect your own intelligence has identified this group operating under the guise of Cuban foreign aid for the purposes of cultural enrichment. Load of balls.' Manuel paused for Wynton's confirmation or denial.

'Yes. What we know is this cultural and educational group are a front for some Cuban Insurrectionist Movement. We estimate there are about 40 members or delegates, whatever they are called, and include specialists in what we describe as urban warfare. I deliberately didn't mention it at our last meeting because I needed a second opinion. Now you have provided it.' Wynton was no longer playing games. 'So please carry on but, please, no more surprises.'

'There are, as you say, about 40 involved. Let's call them by their proper name – terrorists. They come and go so at any one time the maximum number on station is about 20. The rest are back in Cuba. We know some of them – they have been on covert operations around the world and are highly experienced. Bomb makers, assassins and murderers, senior army commanders, saboteurs, propaganda specialists so added together they present a formidable detachment. One works in the Ministry of Justice, one in National Security and one in the Ministry of Economics and Commerce and others have been circulating around the townships in the company of known PNP activists. Violence is growing in a number of the townships and there is probably a close link.' Manuel leaned forward onto the table, drained his cup, took a long drag on his cigar and waited to see how Wynton would respond.

For once Wynton was on top of the intelligence – this was only a slightly expanded version of Carlton's report. 'Two questions if I may. Is there a link between the cultural delegation and this new commander unit? What are the names of those controlling the cultural delegation?

'You should presume there is a link – it is my opinion the cultural team are recruiting local Jamaicans, those recruited are first sent for some preliminary training, and probably indoctrination in Cuba before being shipped to this camp at May Pen. The names of those in charge of the cultural delegation are Rafael Gallegos, Felipe Fernandez and Raul Garcia. Take these three out and I am sure you will diminish their operational effectiveness. You will also be doing us a very big favour too.'

Wynton didn't say any more at this stage in case it emboldened Manuel to up his fee. He also wanted to escape before he found any more downside risks. 'OK Manuel – what do we owe you?'

'With expenses, the pay-offs, the risks, the time and effort let's call it a round $60,000. It's been a dangerous mission and I think we delivered more than you expected.' Manuel was now piling on the agony knowing Wynton was fully preoccupied.

'We could manage a round $40,000' responded Wynton still alert enough to recognise the standard negotiating ploys. There wasn't a published price list and everyone knew money was never an obstacle when negotiating with the CIA. But try it on too often or become too greedy and internal revenue inspectors had an uncanny way of finding out.

'Why don't we cut the dance and settle for the $50,000 it cost us' responded Manuel.

'You can pick up the cash next week. You'll get instructions about the drop point on your answer phone. We must keep in touch but my priority is to work out a plan for dealing with this new commando unit and putting a stop to all this cultural enrichment.' Wynton reckoned Manuel had delivered on his promise. He was now a much wiser man than two hours earlier but also one closer to breaking point.

'I have just one final question for you Manuel - what is your relationship with Joaquin Roselli and Roberto Santos?' Wynton was hoping to catch Manuel off guard. He needed to find out if there was any working relationship and the only way he was going to do it was by surprise.

Manuel was ready for the question - he had been anticipating it and was not going to deny knowing them. 'Yes I know them both. I first met Joaquin as a member of Brigade 56 in the run up to the Bay of Pigs. We meet socially at reunions. I also know Dr Santos – we both arrived in Miami in 1959. Dr Santos has moved up in the world and left us behind.' There was more than a grain of truth in the reply and hopefully enough to disguise the true nature of the relationship.

Wynton thanked Manuel for his help. He was dropped off at Domino Park but before returning to his hotel he took a taxi to the American Club in Eight Street. He had been a member of the club for four years and it was a place that offered a unique insight into all things Cuban. The club had started life in Havana, formed by a group of American businessmen before being reformed in Miami in the 1960's by a group of Cuban businessmen. It was a place that had almost been swallowed up by Miami-Cubans anxious to prove their pro-American credentials. Cuban influence was so overwhelming Wynton thought it should be renamed the Cuban Club. Cuban-Spanish was becoming an unspoken pre-requisite of membership, the Board of Directors did not contain one non-Hispanic name, the club newsletter was printed both in English and Spanish and the menu was exclusively Cuban – this week's specials including such delicacies as Ropa Veija and Bacalao. But the club was important to Wynton – friendly companionship, a place to meet influential anti-Castro contacts and privacy. Today he needed the latter. He avoided the bar, the restaurant and coffee shop and headed straight towards the library where silence was strictly observed.

Wynton was a troubled man. Unanswered questions were stacking up. Was Carlton involved in some drugs scam? Who was behind the Thai's murder? What had Manuel said that made him feel uncomfortable? What should be done about this new Cuban commando force? Was Manuel's denial of a relationship with Roberto and Joaquin genuine? What was the prime purpose of the run down meeting venue and who owned it? It seemed he was always being surprised on the downside – Red Snapper just kept getting more and more challenging and he increasingly out of his depth.

CHAPTER 18

Wynton was beginning to feel the pressure weighing down on him. It was beginning to affect his every waken moment. Red Snapper was his operation but he never once thought it would get this complicated. What had been certain two weeks ago had suddenly and dramatically been undermined from the information he bought from Manuel. He had to press ahead, time was running out, the election date had been set for October 30th and big decisions were needed.

Miami was hot – well into the 90's. Humidity made walking just 100 yards uncomfortable. What pedestrians were about sat or walked in the shade. Dogs lay panting in deserted alleyways. The breeze from the Biscayne Bay instead of cooling just added to the discomfort. The white walls of the Miramar Medical Centre were reflecting and exaggerating the intensity of the heat. Even Luciano the security guard was slumped forward on his forearms but as the Ford Fairmont mounted the pavement to enter the private car park he was on his feet alert for any intruder or interloper.

Wynton parked his car in the 'visitor' bay and introduced himself to Luciano. Luciano was expecting his visitor and accompanied him all the way to the reception desk. Only when he was convinced his visitor had produced the appropriate identification documents, signed the visitors book and under the control of the reception staff did he depart. Luciano was a professional security guard and took no chances with unknown visitors. He would have lain down his life for Dr Roberto Santos.

'Good morning Mr McKenna – it's good to meet you at last. Dexter and Joaquin have mentioned your name and I understand from Dexter you are the one in charge of Red Snapper.' Roberto was laying his cards on the table. He had learned the tricks of the trade – in one sentence he had communicated the key facts he knew about the operation and who the relevant partners were. He exuded an air of confidence bordering on arrogance.

Roberto had worked with Dexter Broadbent long enough to understand the way he operated. His arrangement with Dexter about blackening the reputation of the criminal and mentally unstable Marielitos would not have been shared with Wynton. This is how the CIA created its firewalls. Operations were like circles – some bigger than others. The degree to which these circles overlapped determined how much information and intelligence was shared. Dexter had decided the Marielitos propaganda and Red Snapper operations did not overlap and therefore no need to involve Wynton. Roberto knew this - it gave him a feeling of importance because he was more involved with the CIA than his visitor could have imagined.

'It's good to meet you Roberto' Wynton was keen to set an informal tone – 'the name is Wynton.' He was trying to counteract the slightly overbearing attitude of his host by dragging the tone of the meeting down one notch to match his comfort zone.

'Coffee? I can promise you one of the best cups of coffee in the whole of Little Havana – given the competition it is quite a challenge' said Roberto trying to regain the initiative with his little boast.

Wynton accepted the offer and the two disappeared into what looked like a private consulting room. In addition to all the traditional medical furnishings and sinister looking instruments there was a small round plastic table in the centre of the room together with two tubular chairs with moulded plastic grey seats. The two sat facing each other, neither willing to start before the coffee had been delivered. They were two independent and assertive individuals, uneasy with each other and struggling to find common ground.

'I'll get straight to the point' started Wynton determined to take control of the meeting 'I am making the assumption when Dexter informed you about me he also briefed you about the aims of Red Snapper?' Wynton was sufficiently experienced in the art of communication to know much could go wrong between the original transmission of information and the receipt and interpretation of that same information. Getting Roberto to clarify his understanding would also give him the opportunity to better assess his new working partner. He needed to get behind this confident exterior – to work out for himself his true capabilities and trustworthiness.

'Put simply he wants us to help him make sure the PNP is voted out at the ballot box and we get a pro-western JLP in power. I would add we have agreed to help on the implicit understanding we take whatever opportunity is presented to us to strike a blow directly against Castro.' Roberto was now trying to win approval for an extension to the terms of reference by legitimising a new goal and his tone was more accommodating and less condescending.

'Isn't saving Jamaica from becoming a Cuban satellite sufficient?' questioned Wynton noting the change in Roberto.

'Indirectly, yes of course it is. What you may find difficult to appreciate is the intensity of the hatred we hold towards Castro. Many of us want to return to Cuba – don't get me wrong America has been very accommodating but Miami is not our home. What I was referring to was something much closer to Castro and his government – an action that actually helped to topple him. Red Snapper, if successful, will weaken his influence and prestige but he will still be secure in fortress Cuba. If we are successful we will help drive the Cubans out of Jamaica but will leave them free to emerge elsewhere stirring up trouble' Roberto was more than happy to spell out in great detail his ambitions.

'Our focus has to be Red Snapper – we must not get side-tracked. I do understand these bigger issues but I do need to concentrate minds on what needs doing in Jamaica.' Wynton recognised the tactic and was keen to demonstrate, in as polite a way as possible, he would not tolerate any actions other than those required to defeat the PNP at the ballot box on the 30th October. It was his way of confirming his leadership role in Red Snapper.

The two men were beginning to understand each other. There were perhaps the beginnings of a basis for mutual respect. Wynton continued 'I presume Joaquin has told you about this bogus cultural delegation which has set up its operation in Kingston?'

'Yes – indeed he has. We have our informers in Cuba who have been monitoring their comings and goings – we stepped up surveillance following your meeting with Joaquin' replied Roberto. 'Joaquin and I concluded we might be involved in Red Snapper and should make sure we were prepared. Joaquin is good at what he does but he is only as good as he is because he insists on quality intelligence.'

'In your opinion what do you think they are planning?' enquired Wynton.

'They seem to have a broad range of expertise, the standard range of destabilising tricks you would expect from a CIA operation. They have obviously been well trained' Roberto responded with a broad grin – clearly alluding to all the dirty tricks the CIA had employed and failed in trying to topple Castro. 'One is a political wing – specialists are being seconded into some key government departments. Their role is to influence policy but more importantly to be in a position to take control if it comes to a military takeover. The second is the military wing itself – these are the ruthless bastards that could start to destabilise the country – political assassinations – frightening off the foreigners who are in the country providing technical support – murdering JLP activists in the townships – taking over key army positions and so on. The third wing is the propagandists – those responsible for putting out the lies.' Roberto was now keen to impress Wynton – he wanted to be involved – they had an agenda all of their own irrespective of whether it was approved or not. He was keen to engineer the kind of response he needed from Wynton to make this happen. He was sufficiently experienced to know it was down to him to adjust his tone to the expectations of his client.

'And what would be your suggestion for eliminating this threat or at least rendering it impotent?' Wynton had learned the hard way he didn't hold a monopoly for operational brilliance. He had developed into a good listener and was more than happy to listen to the ideas of others before reaching his decision. He was also fully on his guard.

'Remove the leadership – as simple as that. You have to understand this regime is paranoid – Castro trusts very few of his associates and this paranoia filters down through the whole bureaucracy. Cut off the head of each wing and no one would or could take over. The unit would be paralysed with indecision. It would require a decision by Castro himself and by the time he got around to finding replacements the operation would be in chaos' replied Roberto carefully crafting the discussion along a predetermined route.

'What do you know about the leadership of this group?' It was now Wynton trying to draw Roberto to confirm or contradict the information offered by Manuel earlier.

'We know quite a lot. There are three key men – one for each of the three wings of the delegation. Rafael Gallegos – the political commissar, Felipe Fernandez – the military supremo and Raul Garcia – ex professor of political science in charge of communications. They are close to Castro – all trusted and clearly been promised key positions in any new PNP administration. They all go back a long way.' Roberto was well informed on the cultural delegation – he was being supplied with information from within by 'Almeria'. He had no intention of disclosing the identity of 'Almeria' or even admitting to his existence. His aim was to use his information judiciously, to establish a rapport and build trust but he was not going to make things too easy for Wynton.

'More coffee?' Roberto was planning for a lengthy meeting.

'Is Joaquin the man for this task?' asked Wynton accepting the refill without acknowledgement.

'May very well be the only man up to the task. He can't do it alone but I am confident we can put a unit together. Are you asking us to undertake this task?' It was Roberto's turn to seek clarification.

'Dexter seems to hold you in high regard and therefore you tell me, are you the people for the job? What other options do we have?' again Wynton was keen to explore all possible options.

'Thank you for that vote of confidence – I never quite know where I stand with our friend Dexter.' They both laughed. They were on common ground with respect to Dexter Broadbent. Dexter had his uses – the mention of his name helped to reduce the prickly formality.

'I can think of no other effective way of neutralising, sabotaging or eliminating this group. To take on the group as a whole would take a small army and I have to admit we don't know what internal support we could rely on from the defence force – far too risky.' Roberto was keen to rule that option out. There was absolutely no way he could control such an operation. 'So elimination of this deadly trio is your only option or should I say the only option we can provide. You could call in the marines.' Roberto was fully aware there was not the remotest possibility of a US led invasion. Joaquin had fully briefed him about Carter's abhorrence of more military action.

Wynton laughed out aloud. They both knew such action was not a remote possibility. 'There is also another problem. We have some reliable intelligence a small Cuban commando unit, totally independent of the cultural delegation, is now operational. They have established a training base west of Kingston in a place close to May Pen and looking to recruit locals for a guerrilla army.'

'I think you might be slightly misinformed on this. I know precisely what you are referring to but events have moved ahead much faster than your so called reliable intelligence is telling you. Have you heard of the Brigadista scheme? Roberto was keen to show Wynton he was fully up to speed with these potential ramifications for Red Snapper.

'Yes – but only as an educational and cultural programme for youngsters' again Wynton was bracing himself for another downside surprise.

'To the outside world that's what Brigadista is meant to convey. Somewhere where you can safely send your kids to learn about the true Cuba or more precisely Fidel's version of the true Cuba' responded Roberto.

'OK where have we slipped up?' replied Wynton anxiously trying to maintain his equilibrium. Red Snapper was an operation looking like it might spiral out of control at any time.

'You haven't slipped up exactly – just got the thing the wrong way round. Cuba is currently playing host to about 300 youngsters from Jamaica aged somewhere between 16 and 22. They are on the Brigadista scheme. Some of it is good – they learn to read and write – they study the history of Cuba and Jamaica. But there is also a subtle indoctrination taking place – everything is slanted towards anti-capitalism and anti-imperialism and pro-socialism. Some of the more vulnerable and gullible are being siphoned off to take part in physical training that includes unarmed combat, weapons training and sabotage. From this group a small but powerful unit of totally brainwashed combat ready soldiers is ready for some action. It is our opinion the commando unit you referred to is not setting up a training operation but a fortified compound with barracks and firing range – everything you would expect for an army unit prepared for action. These young men don't need any more training.' Roberto leaned back in his chair to await Wynton's reaction to his latest revelation.

'Are you saying it is too late for us to do anything about these Brigadistas? Are they primed and ready? Wynton was finding it difficult to contain himself. This was an unexpected development – Red Snapper was expanding beyond all original projections.

'No, I am not saying that at all. Remember they are currently based in Cuba in a camp east of Havana – somewhere in the mountains in Pinar Del Rio Province. The commando unit you referred to are all Cuban and therefore the leadership is Cuban. They would not risk making a Jamaican part of the command structure. Jamaica is a very unhappy place at the moment and so is the PNP. Without Cuban leadership some of this group might not be as brainwashed as we think and could make their own mind up as to what is best for Jamaica.' Roberto had thought through all the potential scenarios and felt he was still on track to controlling the outcome.

'OK here we go again – how do you think we should deal with the Brigadistas?' Wynton was beginning to feel impotent – he was struggling to hold his nerve. At every new turn he was having to rely on those he could neither totally control or trust. The downside risks were increasing and with it his career.

'Same as with the cultural delegation – remove the leadership. This is an easier operation because it is still based on Cuban soil. It is our view they will only move the Brigadista's into May Pen two weeks before the election. What would be the point of them moving sooner? If they were there any longer they would be breaking out looking to shag anything that moved. Even the Cuban's couldn't maintain discipline for longer than two weeks. Remember they are not regulars – they are a bunch of young men given some attention and structure for the first time in their lives' continued Roberto.

Wynton's options were being curtailed. He was being shunted into a siding with Roberto in charge of the points. It was too late to recruit a new assassination team – he didn't know where to look and he was not prepared to admit failure to Dexter Broadbent. He had accepted responsibility and it was time for him to act. 'I have the power to authorise whatever actions are necessary to eliminate the threat posed by the Brigadista's and the cultural delegation. You appear to be well informed and therefore my question is do you have the resources to accomplish the mission - the mission being to remove the leadership of these two organisations?'

'An unequivocal yes is the answer' replied Roberto. 'Joaquin and I have talked through what's needed. Joaquin would take command of the operation. There is no one more loyal and trustworthy. I know he has his problems with Dexter but he is not the only one who has failed to assassinate Castro. I've lost count of the number of attempts. I am pleased he was not the one behind the exploding cigar' an attempt that always had Roberto chuckling.

'I don't have a problem with Joaquin. It's my decision if I want to work with him.' Wynton was more than happy Joaquin was on board. In fact it was a relief. He was after all a contract employee of the CIA and whilst Dexter had his issues Joaquin did have a string of notable successes.

'Joaquin needs support. He reckons he needs a team of three. The one problem we have is they still live in Cuba. They are a bunch of disillusioned mercenaries still employed by the military who want to escape Cuba. Part of the price of using them will be a residency permit in the US with no questions asked. As things stand the US authorities would rather welcome the criminals and mentally insane than these three. They have been in Angola, Nicaragua, and Grenada but are sick and tired of it all – they would happily do our bidding.'

'It strikes me all kinds of criminals and reprobates are being allowed in so three more won't make much difference. The Mariel boatlift is the obvious cover. Do you need us to provide transport?' replied Wynton trying desperately hard not to show the relief he felt he now had a workable solution to a problem spiralling out of control.

'No – we have done three runs to Mariel to pick up friends and relatives – so we are known to the guards at Mariel. We still have to work on new identities for the three but its best if you leave it to us. It's been sometime since we have had such an opportunity to hurt Castro.' Roberto responded enthusiastically. It was time to show confidence in the plan and reassure his paymasters the cost would be money well spent.

Roberto continued 'So that we fully understand each other we will eliminate the leadership of both the cultural delegation and the Brigadistas. In this way we eliminate any potential for a military take-over of Jamaica in the event of the PNP looking likely they will lose the election. How we do it need not trouble you. Your ass, which you guys are so desperate to protect, will not be exposed. Some may suspect the culprits but no one will be able to track the deed.

'I think we understand each other perfectly' for the first time since he took command of Red Snapper he felt he was starting to feel he was regaining some control. 'Do you know Manuel Franqui?' Wynton was anxious to resolve this nagging concern about his other Cuban contact and tried to use this unguarded moment to test Roberto.

'Why do you ask?' Roberto was not expecting this inquiry at this juncture; he had lowered his guard and stalled for time to regain his composure.

'He is someone I met some years ago in my university days – he was involved in the Bay of Pigs operation' Wynton noted the surprise in Roberto's response but couldn't decide whether it was based on guilt or disconnect with the subject under discussion.

'Yes I know Manuel Franqui. Our paths cross at different social functions. A somewhat scruffy and lazy individual' Roberto was anxious to close this conversation topic and to move on without disclosing his anxiety 'can we discuss the financial and other arrangements for our little ventures?'

Roberto's response had not provided the reassurance he was hoping for but concluded nothing more could be gained from pursuing it. 'Fire away – I assume you have it fully worked out. I will leave the detail to Dexter – he will arrange payment through the Miramar Medical Centre and I will happily leave it to the two of you to resolve any financial disputes.' Again they laughed – Wynton happy for the first time to have kicked a problem on to someone else's patch and Roberto at the thought of further trials and tribulations with Dexter Broadbent.

CHAPTER 19

A tropical storm with torrential rain, thunder and lightning was an appropriate send off for Carlton as he headed back to Jamaica. It was the perfect accompaniment to Naty's mood which turned swiftly and unexpectedly when he informed her he was returning to Jamaica on a matter of some urgency. The flying plant pot aimed directly at his head was evidence enough she was not pleased with this latest turn of events.

In between his routine trips to Guyana, Trinidad and Barbados, studiously avoiding Grenada and Jamaica, Carlton had spent every available moment with Naty and her two children in Little Havana. Trust and security were slowly building as both secretly hoped and openly planned of a future life together.

Grenada was off Carlton's itinerary because Uriah Jagan was in custody – held in solitary at the guard house in the military barracks at True Blue. Carlton had no way of knowing what Uriah was telling his captors but common sense told him to keep his distance. Whatever Uriah was revealing would however, in CIA parlance, be 'plausibly deniable'.

Jamaica was also temporarily off his list until either he received further instructions from Wynton or opportunities arose directly connected to his original tasks.

His return to Jamaica was prompted by such an event. Carlton, on one of his routine but highly visible visits to the Miami Chamber of Commerce had received a facsimile from Jamaica. It read:

FOR THE ATTENTION OF CARLTON DAVIES – EXPORT DEVELOPMENT EXECUTIVE.

FOLLOWING RECENT SYMPOSIUM WE HAVE IDENTIFIED TWO MANUFACTURERS INTERESTED IN DEVELOPING EXPORT ROUTES INTO EASTERN SEABOARD STATES. OTHER DEVELOPMENTS MIGHT FURTHER HELP WITH YOUR TRADE MISSION. KEEN TO HELP ANYWAY WE CAN. HOPE TO MEET UP ON NEXT VISIT SOON.

MURIEL SHARMA – BUSINESS EDITOR.

His early morning Air Jamaica flight to Kingston was bang on time. Everything this airline did seemed designed to cause Carlton maximum inconvenience. His faxed response to Muriel had included a request for a pick-up approximately one hour after the timetabled ETA. He was now destined to spend another one hour of wasted time hanging around Norman Manley Airport.

During his flight he speculated about Muriel's coded message. Something had clearly happened. The principled journalist appeared to have had a serious change of mind.

Just occasionally two people take an instant dislike to one another. This morning the Jamaican immigration officer did not like what he saw when Carlton presented his passport and immigration card. Maybe he wasn't paying due respect to authority but the elderly sour faced official was clearly offended by something. For the first time ever he was questioned about the purpose of his visit, how long he would be staying, where he would be staying, what other countries had he visited recently, was his Yellow Fever jab up to date? Carlton remembered the Berretta in his toilet bag and decided to fall in line. A respectful 'sir' at the end of each response softened the man's attitude and he was eventually waved through.

This twenty minute interrogation had the benefit of filling in time. By the time he left the Arrivals Hall Muriel Sharma had arrived early, parked her car in the short stay car park and was now brushing off the unwanted attentions of a couple of young porters.

'Thank you for coming' was all Muriel said as she flung her arms around him.

Not one to miss the opportunity of an embrace from a beautiful woman Carlton responded enthusiastically. To the neutral observer this was a loving couple happy to be reunited after a very lengthy absence. But Carlton could sense the tenseness in Muriel's body. This was a hug of a frightened woman seeking protection and reassurance.

Not another word was spoken as they walked hand in hand to Muriel's white three year old Volkswagen Polo – the result of an unofficial deal with a departing embassy employee. Muriel was obviously not one to let her principles get in the way of a good financial deal!

'I am being targeted. Look at the bonnet' Muriel pointed to the scratched markings on the bonnet – the initials JLP with a crudely drawn dagger through it.

'This could be the work of kids' Carlton said trying to reassure her.

'Get in' instructed an unsmiling Muriel unimpressed with Carlton's patronising response.

Carlton got in but kept his battered holdall on his knee. Muriel was making him nervous and when anyone did that to him he needed the reassurance of having his gun close by. He waited for Muriel to talk. The apparent abandonment of normal highway rules combined with sets of confusing road signs, making it virtually impossible for the occasional visitor to exit the airport, suggested it was not a good time to put the pressure on with his intrusive questions.

With the airport finally behind them Muriel started to open up 'my apartment was broken into and ransacked. Photographs of me and Faith were smashed and one had a knife through it pinning it to the wall. Nothing was taken. This was clearly a warning. You know where I live – it is as secure an apartment block as there is in Kingston. A 24 hour guard supposedly covers the one and only entrance. The person or persons who did it must have been in collusion with security.' Muriel was desperate to talk to someone she could trust and the relief of unburdening herself caused the tears to flow. 'I am frightened Carlton.'

'Why have you been targeted? What have you done lately that is different or outside of your normal routine?' queried Carlton looking for some rational explanation.

'All I do is my writing or commissioning articles for the Gleaner or interviewing people. I get out and talk to businessmen and some of the politicians – both PNP and JLP. I try my best to find out what is going on in the business community and what impact government policy is having and might have on them in the future. All negative stuff and perhaps they have started to take exception.' Muriel had obviously been through all possible causes and explanations in her mind and concluded some PNP activist was trying to frighten her off.

'Where are we going now?' enquired Carlton not certain how he should respond to this turn of events.

'Back to my apartment - this break-in has changed my plans about living in Jamaica. I want out. I would like to take you up on your offer of a Green Card – I am not prepared to live like this – I don't care who wins the election. I don't care what happens to Jamaica.' Muriel clearly had had a serious change of mind.

Carlton didn't know what to say. He was powerless to organise a Green Card without the appropriate quid pro quo. He couldn't find an appropriate conversational topic for a time like this but the coded message suggested there was much more to come.

Muriel sensed Carlton's discomfort. 'I am prepared to help you – I don't want you sticking your neck out for me and getting nothing in return. I will arrange for stories to be published but I think I can provide you with something more valuable.'

This is what Carlton wanted to hear.

'I have recently met with a young guy from England. He has come over on secondment from some university. He has brought with him the first IBM PC on the island.' Muriel wanted to impress Carlton – she desperately wanted a new life in the US.

'And what exactly is an IBM PC?' responded a puzzled Carlton wondering how on earth this could be connected to anything of relevance to his tasks.

'You have clearly not been paying attention on these courses you have been attending' replied a now more relaxed Muriel. 'It is a small powerful desk top computer – PC stands for personal computer.'

'So?'

   Conversation came to an abrupt end. Night time curfews had been in operation in downtown Kingston for about six weeks. Anyone breaching the curfew was likely to be shot on sight. Curfews were normally lifted by 7 am but today roadblocks were still in place four hours later at 11 am. A dozen fully armed soldiers in combat gear were manning a check point with randomly selected cars being searched. The queue stretched about 200 yards and Carlton could see occupants of selected vehicles' being required to vacate their car while a thorough search was made.

'Do you see why I need to get out of this place?'

'What are they looking for' asked a concerned Carlton. First a lengthy interrogation at the airport and now this – paranoia was starting to creep up on him.

'Drugs, guns, kidnapped victims, stolen loot – who knows? This is a first time this has happened to me.'

After a thirty minute wait they eventually reached the check point, chosen for a random search and ordered out of the car at gun point. Nothing was said and two young soldiers made a thorough search of the car – looking under seats, spare wheel compartment, glove box, behind sun visors, under wheel arches and were about to search Carlton's holdall when an officer joined the search team 'good morning Miss Sharma. Can I ask where you are going?'

The two soldiers were left in two minds and stopped what they were doing. If this was a friend of the officer then the last thing they needed was to get on his wrong side and awaited further instruction.

Muriel recognised the officer as one of the guest speakers at a business security seminar organised by The Gleaner in response to the growing lawlessness against the business community. His on-duty manner was of the no nonsense variety – stern, officious but very professional. It was in stark contrast to the genial, friendly but very professional speaker who reassured delegates about the additional measures being taken to protect factory and commercial property. 'I'm returning from the airport with my guest Carlton Davies from the US Chamber of Commerce. Is there a problem?'

The officer eyed Carlton before demanding 'can I see your passport?'

The officer examined every page before ordering the two soldiers to stand aside and without a word waved Muriel and her passenger on their way.

Back in her car Muriel banged her fists on the steering wheel in frustration 'this country is descending into chaos. No explanation, no nothing.'

Not another word was spoken until they pulled up at the security gate outside of Balmoral Castle apartments on Balmoral Drive. The security guard recognised Muriel and immediately raised the rusting traffic barrier giving access to the private numbered parking bays.

'I now look at these security people differently. I have known this guy, his name is Douggie, for two years but I now question whether he had something to do with the break-in. They know my movements inside out – I am a creature of habit.' Muriel drove past the guard acknowledging him with a brief smile.

Inside the modern and tastefully furnished apartment, still showing the scars from the break-in, Muriel went straight to the fridge and brought out a bottle of Appleton's Light Jamaican rum and a bottle of Ting. She never forgot that Carlton, whatever time of day, would always welcome his rum and Ting. Her apartment was full of black wooden carvings and framed paintings, all by local artists, of iconic images of Jamaica – Bob Marley, Rastafarians, Higglers, Dunns River Falls and many others. Muriel had desperately wanted to make Jamaica her home.

'Thanks. It's great to see you but not under these circumstances. Your coded message was very clear to a point – do you want to tell me the rest? By the way where is your daughter? Is she OK?' asked a genuinely concerned Carlton.

'Yes no problems there thank God. She is at nursery school – my cleaner is very good and quite happy to look after Faith or pick her up from the nursery for a few extra dollars. She very often stays over at her place if I need a baby-sitter' Muriel replied joining Carlton on the sofa.

'Right, are you listening? Let me explain in clear and simple terms for you. This English guy is over here with his wife and three children. He is being sponsored by one of these international aid organisations and his task is to train someone up on this latest gadget called a PC – a personal computer. It sits on your desk. Got it?' asked a smiling Muriel. She liked the idea of having a man in the house – one she could rely on but one she still needed to be on her guard against. One rum and Ting had been known to power up his testosterone but sex was far from her mind today.

'No, but no doubt enlightenment will follow soon.'

'I thought I would have trouble' laughed Muriel. She was beginning to enjoy teasing him. 'Guess where this PC is parked? It sits on a desk in the Ministry of Foreign Affairs – Import/Export Statistical Section under the control of our new found friend.'

'No, no enlightenment yet' replied Carlton beginning to feel a touch stupid.

'This PC is now processing Jamaica's import and export statistics. It has just gone live and government officials and planners have started to use the information generated from the computer. Standard press releases are now based on statistics generated from this mighty little PC. It has replaced the manual systems and grossly inefficient mainframe computer. Are you getting warm?' enquired Muriel.

'I have just moved from ice cold to tepid - I'm struggling to get warm.'

'Don't you see, if we can find a way of manipulating this data to our advantage the government will continue to issue regular press releases containing this mis-information and we can then legitimately use it as the basis of a good lead story.' Muriel thought she had done sufficient to convince Carlton but his response suggested enlightenment was still some way off.

'You are going to have to talk me through this' said Carlton.

'God, you are thick' laughed Muriel. 'Let me ask you what would be some of the consequences of a big current account deficit – what would happen if Jamaica went millions of dollars into the red where the cost of imports well exceeded the revenue from exports?'

'OK let's see. I'm beginning to see the light. If this really happened then Jamaica wouldn't be able to pay for its imports. The only currency acceptable to its creditors is the US dollar or sterling. If it is not selling enough overseas then it won't be able to generate the hard stuff to pay them.'

Muriel was now getting more excited by the minute. 'Well done. In addition, the PNP, much to the disgust of the extreme party members has gone cap in hand to the IMF for loans and credit lines to overcome what it sees as temporary difficulties in paying for imports. But if the IMF or World Bank take the view Jamaica will not be able to repay the loans then they will, at best, reject their application or at worst, seek more reassurances. We can then quite legitimately write headline grabbing lead stories about the incompetence of the PNP's economic strategy. If Jamaica cannot generate the hard currency then it can't afford to buy oil and there will be blackout's, if there are blackouts factories will close and unemployment will rise, it won't be able to afford drugs and equipment for hospitals and the young and old will suffer. I could have a field day with a press release like this.'

'I'm now following this but can we rewind back to this PC thing – where does this come into it' asked a still puzzled Carlton.

'I know where this PC is located. If we can gain access we can cook the statistics and make the trade deficit even bigger. Timing is critical – we need to time this for about 6/8 weeks before the election giving us time to receive the official press release and to make certain it is circulated far and wide. Discredit the PNP both locally and internationally.' Muriel had clearly thought the plan through. 'If my little plan is going to work then we need to get busy.'

'I also know some big Jamaican exporters, the food processing cooperatives, clothing manufacturers and others are working fiddles with some corrupt bankers. Exports are loaded onto ships going to Canada and UK with bogus documentation. Bills of Lading are issued with accurate descriptions of goods and tonnage but accompanying Letters of Credit are for approximately half the true value of the cargo. When these Letters of Credit are presented, Jamaican banks receive US dollars or Sterling on behalf of the exporter – the other half of the value of the consignment is paid by the recipient of the goods directly into a US or UK bank for the benefit of named individuals. All involved take a cut and those already in possession of a Green Card have set themselves up with dollars or sterling to fund a lifestyle in their country of choice. This is one way the rich are getting their capital out of the country.' Muriel was finding it difficult to conceal her excitement. It was not just the possibility of earning her Green Card for herself and Faith it was also a high degree of self-satisfaction with the sheer simplicity of the plan.

'If this is already happening why do we need to take any action with the PC?' queried Carlton.

'Because it is not happening on a big enough scale or fast enough to generate the headlines. Coming back to our computer genius – this is where we can make the biggest impact. We can either help mislay or delay the arrival of legitimate documentation about export consignments or we crack the security codes on the PC to adjust some of the figures. I'll simply work on the sugar and bauxite export statistics because both are already in decline for a whole range of reasons. Banana exports will be hit next month because of Hurricane Allen which has virtually wiped out the whole of the industry.' Muriel had it all worked out.

'And just who is going to crack the security codes on the PC and how are they going to get access to it?' Carlton asked. He was beginning to see the potential of the plan but also the obvious risks.

'I have attended some of the workshops run by Derek and he is keen to show off his knowledge and expertise. Like many of these consultants he hasn't a clue about local politics. He is so naive and innocent and just assumes everybody is keen to work with him to develop a more efficient system. Unlike many of those forced to attend his boring workshops I have shown a genuine interest – I have got to know how it works – it is simplicity itself. He has actually let me enter some of the data into the spreadsheet. I have even written and published an article on it in the Gleaner. All I need you to do is to get me access to it over a weekend – a simple little break-in.' Muriel stunned Carlton with this last request.

'Won't your friend notice someone has been tampering with his machine and statistics?' asked Carlton.

'There is a slight risk but he is not familiar with the pattern of imports and exports. There are huge seasonal swings in any case and there are thousands of different entries. I would delete a number of export entries and duplicate a number of import entries.' Muriel was bargaining no quality control procedures had yet been put in place. 'Backup copies of the data are made and stored securely in a safe but they are only likely to be used if the PC malfunctioned.'

Muriel dropped Carlton off at the Mayfair. They both agreed for security reasons it would be better not to be seen to be too close. He had agreed to give the plan some serious thought and do a preliminary reconnoitre of the building housing the IBM PC. He was familiar with the office compound on Waterloo Road simply because he was a frequent and welcomed visitor. He knew many of the managers and supervisors and another visit would not be seen as suspicious because all would assume he had an official appointment with someone or other.

Jim was surprised to see Carlton. 'How do you know we wouldn't be full to the rafters?' he joked.

'You have to take risks in life' responded Carlton.

'We'll squeeze you in then. By the way a member of the JCF [Jamaican Constabulary Force] was round asking a few questions about you – it was the day after you left on your last visit' Jim nonchalantly informed his guest.

'Any idea what it was about?' asked Carlton.

'No. I presumed it was about Toffy. I kept my mouth shut' replied Jim. 'You don't know who you are dealing with these days - best not to volunteer anything.'

Carlton was unsettled by this new revelation. First a lengthy interview at the airport, next his passport scrutinised at an irregular checkpoint and now this. Coincidence or was the PNP intelligence service more sophisticated than given credit for? Were his movements being monitored and if so, why and by whom? Had he been careless or, more seriously, was someone informing on him.

CHAPTER 20

One of Derek Goulding's key innovations was to introduce discipline into how the import and export statistics for Jamaica were calculated for the previous month. Never an exact science given the arbitrary and casual way data was collected and delivered to the office on Waterloo Road but by agreeing a final cut-off date some basis for consistency had been established.

Muriel knew this. She had spent a number of hours listening to Derek's proposals for the new computerised system. She had received an invitation from Derek to preview the system, as it ran in parallel with the existing chaotic system and before it was given approval as the country's trade statistical data base. This data base would now provide the balance of trade statistics and the basis of the routine press release. It was this document that provided Muriel with the information with which to applaud, or more likely criticise, the government's economic policy.

Muriel had targeted Sunday 17th August 1980 as the day they should break into the offices of the Statistical Section of the Ministry of Foreign Affairs. 21st August was the agreed cut-off date for computing the balance of trade statistics for the month of July. The press release was routinely distributed approximately 10 days later after authorisation by the Minister. This would be the final press release before the election on Thursday 30th October and giving Muriel the ammunition to mount a withering attack and condemnation of the PNP's economic strategy. No one could argue if such an article was based on the Government's own statistics! That was the plan she agreed with Carlton.

At 21:00 hours weather conditions provided the perfect cover for the clandestine operation. Intermittent cloud helped block out light from a full moon and a gusting wind with squally showers would discourage the casual walker who might witness the break-in. Casual walkers at this time of night were a very rare sight indeed – at least the honest casual type.

'Are you ready?' Carlton whispered to Muriel. There was actually no reason to whisper as they were sitting in Muriel's car parked immediately behind the colonial styled wooden office building in a deserted cul-de-sac off Kingsway Road. But both were feeling the tension.

They had driven past the front of the building facing onto Waterloo Road a number of times confirming their expectation no permanent security men were on site. The fences surrounding the complex were in need of repair and therefore no unfettered guard dogs would be roaming freely. They didn't expect to encounter any of the local petty thieves neither– they would have established long since there was no local demand for stolen statistics!

'Yes – let's go.' They got out of the car and stood in the darkness of the overgrown hedgerow and waited. After two minutes of watching and listening they entered the rear gardens of the building. The only precaution they took was to dress in casual dark light-weight clothes and wear soft soled shoes. Their first line of defence, if caught, was to claim a mechanical breakdown and taking a short cut to avoid being caught out during the curfew. A pretty feeble excuse as the curfew did not extend to this part of Kingston but better than nothing.

The buildings were not alarmed. Carlton had done his survey. The wooden doors were however very securely locked and the only option of gaining entry by this route was by destructive force. The locks were at least 50 years old - an invisible legacy of colonial rule. They certainly knew how to keep the natives out in those days. For this reason his preferred entry route was through a side window. It was absolutely critical no tell tale signs of entry were left behind.

Carlton slid a thin bladed knife in the gap between the two interlocking sash windows and forced open the locking bar. The window was normally open all day long and was very loose in its mounting and as soon as it was released the top window crashed down onto the windowsill below with a loud bang. The window sashes had probably perished many years before.

'For Christ's sake – what the hell are you doing' whispered Muriel through gritted teeth.

They both stood motionless. A dog started barking. The wind made it difficult to determine the exact direction of the barking. Ten minutes passed. They were just about to enter the building when car headlights started lighting up parts of the rear garden. The car headlights continued moving suggesting a car driving and turning in the front car park. Car doors slammed. Voices could be heard then laughter. A further ten minute wait and then car doors slamming and an engine being revved.

'Could have been police or security guards making a cursory inspection - their arrival had nothing to do with the noise from the window.' Carlton was used to these situations and the one thing he had learned was not to panic. Stay absolutely still – fade into the shadows – breath slowly and deeply but be ready for the unexpected. He held Muriel's hand and he could feel her shaking. He smiled reassuringly at her.

All sounds were being magnified in the silence left when the wind dropped. They carefully eased their way into the central reception area of the office building – the dark wood stained floor hopefully hiding any damp left from their footsteps. Carlton closed the window behind them and walked to the small adjacent lean-to extension housing the PC.

'Are you OK now? Do you know what to do?' enquired Carlton as he prepared to keep a watchful eye for any further security searches.

'Yes. I have brought a thick blanket and I'll enclose myself with the computer to avoid any light escaping from the screen' replied Muriel. 'Just stay there until I check the power cable – make sure it is plugged in.'

Muriel traced the cable from the back of the computer to the wall socket. Having confirmed the connection she returned to the computer desk, sat down and switched on. Nothing happened. 'Carlton, I need your help – quick.'

'The power is probably switched off at the mains as a basic fire precaution. Where is the master board?'

'How the bloody hell would I know. Look for it.' Muriel was beginning to panic. This simple little break-in was turning into anything but.

'I need to find where the mains cable enters the building. Come and hold the window while I search the outside.' Carlton was beginning to regret agreeing to this venture but having come this far he was not prepared to give-up. He quickly checked each side of the building not knowing whether it was an underground feed or one dropped from an overhead line. Twenty minutes passed and Muriel, with nothing to occupy her mind, was on the verge of something close to a panic attack.

'Found it. It is directly opposite the window you are holding.' Carlton scrambled back in and spotted the thin oblong cupboard that could have no other function than housing the electricity meters and master switch - he hoped. 'Yes this is it. Get ready – there. Shit.' Half the lights in the office came on momentarily before he switched it back off. 'Go round all the light switches and make sure they are off.'

After another ten minutes of searching Muriel said 'I think I have found them all – try again.'

This time complete darkness. Muriel powered up the IBM – PC, settled down under the cover of the blanket and got to work. The entry password was the nickname of his daughter 'loopyluce' – they had had a good laugh at it when Derek was demonstrating the system. Muriel calculated she needed to depress the value of exports by about $10 million US dollars and increase the value of imports by about $3 million US dollars thus engineering a massive $13 million US dollar monthly deterioration in Jamaica's current account deficit - more than enough to spook both the educated electorate and international financial institutions.

It took Muriel twenty minutes to accomplish the statistical 'adjustment'. She closed down the computer, slipped out of the blanket, turned off the mains and turned on the light switches that had startled minutes before. The blanket was used as a floor mop to get rid of any tell-tale footprints before exiting the building. Carlton gently lowered the bottom half of the window and trusted to luck no one would notice the unlocked catch on Monday morning.

Back in the deserted cul-de-sac Muriel and Carlton quietly hugged each other – an embrace driven by a combination of relief they had not been discovered and the decision made earlier they would not meet again in Jamaica. There was nothing more to be gained from the partnership and any closer friendship might be viewed with suspicion.

Muriel got into her car and set off back to her apartment. Carlton was just a few hundred yards away from the Mayfair and had decided to walk back and join the expats in the bar for a nightcap.

Any thought of a quiet relaxing drink was quickly denied – the car park at the front of the Mayfair contained three police cars with flashing warning flights. Jim was being questioned by two burly individuals – one in uniform and one plainclothes. Carlton took the immediate decision to abandon any thought of returning to the hotel – his coincidence theory was now being stretched beyond the plausible.

CHAPTER 21

At 13:00 pm on Friday 5th September, Mitch received a coded radio message from the CIA agent based close to the Cuban port of Mariel. 'TROJAN LOADED. CREW OF FOUR ASSEMBLED. PROBABLY LEAVING MARIEL WITHIN HOUR. ESTIMATED ARRIVAL JAMAICAN TERRITORIAL WATERS FOUR/FIVE HOURS.'

He switched frequency and relayed the encoded message to the Miami University Marine Biology Deep Water Research vessel with the added caveat 'IN PLACE TO RECEIVE LANDING COORDINATES 1700 HOURS.' The deep water research vessel was bristling with the latest electronic surveillance equipment, funded by the CIA and tasked with monitoring all military communications and the movement of non registered shipping heading to and from Cuban territorial waters. Tracking a 44' cabin cruiser was trivial compared to other tasks asked of the specialist crew.

This was the message Mitch was waiting for. He was getting bored just hanging around the apartment block eyeing up the female residents lounging beside the pool in their revealing swim suits. Frustration was building on all fronts. They were now finally up and running. His first act was to phone Christian and Ebeneezer who were renting a small wooden bungalow in a country village called Moneague, just a few miles from the north coast. Mitch doubted they would just be eyeing up the local talent!

Everything they could think of had been talked through and practiced. They were now expected to be ready to move and take up their position overlooking the most likely of the three predicted landing areas. If the coordinates did not confirm this landing site then the operation would be cancelled. The plan was for them to make their way to the rendezvous point on an old and battered but still reliable 1960's BSA 175cc motorcycle. Both were armed with knives and Walther P38's.

Mitch had swapped his white Honda Accord for a 1978 two litre faded yellow coloured Toyota Pickup. Operational necessities had meant he had to sacrifice some of the luxuries of life. The Toyota was fuelled up – Mitch took every opportunity to keep it in this condition because he never knew when fuel supplies would run out or be rationed. A portable radio receiver and transmitter was stored securely in the foot well on the passenger side and a bag of Jamaican patties and six Red Stripe were parked on top to help see them through, what might be a long wait.

Thirty minutes after receiving the message and securing his apartment, Mitch was on his way to the north coast. He estimated a journey time of approximately one hour and forty minutes to cover the 66 miles to Columbus Park. This journey time anticipated the usual impediments - the odd traffic jam, slow moving wagons laden with bauxite or sugar cane but excluded the possibilities of hijackings and army road blocks.

Columbus Park is an ideal place to assess coastal weather conditions but more importantly it provides the necessary cover to receive the radio message without risk of being disturbed by curious security personnel. Columbus Park is popular with tourists. It is an open-air museum with a whole series of artefacts from the days when the Spanish and British first came to the island. Travellers between Montego Bay and Ocho Rios frequently stopped off to take in the spectacular sea views. A white man sitting in his car looking out to sea looks more ordinary than exceptional in this tourist Mecca.

Today the weather was perfect for the gun runners – clear blue sky, powder puff winds and a gentle sea swell. But not so perfect for those hoping to secretly track whatever consignment was landed. Just three weeks before, this coast had been battered by Hurricane Allen, the first of the 1980 season and one of the most ferocious to hit the island for many years. The shore was littered with lumps of white coral wrenched from the reefs by a 36′ tidal surge and piles of rotting stinking vegetation.

At 16:22pm precisely the radio sparked into life transmitting the encoded message '77-26 longtitude,18 -25 latitude'. A quick glance at the chart confirmed his hopes and earlier prediction the 44′ Trojan was heading for a landing somewhere between Runaway Bay and Rio Bueno. The actual landing areas were restricted to coastal inlets and caves stretching approximately two miles – the other parts of this coast line were just too dangerous to navigate because of jagged limestone outcrops and inaccessible cliff faces.

As the sun dipped towards the horizon the tourist buses and private cars started to exit Columbus Park. Mitch walked to the farther most point and scanned the horizon with his powerful Docter 10 x 42 military issue binoculars – still looking like a tourist desperately using the dying minutes of daylight to soak up the view. Nothing, as yet, resembled the 44 foot Trojan cabin cruiser. Mitch was not too surprised – he didn't expect the boat to come within sight of land before the sun had disappeared over the horizon.

His next action was to drive the Toyota pick-up to a point closer to the beach, park off road and walk the remaining mile to the rendezvous with Christian and Ebeneezer. He carried the beers and patties in an ordinary shopping bag – now looking like a self-catering tourist. When he was absolutely certain no one was about or any traffic approaching he casually slipped off the road onto a path leading up to a promontory overlooking the bay. They had created a hideout within dense bushes roughly at the centre of an arc containing within it what looked to be the safest landing points. Making certain the area was deserted Mitch quickly and quietly slipped into it to join his two colleagues.

Each took it in turn to use the night vision binoculars. It was Ebeneezer who first raised the possibility the Trojan was approaching. It was 23:00 hours. Each had been given photographs of the cabin cruisers and airplanes and told to remember and recognise their silhouettes. The advantage had now switched to Mitch and his team – the black but clear sky and a three quarter moon was beaming sufficient light for Ebeneezer to first pick up the wake of the blacked out boat and secondly, as it got closer, the silhouette. The binoculars were passed around and all agreed it was a Trojan cabin cruiser and very probably the targeted one.

The cruiser slowed – probably cut its engines completely allowing it to drift towards the shore – still about half a mile off shore. After, what seemed an eternity, three bright flashes were observed coming from a pencil thin torch on the boat. It was impossible to know whether this was a request for or response to a coded signal.

Three more minutes passed before Ebeneezer spotted the white foam being churned up by the boat's engines. The boat was slowly heading in towards the shore and the signal for Christian to disappear. With back pack, flippers in hand and wearing a black short cut diving suit he headed towards the shoreline. Mitch also disappeared, heading back to where he parked the Toyota leaving Ebeneezer with the task of monitoring all that followed.

The Trojan sailed to within 20 feet of the shore line before swinging round, presumably to facilitate unloading. A rope was thrown from the boat towards the shore and for the first time the shore based team started to emerge from their seclusion. A second rope was thrown and both were tied to tree trunks to hold the boat steady for unloading. As soon as this was completed two men were seen approaching the rear of the boat – and two men on board started hauling boxes from within the rear cabin. The men greeted each other and immediately started the transfer with each box requiring two pairs of hands to shift it.

'What do the i haffinight?' asked the tall skinny Jamaican dressed in a dark coloured t-shirt and shorts.

'10 boxes of Kalashnikovs – these are part of the replacements for those lost in the hurricane. You need to be more careful' responded the man standing on the side decking of the Trojan. He appeared to be the one in charge as he made no attempt to lift or carry any of the boxes.

'You have no idea i-dren what dat that storm was like' answered the skinny Jamaican.

Ebenezer had now left his hideout and had crept to within 150 yards of the unloading operation. He could just about follow the conversation and it appeared they were not too concerned about being disturbed. Clearly complacency had set in – they had made so many journeys without any hitch and had certainly no reason to think tonight would be different.

The boxes were being piled up on the shore by two teams each of two men. Ebenezer began his search for the transport the men would be using to move the boxes and also for any lookouts posted. His task was to identify the vehicle and make a record of any markings or other unique identifiers that would enable him to recognise it again and then make his way back to pick up his motorcycle. He would then wait for whatever transport they were using to emerge loaded from the shore. The expectation was they would be heading back to Kingston via the A1 through Fern Gulley. Mitch was parked off the road in Fern Gulley in anticipation. Ebenezer would run the BSA into the back of the Toyota and then settle down to follow the gun runners close to their final destination.

CHAPTER 22

Christian quietly slipped into the water half a mile east of the Trojan cabin cruiser. A Jamaica Defence Force trained and champion swimmer it took him just 40 minutes to swim in a wide arc enabling him to approach the boat at a 90 degree angle from the shore. His task was to fit a powerful explosive device to the boat timed to go off in 180 minutes. The hope was the crew would not hang around after unloading but would head straight back to Cuba at maximum knots. The explosive material was calculated to obliterate both crew and boat – to raise questions back in Havana but leave no forensic evidence to point the finger. Semtex-H, smuggled out of Libya, being used in preference to the American manufactured C-4 plastic explosive as an insurance policy.

Christian took some time out to observe the activity on board and it appeared only one person was not physically involved in discharging the cargo. This crew member seemed preoccupied with supervising the operation and spent as much time on shore as he did on board. Christian was about 40 yards from the boat when he could hear raised voices – his interpretation was an argument. This, he thought, was his opportunity.He dived underwater and swam the distance surfacing under the clipper bow. He was invisible to anyone immediately above him on deck but as he could observe the shore based activity it was also possible for them to see him.

Christian carried with him two explosive devices – one magnetic and one attached to a fifteen foot rope. The Trojan's hull was constructed of fibreglass and this presented a technical problem – there was no reliable way of attaching an explosive device to fibreglass in the short space of time available. The plan was to attach a magnetic device to the steel transom at the rear of the boat if they were off loading via the bow. This was the easiest and preferred option. If they were off loading at the rear then the plan was to hook one end of the rope to the central stanchion of the steel 'pulpit' and let the movement of the boat drag the second explosive device under the front cabin. Christian was now faced with the more difficult of the two tasks.

Suddenly someone started running to the front of the boat – the boat started to rock. Christian, still holding onto the bow slid below the surface. 60 seconds was the maximum he could hold his breath and slowly resurfaced. He had made his first mistake – he had no way of knowing where the runner was – was he above him? To attach the rope he had to reach out of the water and slip the rope around the central stanchion – this was too far out of water to reach by hand and he had brought with him a specially adapted aluminium rod – part of an old television aerial. He had connected the metal clasp at the end of the rope to the rod but could not take the risk of moving it until he was certain the crew member had disappeared.

Five minutes passed and Christian was about to make his move when the water was disturbed by a torrent of vomit from above. This startled Christian and he lost his grip on the sharp edge of the bow and started to drift away from the boat. He could now see the crew member – he was leaning over the 'pulpit' just feet away from him – he started to wretch again and another mouthful of vomit cascaded down just inches from his face. Christian put his head under water and with one flip glided under the boat. He surfaced 20 feet away on the port side of the cabin cruiser. He could hear the man shouting something and other crew members were running towards him. He assumed he had been spotted.

Christian was quick to seize the opportunity this presented. With all of the crew now located at the bow end he dived and swam towards the rear of the boat. Having located a propeller shaft he partly unslung his back pack, extracted the magnetic explosive device, slipped the safety loop around his wrist and glided the bomb until he could feel the tug of the magnets attaching themselves to the steel transom. He slipped the nylon safety hoop off his wrist, still keeping his other hand on the bomb and carefully checked to see it was securely engaged. The magnet would have to withstand the pressure of the swirling water churned up by the powerful outboard motors and therefore important the magnetic strips were in the correct position.

He now needed to make his escape. He had to presume his presence had been discovered but if he could escape without further visual contact then the crew might just think the vomiting crewman was hallucinating or it had been a Caribbean Reef shark.

Christian took in a lung full of air, lined himself up to head directly away from the boat and attempted to dive to the sea bed only to find himself being forcibly restrained. The air rushed from his lungs due to the force of the restraint and sudden surprise. He twisted round to surface only to find he could neither move up nor down. His twisting merely tightened the restraint. His lungs were close to bursting at which point his army training kicked in – training that taught him not to panic. He located the main pressure point and discovered his back pack was snagged on a broken ladder rung which he estimated was about four feet beneath the surface. There was no time to work out how to untangle the strap but reached for the knife strapped to his leg. He cut the straps, freed himself and surfaced. He gasped in the air and listened – his twisting must have caused some motion. Panic now set in – his training had never envisaged this scenario. He dived again leaving his back pack still entangled. The adrenalin gave him the energy to swim 35 yards before a quick surface and a further 35 yards. He continued for another four bursts before risking a quick look back.

The shore crew had unfastened the ropes anchoring the boat and flung them to waiting hands. The powerful Chrysler outboard motors started, the captain swung the boat round 180 degrees and started an arching sweep of the bay. Christian decided his best strategy was to head to the rocky coves – no captain of a Cuban cabin cruiser would risk his boat and crew weaving between jagged limestone outcrops. Thirty minutes later the cabin cruiser headed out into the open sea. Christian collapsed exhausted wondering what he would say to Mitch? He had accidentally managed to attach two explosive devices and providing they remained undiscovered were likely to cause the mother of all explosions. Someone, in addition to the Miami University surveillance vessel, was bound to hear or witness it.

CHAPTER 23

Ebenezer crept silently down the path leading to the shore where unloading was taking place. He had mentally mapped out the links in the supply chain. Boxes containing whatever were being quickly manhandled from boat to shore and stacked about 30 feet from the water's edge. He anticipated a van or small pickup would be located hidden from view but close enough that the armaments could be quickly loaded and spirited away. He also expected a guard posted between the vehicle and the main road – they would not be expecting, he hoped, an intruder approaching from a coastal path at this time of night. How wrong he was.

Still some 30 yards from the unloading, moonlight was just sufficient to make out the path but not enough to expose the individual casually leaning against the rocky outcrop. The two came face to face, Ebenezer was first to react. Palm of his hand smashed hard up against the individual's nose followed by two hands around the throat smothering any possible cry for help. In that brief moment he had squeezed the life out of a skinny youth of no more than 17 years of age. Ebenezer was not even certain he was connected to the arms smugglers. But whatever his connections Ebenezer wasted neither time nor compassion in disposing of the body. He carried the youth back along the path to the edge of a 40 foot cliff top and dropped the body onto the rocks below. There was just a slim chance whoever missed him would interpret it as an unfortunate accident.

He retraced his steps, more alert than he could ever remember, back to where the confrontation took place. Instead of heading to the shore he moved in land towards the main road. He had lost valuable time and needed to at least identify some memorable characteristic of the transport vehicle. There was also a very big possibility a search party had been sent to find the missing youth.

Just yards from the main road he dropped to his knees and crawled parallel with it until he found a track capable of taking the truck. He didn't have to wait long. A light blue Chevy truck crept slowly forward, no lights, a driver and two passengers in the cab. It stopped momentarily at the junction before switching on its main headlights and racing off at speed towards Ocho Rios.

Ebenezer had hidden the BSA about 800 yards west of the point the truck had emerged from – just outside the village of Bengal Bridge. He ran as fast as he could but it still took about six minutes. He fired up the BSA and raced after the Chevy – the road was completely deserted and he could see no distant lights. He started to suspect the truck might have pulled over to check to see if anyone was following. The aim was to get to Mitch's parked Toyota in Fern Gulley as fast as he could. Mitch would be monitoring all traffic heading towards Kingston. He just needed to make a match with the vehicle before setting off in pursuit. If they couldn't make a match then quick decisions were required.

It took Ebenezer 30 minutes to reach Mitch's parked pickup hidden off road about half way through Fern Gulley. 'Did the i see a blue Chevy pickup with dree people in de cab?' asked Ebenezer.

'Yes it passed here going flat out about ten minutes ago' replied Mitch. 'Run your bike into the back – the ramp is in place.'

Two minutes later they were on their way heading towards Kingston with headlights on full beam. The road was too dangerous to drive without them. A ten minute gap equated to about four or five miles so there was very little chance their headlights would be noticed. Their headlights would only be a problem if they made it obvious they were tailing them. Traffic was very light at this time of night and the betting was those out at this time were as anxious to avoid recognition as the drivers of the Chevy and Toyota pick-ups.

'Any problems?' asked Mitch.

'Yeh man' replied Ebenezer, 'had fe silence someone who was keepin guard.' 'I dumped his structure over de cliff fe make it coo pon gaan fe bed an accident – nobody saw i. His mates didn't hang around too tall lookin for him.'

'Well that's one more added to the tally' commented Mitch. 'Judging by the speed they were going they were either behind schedule or just so anxious to get away before someone saw them. It concerns me as to how they are going to avoid the curfew in Kingston. It never occurred to me before but I don't think they will be heading into Kingston. Did you see anything of Christian?'

'No, nothin – dere was a bit of rumpus on board de Trojan but impossible fe work out what caused it' replied Ebenezer.

At that very moment Mitch noticed out of the corner of his right eye two men having a piss beside what he took to be the blue Chevy. He almost braked but corrected himself just in time and carried on at about 50 mph – slightly too fast for driving on these roads at night. He never anticipated this but decided he had no option but to continue. The two men would most certainly have noted the yellow Toyota. Mitch decided they could not continue in the Toyota – too big a risk – they needed to ditch it.

'Let's drive to Ewarton, just before the road junction, dump the Toyota you get on the motorbike and wait for them there. There is just the odd chance they might branch off at Ewarton and head to Lluidas Vale otherwise I think they will be heading to Spanish Town'

They didn't have long to wait. The blue Chevy sped past them. Ebenezer eased the motorcycle into first and took off after them. He heeded Mitch's advice and agreed the likely destination was Spanish Town. His strategy was to ignore the need to keep the truck in site but to follow at a steady speed of about 45 mph. After Bog Walk Ebenezer upped the tempo and increased his speed by about 10mph and by the time he saw the road sign for Angels could see tail lights in the distance.

He approached to 400 yards and cut his lights. He knew Spanish Town well. The lights ahead turned into Cumberland Road – he closed to 200 yards and heaved a sigh of relief when he could confirm the lights were indeed the blue Chevy. The Chevy then did a sharp left down Old Market Street and pulled onto the driveway of a wooden bungalow located somewhere between Young Street and Hanover Street. Ebenezer increased speed and sped past the arms smugglers but not before he knew precisely where the truck was parked. Mitch had been right – Spanish Town was either a temporary or permanent home. Ebenezer needed to hang around to see if the truck was moved to Kingston after the curfew had been lifted. He made a surprise visit to his Aunt Primrose.

CHAPTER 24

'I'm not clear about the purpose of this meeting or what possible good it will do. Events are moving so fast I need to be in Jamaica' bemoaned a worried Wynton doing his best to put on a brave face and feed the impression everything was under control.

Events had indeed moved faster than anyone expected following trajectories neither planned nor controllable.

'Dexter called the meeting, which is in itself unusual. Normally if he has handed over control the onus is on the operations leader to brief him. He must have got wind of something.' George T Rosenberg replied trying his best to interpret the motivation behind Dexter's request. 'We still have some time to play with before the people of Jamaica go the polls and there is still one thing in our favour.'

'What's that?' responded Wynton looking for any morsel that could bolster his mood.

'It means Dexter is still on board. His name is still connected to Red Snapper. If he was so worried the operation was going to be a mini Bay of Pigs then we would not have heard from him. He is still accepting overall responsibility. So stop worrying until we find out what, if anything is troubling him' replied George trying his best to lift the spirits of his colleague before the scheduled meeting with Dexter.

'Thanks George for your support but this meeting is not going to be easy. I am going to have to come clean about Carlton or as clean as I can be given the circumstances. The truth of the matter his absence is still a mystery.'

The two were hunched over a coffee in a rundown Wendy's Diner off Ocean Drive trying to gather their thoughts before travelling to meet with Dexter at a CIA safe house – a cheap bed and breakfast hotel. The skinny elderly waitress with wild bleached hair beyond repair, fiery red lipstick and black pencilled eyebrows set on top of a white matt emulsion foundation had given up on her carefully crafted customer request 'you guys want anything to eat or not?' The two were in a world of their own. What six months before had been a seemingly straightforward operation was now anything but.

'Come on, it's time to go. We can speculate all we like but the chances of second guessing Dexter are remote' said George.

The taxi dropped them off a couple of blocks from 'Daisy's B & B' and they walked the rest. The red neon sign in the centre pane of the grubby window flashed 'No Vacancies' as it always did, lighting up the 'Satisfaction Guaranteed' deal sealer for any passing punter. An enormous woman called Miriam ran 'Daisy's B & B'. About 5' 6", a pleasant demeanour supported by three chins and framed by riotous black curls, Miriam was a low level CIA contract employee. Her job was to entertain CIA clientele, keep a small arsenal of weapons ready for deployment or storage, provide a respectable menu of Cajun meals and keep unwanted guests at bay. She also maintained a bug free meeting venue. 'Daisy's B & B' was another of George's outlandish creations.

George rang the bell and the electronic security lock was released allowing the two of them in. Miriam tracked callers through an external camera linked to a monitor in her front room. She recognised George and didn't bother to expend energy in greeting him in person. She remained seated in an arm chair covered by a threadbare army issue blanket situated just six feet from her bank of security and TV monitors. The two understood each other perfectly well. George would not be offended by the impersonal greeting.

'Good to see you George' said a smiling Miriam ignoring his guest.' You know your way and your colleague is waiting for you.' Names were kept to a minimum and Miriam did not engage in trivial conversation. This was the best paid job she ever had and she knew the limits of her role.

Up one flight of creaking dark stained wooden stairs on to a landing with eight black painted doors along three walls. George knocked at number seven and entered. Sitting at the mid-point of the table facing the door was an unsmiling Dexter Broadbent, his podgy hands resting on a slim manila folder and his flask of scotch within handy reach. Two leather upholstered straight backed chairs had been arranged opposite about eight feet apart. Dexter would not be allowing any collusion between his guests – he wanted the unvarnished truth.

No welcome, no greeting – what you see is all you get from Dexter Broadbent 'right gentlemen looks like Red Snapper is heading for one almighty fucking cock-up. Please convince me I have got it wrong. Please convince me that bastard Castro is not going to put one over us yet again.'

George and Wynton were immediately wrong footed by Dexter's opener. Neither knew what Dexter knew. Neither knew where to start. Both had expected an insight or accusation that they could respond to.

After two very long minutes of silence Dexter exploded. 'Do not play games with me. I am sticking my fucking neck out for you so the least you can do is level with me. If Jamaica goes red we can all kiss bye to a future.'

'Sorry Dexter, I thought you called the meeting and therefore had an agenda' responded Wynton somewhat nervously. It was his operation and was clearly expected to provide chapter and verse. 'Yes I do have a problem. Carlton has gone AWOL and I don't know why or where he is. I am no longer sure which side he is on or whether he is in trouble or setting up deals to feather his own nest.'

'This is fucking marvellous. Why wasn't I informed – a rogue agent – is that what you are saying? Red Snapper could be compromised.' Dexter was turning a colour that indicated this was news to him. This was clearly not the topic that was on his mind when he called the meeting.

'No I am not saying that. I said I don't know and I mean I don't know. I got a message saying he was returning to Jamaica on urgent business but didn't say what business or with whom. After seven days with no contact I started to worry so I visited his office at the Miami Chamber of Commerce. They had booked him a 72 hour return flight to Kingston. They were not concerned – not unusual for Carlton to disappear – he is not part of the formal organisational and therefore not answerable to any of the full time managers. I asked if there had been any phoned or other messages and they dug this carbon copy up of a facsimile received 18 hours before he left. He was clearly in a hurry.' He passed the crumbled message to Dexter.

FOR THE ATTENTION OF CARLTON DAVIES – EXPORT DEVELOPMENT EXECUTIVE.

FOLLOWING RECENT SYMPOSIUM WE HAVE IDENTIFIED TWO MANUFACTURERS INTERESTED IN DEVELOPING EXPORT ROUTES INTO EASTERN SEABOARD STATES. OTHER DEVELOPMENTS MIGHT FURTHER HELP WITH YOUR TRADE MISSION. KEEN TO HELP ANYWAY WE CAN. HOPE TO MEET UP ON NEXT VISIT SOON.

MURIEL SHARMA – BUSINESS EDITOR.

'What the hell does it mean?' barked Dexter.

'It's obviously a private and coded message. May not be anything sinister but on the other hand it might be to do with drugs. Carlton has dabbled in some low level dealing in the past. Some of the intelligence coming out of Havana suggests, and I must emphasise this is by no means confirmed, that our Thai friend, Toffy, was discovered poking his nose into a drug smuggling syndicate and that is the reason why he was killed. The question is was Carlton involved in his death - do the 'export routes' referred to in the message mean drugs?'

'I spoke to Santos the other day and he didn't mention anything about this. Where did the intelligence come from?' snapped Dexter. Dexter never left anything to chance.

Wynton had just dropped himself into the shit big time. There was no way back. Dexter had caught him out. 'I have been using an old acquaintance to get corroboration of some of Carlton's exposes. The guy's name is Manuel Franqui. I have not mentioned this to anybody – even George.'

George was surprised and disappointed about this latest disclosure but kept his composure. He intended to have a very serious conversation with his junior after the meeting if there was anything left of him after Dexter vented his anger.

'Jesus Christ - I know Manuel Franqui, the biggest two timing bastard in Miami. I need to know how you even know this guy, what the two of you have discussed and who else you have been plotting with.' Dexter's demeanour suggested an explosion of apocalyptic proportions was but just seconds away.

Wynton spent the next 30 minutes providing his two colleagues with a full and detailed description of his two meetings with Manuel Franqui and his recent meeting with Roberto Santos. Dexter never once took his eyes off Wynton.

'You realise you have been discussing Red Snapper with Franqui who would sell his mother into prostitution if he could make money out of it' said Dexter curtly.

'I was very careful not to mention Red Snapper to Manuel' at which point Wynton suddenly stopped talking, the blood draining from his face as he suddenly realised what precisely had unnerved him at his last meeting with him. 'Christ Almighty – Manuel knew about Red Snapper. That's what troubled me at our last meeting – I couldn't figure it out at the time but he accidentally let it slip he knew about Red Snapper. How the hell did he find out?'

'Lesson one – you can't trust a Miami based Cuban if you have nothing on him. Franqui has been up to his neck in all kinds of criminal activity including drugs and murder but we have nothing on him. His '201 file', which we can all access, is full of crap and wouldn't support any criminal charges and I know he hasn't got a 'Softfile' – I've looked.' Dexter was still showing an explosive tendency and continued in this vein. 'Lesson two – Miami based Cubans look out for each other but if it's in their interest to deny knowledge of each other they will happily do so. They first look out for themselves and family, they next look out for their friends, then it's their criminal associates and then it's us, unless of course you have enough on them to put them in the electric chair or jab a lethal injection up their ass. That's where I've got, and will keep, Roberto Santos and Joaquin Roselli.'

George and Wynton had both been stunned into silence. They waited. This was a new Dexter Broadbent. He was not pleased, which was fairly normal, but not expressed with such venom. The table in front of him was speckled with minute spit bubbles.

'What you did Wynton was stupid and hot headed. I reckon you have learned a valuable lesson so let's move the agenda forward' said Dexter after a moments silence and in a tone that suggested he was returning to his more normal aggressive self.

Addressing Wynton, Dexter said 'irrespective of whether you involved Manuel Franqui or not he would have been brought into the loop sooner or later. These three work together. They don't know I know or I don't think they know.' There was now a more relaxed atmosphere in the room. Dexter had found out what he needed to know even if his methods were a touch brutal.

'You were quite right I did have an agenda. The first item was the Manuel Franqui issue, I just had this feeling the greasy bastard's name would crop up. The second is another fat undesirable - you may not have heard of a Marcello Mancini but he is a Mr Big in the local Mafia. He provides us with certain services for which we pay him rather handsomely. Our last safe house meeting on that cabin cruiser was organised by a business partly owned by Marcello Mancini - another slippery fat bastard. Well it looks like Marcello has just got himself arrested by the FBI. They had been monitoring him for weeks – running arms shipments into Jamaica and returning with a shed load of Columbian drugs.' Again Dexter startled the present company.

'Whose he supplying the guns to?' asked an astonished Wynton.

'I'll come to that in a minute' replied Dexter

Wynton again felt the colour in his face change. He had forgotten Manuel's comment about the Mafia. Dexter noticed the change and stared at Wynton.

'There is one thing I forgot to mention. I didn't take it too seriously at the time. It was the first meeting with Manuel – he let drop in a casual way the Mafia were hoping to set up their casino operations on the north coast and were not banking on a PNP victory. They were going to use their 'slots' as a base for other activities – presumably drugs and prostitution. Could it be something to do with that?' said Wynton tentatively trying to slide this latest revelation in unnoticed.

Dexter paused, the latest comment catching him off guard. 'You seem to be running your own bloody intelligence service – are you sure there is nothing else you would like to share with us?'

'Absolutely and verifiably no, all other intelligence has come through or been corroborated by Roberto Santos' Wynton responded thinking he detected the beginnings of a very brief softening in Dexter's tone.

'We are going to have to get Mancini off this drugs smuggling charge - we'll make sure the case doesn't get to court or failing that get it thrown out on a technicality or if all else fails claim national interest. We need the fat bastard and we don't want him shouting his mouth off in open court. Bridges will need to be burned. Things will be different if Reagan wins but for the time being we need to keep Mancini's mouth shut' said Dexter.

For the first time in the meeting George spoke and repeated Wynton's question 'who is Mancini supplying arms to in Jamaica?'

'Well' and Dexter seemed to hesitate for a moment before adding 'maybe Wynton has just provided us with the answer. Maybe he is setting up the foundation of his new criminal empire with the firepower to discourage the competition.'

George muttered an unconvincing 'ummm.'

---------000000--------

After leaving 'Daisy's B & B' Wynton and George took a taxi to Ocean Drive. It was late in the afternoon – the heat was fading – sun lovers were leaving the beach. They walked for a mile before Wynton decided to break the silence 'I am sorry about not keeping you in the picture about Manuel Franqui. It seemed a good idea at the time but I felt Carlton's report was too short on detail to raise the alarm. I totally forgot about the Mafia comment – it struck me as odd at the time but could not see any possible connection with Red Snapper.'

'I am puzzled by this meeting. Thinking about it for a moment in the absence of Dexter's ranting and raving, I would have done the very same thing. I would have 'worked' those in the know and so would Dexter. Since when did he stick to the rules? It goes with the job' George replied reassuringly. 'My only concern is that you could have mentioned it before our meeting with Dexter because he will now begin to question the nature of our working relationship. This is one ugly dirty business and he'll have lodged it away for possible use at some future day. He could use it against either of us whether fellow Bonesmen or not. Providing you come through this unscathed there will be times when you need to trust someone – if only to cover your precious ass.'

Wynton was left to absorb George's advice before being asked 'let me ask you a question. What new information did you learn from Dexter this afternoon about Red Snapper?'

Wynton pondered the question for a few minutes before replying 'nothing, in fact absolutely nothing, sweet fanny adams.'

'OK let me ask you another question. Why was Dexter so bloody angry when we entered the room and why did he set up the room to separate and isolate us – eliminate any comfort zone?' continued George.

Again Wynton pondered the question for a few minutes trying to recollect the sequence of events before answering 'I don't know, I haven't a bloody clue. It always seemed to be me on the back foot trying to defend or explain myself.'

'Now turn this whole meeting round and tell me what Dexter discovered about Red Snapper?

Wynton could now see the point of George's questions 'absolutely everything I know or suspect about what is right or wrong with the operation.'

'Exactly. You have just been professionally sand bagged by Dexter Broadbent. He wanted to make sure he knew everything about Red Snapper and he did it by bullying you into revealing all you knew. He knows full well we all keep secrets. The question on my mind is why?' concluded George.

'One thing is troubling me, why Dexter didn't make more of Carlton's disappearance.' It was now Wynton's turn to raise questions about Dexter Broadbent. 'An agent goes AWOL, he starts blaspheming and then drops it. And another thing why was he so evasive about what Marcello Mancini was up to – why even mention it in the first place?'

George didn't respond to Wynton's question about Marcello Mancini. He was equally puzzled by it – it was not normal for Dexter Broadbent to disclose anything voluntarily and particularly when there was no connection to Red Snapper. He was up to his old tricks again of trying to bully information out of people but there was nothing to disclose – and Dexter now knew it.

They were both left to ponder the mysterious workings of Dexter Broadbent.

CHAPTER 25

Wynton had to be prodded into action by the Jamaican couple standing behind him as he waited to check in for his late morning flight to Kingston. His mind was preoccupied with Red Snapper but his big concern was Carlton. He was uncertain what his action plan was but he alerted Mitch by radio he would be staying at the Pegasus for a few days. He also decided to keep his visit as low profile as possible, not visit Devon Place but suggested to Mitch they meet up at the Pegasus's Sunday night poolside barbecue. Whatever the weather you could always rely on their chicken and lobster barbecue to the accompaniment of the resident steel band. It was one of the few reputations still intact after the months of crime and deprivations.

As soon as he completed registration at the Pegasus he made his way to a public telephone booth located in the hotel lobby and dialled the number staring at him from the front page of the Gleaner. 'Do you have a specialist reporter that deals with business issues – I need some advice?' Wynton tried to give the impression of an uninformed nobody looking for some general information.

'And your name is?' enquired an efficient and friendly receptionist.

'Rodney Bailey – I run a small cosmetics manufacturing business and follow your business advice column' lied Wynton.

'Thank you. I will try to connect you with the business section. Please hold.'

'Business desk – how can I help you – Dorothy speaking?'

'Could I speak with the Business Editor, Muriel Sharma? I was told by your receptionist she was best placed to help me with my query' continued Wynton, his confidence growing as each stage of his story slotted into place.

'Muriel Sharma speaking – how can I help you?'

'Good afternoon. My name is Rodney Bailey and I was wondering if you could help me with my business development plan. I would like to open up a new export route into the eastern seaboard states and desperately need some expert guidance. I did have a consultant working on the project but he is a busy man.' Wynton held his breath. There was an unnaturally long silence at the other end of the line.

'Can you give me some background? Any advice I give might depend on the type of product you are hoping to sell and the potential volume of exports.' Muriel Sharma was clearly stalling for time. She had made a connection with Carlton but she was highly suspicious of the motive of the caller. 'It would also help if you could tell me what contacts you have already established in the US' Muriel added as an afterthought. Her mind was catching up with events and she was now starting to set her own traps.

'I have all this information to hand but it is difficult over the phone. I had hoped to attend the symposium run by the American Chamber of Commerce some months back but was too busy. Running a business in Jamaica at the moment is proving very challenging. Could we meet for a preliminary discussion at the Pegasus this evening – I have all the information you require.' This was Wynton's only option – to try to make the connection with Carlton as credible as possible but not raise the suspicion of anyone who might be taking an interest in the movements or conversations of Muriel Sharma. Wynton simply had to tread carefully. The question on his mind was could he trust Muriel Sharma?

'I could make a meeting in two hours – say 17:30pm. I will meet you in the coffee shop. I may bring a colleague. Is that OK with you?' Muriel's mind was in overdrive – highly curious but at the same time nervous and frightened. She was also mindful without Carlton she had no hope of obtaining her Green Card.

'Yes do please bring your colleague – I look forward to meeting you both. I will be waiting for you at a table in the coffee shop. How will I recognise you?' Wynton could not take the risk of Muriel enquiring about a Rodney Bailey. An atmosphere of distrust was steadily percolating its way through Kingston as election day approached.

'Black briefcase and three inch heels – that should be sufficient. Thank you for your enquiry and I look forward to our meeting. Goodbye.'

Wynton had ninety minutes to occupy before his meeting with Muriel. He was intrigued by her request to bring a friend. Was it a feint to test his resolve because if she had been working closely with Carlton it was very unlikely anyone else would be involved? He would have to wait and see. To fill the time he casually wandered around the grounds of the Pegasus, the jogging track, the pool area, the garden cafe and lobby assessing the best places to position surveillance if someone wanted to monitor a meeting in the coffee shop. He needed to be on his guard. The hotel had few guests – the best hotel in town and probably only 25% occupancy due to the troubles.

He returned to his room, checked the phone and other obvious locations for bugs and switched on his TV to watch news footage of a shooting at a political rally in Tivoli Gardens. The country was close to civil war.

At 17:00 hours he entered the coffee shop and selected a table with unobstructed views of the hotel entrance, lobby and service doorways. He ordered a pot of Blue Mountain coffee and two cups – he anticipated a twenty minute delivery schedule. Service was always casual but friendly. He used his time to monitor the potential surveillance positions he identified earlier but saw nothing to be alarmed about. At 17:27 hours a car with one occupant drove up the ramp towards the rear car park. He concluded her request to bring a friend was probably designed to check him out in some way.

Two minutes later a lady with a black briefcase and three inch heels entered the coffee shop. Wynton was impressed - tall, full figure, smartly dressed in white silk blouse and black pencil thin skirt and impressively good looking. He thought to himself Carlton knew how to recruit his operators. He got up and she immediately headed in his direction. There was no risk of mistaken identity as they were the only two customers.

Muriel held out her hand 'Good afternoon Mr Bailey.'

'Where's your colleague?' queried Wynton noticing the firm grip and steady eye contact.

'Waiting in the car – I told him I wouldn't be long. Now Mr Bailey how can I help you?' said Muriel Sharma business like but smiling.

'Well I do have a problem – the gentleman who was helping me suddenly decided he had better things to do leaving me with many unanswered questions. He was the one who organised the symposium held in this very hotel some months ago which I believe you attended. You reported on the event and your photographs were in the Gleaner. I am a regular fan of your articles. His name was Carlton Davies.' Wynton was now studying Muriel's expression to see how she would react to the disclosure of his name.

'Who are you Mr Bailey? I am a very busy person with a lead article to write for Sunday's edition.'

'A close but worried colleague.' Wynton saw no point in continuing the charade.

'Working for whom may I ask?' enquired Muriel. If she was nervous or suspicious she was certainly not showing it.

'Carlton works for me and he has disappeared off the radar. You were the last person in contact with him and it was your fax that brought him back to Kingston. I am here to find out what happened to him. My name is not Rodney Bailey but Wynton McKenna.' That's as far as Wynton was prepared to go at this stage – it was Muriel's turn to react.

'I am being followed and I know my home phone is being bugged. They don't follow me when I finish work – they presume I will go straight home or pick up my daughter but I cannot go out at night or weekend without some very obvious security guy following me. It has to do with Carlton – I know.' Muriel's reaction was a mixture of relief and concern. Concern as to how trustworthy Wynton McKenna was but relief there might be some end in sight to her torment.

'Do you know where he is?' asked Wynton.

Muriel didn't answer. She had been so unnerved by recent events she barely knew who she could trust.

'Listen Muriel these are very difficult times in Jamaica. I don't know what your relationship is with Carlton but he seemed to be in a very big hurry when he received your fax. Now why was that?' Wynton was desperate for Muriel to open up.

'You tell me Mr McKenna – why would Mr Davies hurry to Jamaica just to see me? What do you think the motive could be? Muriel was regaining some confidence but decided she needed some extra proof of his identity.

Wynton was taken aback by this aggressive response 'I expect he was encouraging you to write articles prejudicial to the PNP and supportive of the JLP. Am I right?'

'And who do you work for?' asked Muriel.

'The CIA so can we stop playing games' responded an increasingly frustrated Wynton.

'Carlton is safe. He is looking for a way to get out of the country. He suspects the authorities are after him – in fact he knows they are. By the authorities I mean police, PNP thugs or their Cuban friends. He cannot leave by air and is looking to hijack a boat.'

'Can you get a message to Carlton for me? That way you can verify who I say I am and perhaps when you are both convinced you could suggest a time for a meeting and a secure venue.'

'I have put myself at considerable risk for Carlton, the CIA and in fact the bloody US. I have been persuaded by Carlton Jamaica needs to get rid of this PNP government and install a more US friendly one. I have willingly done this because Carlton promised me a Green Card one day after the Jamaican election whoever wins' Muriel was now ramping up the rhetoric and was determined not to be sidelined. Once Carlton had been spirited out of Jamaica what chance did she have of getting her payoff?

'I don't know what deal you had with Carlton but we just can't spirit up Green Cards at will,' replied Wynton.

'So the CIA goes back on its word' said Muriel her anger growing at this betrayal.' I have not yet written the article which is designed to destroy the economic credibility of this government both here in Jamaica and in the IMF, World Bank and others who keep Jamaica afloat and if you go back on your word then it won't get written. Carlton and I have gone to unbelievable lengths to get this government to issue statistics that will shoot a bloody great hole in their own foot.'

Yet again Wynton found himself out of his depth. Facts, or what appeared to be credible propositions, had been presented to him told him he was out of touch with the events unfolding before him. In the last 72 hours he had seen the credibility of Manuel Franqui shot from under him, next he had Dexter behaving in a most unlike Dexter manner and now he has had Carlton's soiled reputation partly reinstated. He began to doubt his suitability for his task.

Wynton was getting used to apologising 'I asked Carlton to try to find someone in the media who could help us get the right messages across both locally and through the likes of the influential Wall Street Journal or The Economist. I guess you are that person.'

'Tell me something, that copy of the fax you got from the Miami Chamber of Commerce, what do you think it meant?' asked Muriel her composure and confidence swinging violently between extreme highs and lows.

'We knew it was a coded personal message but one interpretation linked it to drugs' replied Wynton casually. Wynton was low on empathy and never once considered what such a casual observation might have on Muriel.

'You are unbelievable you lot. Only a twisted mind would automatically think the worst of the people you work with. Carlton puts his life on the line and because he goes missing you think he must be up to something that's not in the national interest. Well let me spell it out to you. The 'two manufacturers' referred to my daughter and myself and the 'export routes' was a reference to the Green Cards Carlton promised us if I agreed to help him.' Muriel's anger had returned with a vengeance.

'Seeing what a bloody duplicitous bastard you are Mr McKenna the article will not get written, I will not help you find Carlton and first thing tomorrow I will book a flight back home. I won't tell you my home country in case you blow the bloody plane out of the sky' Muriel had now lost total control. Staff were coming out of the kitchen to see what the commotion was. Cups had slid off the table and smashed on the blue tiled floor. Wynton was juggling with the coffee pot and milk jug with the contents sloshing in his groin area.

'Wait, wait, please' pleaded Wynton. 'I apologise if I have upset you – that is the last thing I wanted.'

'Will I get my Green Card? A simple yes or no will suffice' barked Muriel glaring at Wynton completely oblivious to the gathering audience.

'You have my word, now please sit down so we can discuss it' asked a chastened Wynton.

'There will be no further discussion Mr McKenna. I will write an article based on a government press release made available to the media yesterday which shows a huge decline in the value of exports and an increase in the value of imports. This will have a major impact on the international financial organisations and aid agencies and will further undermine the confidence of the local business community in this current government. The implications will be catastrophic for Jamaica – my article will spell out very clearly what those implications are.' Muriel had developed a sort of aggressive composure which suggested the other party should remain quiet and hear her out. 'This extremely clever ruse was designed by me and which Carlton helped me implement. I did this so my daughter and I can start a new life in the US.'

'You will have your Green Card – I will authorise it immediately on my return. If this article appears this Sunday then all you need do is present yourself at the American Embassy with your daughter next week. You have my word.' Wynton, whilst extremely sore and uncomfortable around his genitals, was mightily relieved everywhere else. If this article was as significant and influential as Muriel suggested he would finally have accomplished the first of his prime objectives.

'Thank you. Now let me tell you what I know about Carlton and his predicament. His name has been linked with the murder of a Thai national visiting Jamaica. The police want to talk to him and Carlton doesn't want to speak to them. End of story.' Muriel got up to leave but as she did so she gave Wynton a folded piece of paper 'he is staying in a holiday home owned by a friend of mine in Oracabessa on the banks of Jacks River. Nobody wants to rent them in this climate but it is just a matter of time before someone spots him. You can get him on this number.'

Without another word, or glance back, Muriel Sharma left the coffee shop.

CHAPTER 26

'Did you read the article in today's Gleaner about the calamitous drop in export earnings and the likely reaction by the World Bank and IMF?' Wynton asked Mitch as they queued to pay for their barbecue at the cashier's window.

'Yes it was a devastating article for the future of Jamaica. I mean devastating to the PNP and their chances of re-election. Manley must be having nightmares. The timing couldn't have been worse for him. I bet the Minister responsible will be in the hot seat – after all he released the statistics. Wouldn't you have thought they would have buried the statistics until after the election or at least twisted them?' replied Mitch.

'Yes – quite surprising such an article like that has appeared so close to the election. I am just waiting for the backlash but the reality is it is entirely of their own making' Wynton was not going to let on this was partly Carlton's work. This operational 'circle' didn't overlap with Mitch's activities and therefore no need for him to be included.

Wynton's motivation for Red Snapper had been given an enormous boost by the article. Someone had delivered and something had gone to plan. He winced as he recollected Thursday's meeting with Muriel. His discomfort came not from his sensitive balls but from the way he had upset Muriel and misjudged Carlton. Whatever else he was up to Carlton had delivered big time on the journalistic front. He had to admit to himself he was both intimidated and attracted to Muriel. He questioned what that said about himself but he desperately wanted to meet her again. He would make absolutely sure the embassy staff in Kingston processed her application as a matter of extreme urgency. He even thought of escalating it to a matter of extreme national importance. In fact he had never stopped thinking about her since she walked out of the coffee shop and out of his life.

'Hey Wynton – come back to earth old chap – what do I do with this receipt? Who do I give it to? questioned Mitch as he tried to stir Wynton from his private thoughts.

'Take it to the chef. He will give you your lobster and you just help yourself to the jacket potatoes and salads. Gee, I was miles away. For once I had something very special and very nice on my mind' said Wynton apologetically.

'Yes there are some fantastic looking women in Jamaica – I presume you were not referring to the food' Mitch said laughing.

They both selected the lobster and piled their plates with everything that was going. A couple of Red Stripe on top of a full stomach and both quite happy to sit back and listen to the Reggae rhythms' being played out on the steel drums - a brief opportunity for them to forget the murderous activity going on all around them.

Mitch was first to break the spell 'you wouldn't believe what is going on throughout the island but especially in Kingston and Montego Bay. Every day the Gleaner is reporting shootings and murders in the townships. They can't run a political rally without it finishing up with bloodshed. Yesterday the security forces shot dead three gunmen in Olympic Gardens and recovered three 38 Smith and Wesson revolvers and a dozen boxes of ammunition. These small arms must be coming in on these shipments from Cuba. Twelve AK47's were seized at Montego Bay airport the other day.'

'What are the polls saying – which of them is in the lead? asked Wynton.

'Depends which paper you are reading. Gleaner has JLP well ahead but if you listened to Jamaican Broadcasting Corporation [JBC] or read the Daily News then it's still all to play for. Now listen to this. The Daily News and JBC ran this poll and the question was' and Mitch dragged a small newspaper cutting out of his wallet and read out 'do you think the CIA may be involved in stirring up trouble in Jamaica?'

Both laughed out loud at the very thought of it. 'And what was the answer queried Wynton.

'JBC Radio News reckoned, and I had to scribble this bit down, 'one out of three Jamaicans believe the CIA is stirring up trouble in Jamaica' answered by those 'who knew something about the activities of the CIA'. Apparently 32.7% could not answer as they were unfamiliar with CIA activities.' Mitch was doubled up by this time. 'This is comical propaganda of the very highest order.'

'Just imagine if Dexter got wind of this. That roughly 600,000 Jamaican's had been privy to details of CIA covert activity on the island.' Again both doubled up with laughter at the thought of Dexter's response.'

'In fairness, and to demonstrate its commitment to balanced reporting it also reported 18.6% felt the KGB had infiltrated Jamaica' added Mitch.

Wynton realised they were beginning to attract attention and added a serious note to the conversation 'what we have to remember is the JBC and Daily News do carry weight and it's this steady drip feeding of anti-imperialist and anti- American stuff that changes minds. All they have to do is add a decimal point and the results take on an air of credibility.'

'What's happening on the security front? How are the police and army responding to all these killings?' enquired Wynton.

'Difficult to gauge but thousands of PNP supporters turned out for a demonstration against harassment by the security forces. It lasted all night and they blocked off Half Way Tree Road' replied Mitch. 'The other story is the PNP have cancelled an order for M16 rifles intended for the security forces. This leaves them vulnerable if the AK47's get into the hands of the PNP gunmen. Makes it critical we destroy as many of these as possible when the time comes.'

Most of the families were leaving the barbecue. Mitch nodded a brief farewell to the English family staying at Devon Place, the father struggling to coral their three children and Wynton again noting the beautiful dark haired English lady. With just a half dozen residents left Wynton pulled his chair closer to Mitch 'I hope you are going to give me some good news – Red Snapper always seems to be one step from total disaster – I now know what it must feel like to be a high wire act without a safety net.'

'Well I have as they say good news and bad news' replied Mitch uncertain with what to lead.

'Oh Christ no – not more bad news?' winced Wynton.

'Let's start with the arms shipments into Jamaica. Everything worked like clock-work' Mitch paused for a moment before adding 'for a time. We accurately identified the spot for unloading the Trojan cabin cruiser. The surveillance vessel gave us accurate coordinates and plenty of time to get ready. We had rehearsed how we were going to blow up the boat but to cut to the plain facts we planted twice as much Semtex – H as we originally intended. The resulting explosion and fireball could be seen for ten miles and the area was crawling with Cuban, American, and every other maritime nation in the bloody world mounting search and rescue. Our plan was for the boat and crew to disappear without trace. The good news is, as far as we are aware, no one is openly fingering the CIA. What they are actually thinking is another matter all together.'

'I can live with that – by the standards of every other aspect of Red Snapper that was a roaring success and no pun intended' Wynton responded, visibly relaxing another objective had been partly completed. 'This might delay other shipments.'

'Now I'll come to the not so good. One of the team, Ebenezer, killed this 17 year old lad. He thought he was part of the arms smuggling gang but it appears he was just a kid snooping around for something to do. The newspapers are reporting an accident – appearing to have stumbled and fell over a cliff smashing his head on the rocks.' Hard as he was Mitch had a conscience when it came to young people but there was no point in blaming or punishing Ebenezer – he knew by his own experience few covert operations went to plan. 'There is nothing in the papers to suggest he was involved in or killed by criminal activity – so that's another item of good news.'

'OK I can live with that but I'm getting very nervous as to what you are about to say.'

'There is no happy ending to this one. Our plan was to destroy one of three light aircraft bringing arms or other supplies in. We reckoned they were using the road at Duncans but the coordinates given to us took us to an airfield – Georges Valley Airstrip in Saint Elizabeth. We knew about it – visited it several times and worked out a plan to sneak a small bomb on board. We set ourselves up but as this plane was landing all hell broke loose – the bloody police were waiting as well. There was also another reception committee waiting so a fire fight ensued. Next thing another light aircraft flew over opening fire on the police – they scarpered and the first plane took off and escaped. We reckon our surveillance vessel got our target confused with an incoming drugs flight.' Mitch took out another cutting from his pocket showing the article from the Gleaner describing the incident and the government promising a major offensive on illegal landings. 'Apparently they have identified 28 illegal airstrips and stepped up their own surveillance. I reckon the Cubans will now suspend all shipments by air. So we have to admit defeat on that one. We could have been so easily arrested or worse and linked with the drugs scam. We hardly had a credible alibi.'

'Or we could look at it more positively the police have done our job for us. Do we know where the guns and RPG's are being stored?' asked Wynton.

'Well yes and no. Ebenezer followed the truck taking the arms shipment from the cabin cruiser and as we expected they headed straight for Spanish Town. This was necessary to avoid the curfew in downtown Kingston. Ebenezer knows his way around Spanish Town and he followed the Chevy to where they parked it. He then paid a surprise visit to one of his relatives – an elderly aunt he hadn't seen for years. Seems they were burnt out the night before by some PNP thugs and attacked with machetes. He was going to use her house to spy on the truck but having seen what happened – he totally lost it. He went after some PNP activists and started his own civil war. Six were killed in the gunfight that followed. Ebenezer scarpered from the scene and is now on a wanted list. His picture is in the Gleaner and Star so has gone into hiding. Somebody must have recognised him.' Mitch slumped back in his chair somewhat relieved to get all the bad news off his chest.

'But you still don't know where the arms are being stored?' questioned Wynton.

'Immediately after the shoot out he got on his motorbike and went back to Moneague – back to this bungalow he was renting with Christian. He met up with Christian before disappearing somewhere in the Cockpit Mountains. He gave Christian a very good description of the truck – a blue Chevy with one or two very obvious distinguishing marks like no back fender. Christian set up surveillance at the docks behind the cultural delegations office block and sure enough 24 hours later that afternoon who should pull up but the blue Chevy with the missing rear fender. Boxes were off loaded and put into the shipping containers. It is our best guess this is one of their main storage depots – handily placed for access and security - outside their backdoor. May not be the only one but we reckon it's the one to destroy when the time comes. We also overheard they lost quite a bit of gear because of the hurricane and we reckon they had another storage depot between Annotto Bay and Buff Bay. The hurricane struck the east and north east coast – Kingston apart from trees and power lines down escaped comparatively lightly.'

'OK Mitch – it's my impression the outcome of this election is too close to call. The violence in the marginal constituencies is getting worse by the day. The PNP are the main perpetrators backed by Cuban terrorists but the JLP are also getting arms from somewhere. Without any of this intimidation and violence my intelligence is telling me the JLP will win. My biggest fear now is a Cuban military backed coup.' Wynton had used his own tactics to elicit everything he could from Mitch. He no longer trusted anyone to the same degree before he took control of Red Snapper and he now looked at Mitch with a degree of unwarranted suspicion.

'I agree with your assessment and from my perspective my task is now more critical. This arsenal has got to be put beyond use' said Mitch trying his best to reassure his boss. 'If we are right then stopping these Cubans is essential.'

'There is something I haven't told you – not deliberately but because I have only recently learned of it. In addition to the cultural delegation we have another mini army of Brigadista's being trained in Cuba and they will travel to May Pen about two weeks before the election. They are a bunch of brainwashed young men trained in urban warfare. They are currently building accommodation for them as we speak' said Wynton. 'Our understanding is they will build and man roadblocks preventing the security forces from either leaving their barracks or from moving around Kingston. They have the firepower to overcome both the JDF and JCF.'

'What do we want to do about them' asked Mitch.

'We need to travel to May Pen and see what is happening. Let's find out how many they are planning to accommodate – there must be some activity and again there is bound to be a weapons store' speculated Wynton. 'And if there is you know what needs to be done.'

'I'm not certain I can do that. I am down to one man. I reckon Ebenezer is not going to show up and if he did would be a potential liability.' Mitch's mood had switched from quiet confident to undisguised concern.

'But we still have a problem – what do we do about Ebenezer and, not wishing to add to your problems, our friend Carlton has gone on the run. Members of the security force are after him in connection with a murder. We need to get to him and find out just what has been happening.'

CHAPTER 27

Roberto Santos punched in the four digit security code opening the door to his underground four car parking lot. A black Buick convertible with dark tinted windows and white walled tyres drove past him. One minute later he was joined by Manuel Franqui and Joaquin Roselli. Manuel and Joaquin hugged Roberto warmly, Cuban style, and made their way to the barbecue area beside Roberto's lavish marble tiled patio. A large pot of fresh coffee and plate of amoretti made an unspoken welcoming statement.

'We are in business my friends. I got the impression McKenna was very relieved to welcome us on board. He appears to have accepted everything I told him.' Turning to Manuel, Roberto continued clearly excited about the prospect of another go at Castro 'our stories dovetailed perfectly – well done.'

'Do you think he has made the connection?' asked Manuel.

'He suspects it but he has no proof. And what if he does – he has given me the go ahead to get rid of our three enemies and those controlling the Brigadistas in Cuba. He can't go back on the agreement and he can't change the plans because we are now operational. He loaded the gun and we are the ones aiming and pulling the trigger' replied Roberto.

'The big challenge is Rafael Gallegos' interjected Joaquin. 'I want him more than any of the others.'

'You can't afford to think like that Joaquin' said Roberto firmly, sensing what was coming next. 'I know how you feel about the man, we all share your pain.'

'I'm sorry Roberto but you don't know how I feel. He murdered my father, my mother lost everything and I'm blaming him for her premature death' responded Joaquin, now finding it necessary to rise from the table to control his anger.

Raphael Gallegos had been a senior figure on the Committee for the Defence of the Revolution at the time Castro took the decision to nationalise all small businesses such as shops, bars, restaurants and repair shops. Joaquin's father complained bitterly to the authorities about losing control of his restaurant business – a business he had spent years building. His complaints were investigated by Raphael Gallegos and he was charged with profiteering, corruption, idleness and immorality and imprisoned without trial. He died in prison and his mother left penniless unable to keep even the most menial of positions in the restaurant. She died two years later. Joaquin vowed he would have his revenge.

'I am going to remind you once again Joaquin, I agreed to including his name on the hit list, against my better judgement I might add, because you gave me your assurance this would not turn into a personal vendetta. Now sit down please' said Roberto forcefully recognising he had to re-establish control over proceedings.

'OK, OK the mention of his name is enough. Yes I know what we agreed' answered Joaquin recognising his outburst helped no one.

'You have to eliminate all three at more or less the same time otherwise McKenna or Broadbent will suspect something. If they suspect what we are up to we can kiss goodbye to life as we know it – we have to do things in a way we leave them with no leads to follow. All three of our enemies have to be liquidated by the first week of October latest. According to our report to McKenna the Brigadista operation will have been completed the week before. That is the one operation we can predict with certainty' continued Roberto still maintaining his forceful grip on proceedings.

'Don't worry my plans are well advanced. 'Almeria' is monitoring their movements and obtained details of future travel plans and scheduled meetings. Things are hotting up on the island – violence in the townships is bordering on civil war and according to 'Almeria' the PNP are becoming very jumpy because they sense the election is not going their way. It appears JLP supporters are starting to give as good as they get – they are getting powerful weapons from somewhere. They are seriously revising their plans about how to control the army and police. They have just cancelled an order of M16 rifles destined for the police saying they haven't the money' Joaquin reported, having now settled down to the business of the day.

'And I presume your plans for dealing with this Brigadista army is equally advanced? enquired Roberto now trying to reduce the tension.

'You can bet your life on it' replied Joaquin. 'I have that fully under control.'

All three looked at each other before bursting out laughing.

Joaquin continued 'there is one problem. 'Almeria' wants out now. He reckons they are watching him more closely than normal. He is not being included in all their planning meetings – unexpectedly sent on errands when key meetings have been scheduled.'

'It is essential he remains in post. If he disappeared now it would confirm their suspicions. Tell him this but reassure him we will get him out immediately after the deed is done' replied Roberto.

'He knows this but it does mean I will have to act soon. I don't know how long he will hold his nerve. It is critical I coordinate the assassinations – they have to occur almost simultaneously otherwise security will be tightened and we will have blown our chance. Either way we will have to get 'Almeria' out of Kingston – evidence or not they will assume him guilty by association' said Joaquin.

'One final thing' continued Joaquin 'do you have the necessary press releases prepared and links with key wire service bureaus?'

'Yes, everything is awaiting your phone confirmation that Gallegos is dead. The confusion should keep the PNP and Cubans guessing for days. The code word for a successful outcome is 'Calle Ocho'.'

Joaquin had made four secret incursions into Cuba since he fled the country and revolution in 1959. On each of these visits his one and only target was the assassination of Fidel Castro and on each of these occasions circumstances had conspired to deny him. Dexter was an unforgiving controller and held these failures against him. His own reputation had suffered as a consequence. This time his target was Raphael Gallegos – a very close companion and supporter of Castro. Gallegos had been constantly by Castro's side in his fight against Batista, spent months in the Sierra Maestra on the run with Castro and two years in jail following his capture by Batista. The assassination of Raphael Gallegos will hurt Castro in much the same way as the death of Ernesto Guevara did. If he succeeded in his mission not only would he have got his revenge for his parent's death but just might get Dexter Broadbent off his back.

'Our three friends will eliminate Felipe Fernandez and Raul Garcia while I take on Raphael Gallegos. I will hold up somewhere in Cockpit country but if the election does go to the PNP I will need an exit route. Airport security will be stepped up and there is no way 'Almeria' can get back from either Kingston or Montego Bay' said Joaquin.

'Mancini is due here in an hour. I think he is working alongside the CIA on some secret and very obviously illegal scam. His tasks are to get the three mercenaries out of Mariel and to hold them in one of his training camps in the Everglades. We tell him nothing about our deal with McKenna' commented Roberto changing the topic of the discussion now satisfied Joaquin was back to his professional self.

'I heard a rumour Mancini had been arrested by the FBI' interjected Manuel.

'I spoke with him the other day and yes he mentioned it. Was furious and reckons someone set him up but the FBI have now dropped their investigation. That to me is Mancini speak for CIA involvement. The FBI do not arrest villains on misunderstandings and then let them go with an apology' snorted Roberto.

'If he is working for the CIA then won't he know about Red Snapper?' queried Manuel.

'Dexter Broadbent doesn't work like that. He is the one controlling Mancini and he may have been given some peripheral task but he will not have been trusted with the bigger picture - simply too dangerous for him to be given too much information. It works the same way with us - McKenna is not party to the deal we have with Dexter to discredit Carter over the Marieletos and if I know Dexter he won't have told McKenna what Mancini is up to either' said Roberto. 'This is one hell of a murky world.'

'McKenna knows the Mafia is looking at Jamaica as a possible business opportunity – I mentioned this to him at our first meeting months ago. I wanted to impress him I knew more than I did – I sensed a pay cheque' said Manuel.

'It's important for us to use Mancini because he can provide the confirmation to Dexter he lifted three Cuban mercenaries from Mariel. This provides the independent confirmation for our story about the Brigadista operation. Mancini won't be able to keep his mouth shut and on this occasion that's precisely what we want. We want everyone to know we were working with three undesirables who were part of a team that assassinated the leadership of the Brigadistas, Felipe Fernandez, Raul Garcia and you know who.' Roberto not risking mentioning Rafael Gallegos's name a second time.

'From my conversation with McKenna I am certain he has not involved Mancini. The relief on his face was so obvious when I accepted the task of eliminating the leadership of the two organisations ' replied Roberto.

Dead on 11:00 Marcello Mancini was shown on to the patio area by Roberto's Cuban housemaid.

'Good morning gentlemen – it's good to see you all again' said Mancini trying his level best to sound sincere.

They all stood to greet him but only with a handshake. He didn't qualify for the full Cuban style welcome. He was offered coffee and greedily consumed the remaining amoretti. 'Didn't have time for my mid-morning snack' he volunteered trying to justify his greed.

Roberto opened proceedings. 'Your first task is to lift our three friends from Mariel. It is still chaotic over there and we don't anticipate you will have too much of a problem. You will have to accept other passengers and God knows who or what they might be. Don't argue with the authorities just accept what you are given.'

'And how do I distinguish the good from the bad?' asked Mancini.

'Tell us the name of your boat and we will radio this on to our friends in Cuba. You will also fly this flag.' Roberto handed Mancini a red triangular flag with one large white dot in the centre. 'They will make themselves known to you and immediately all are on board push off as fast as you can. They will be travelling under false identities and don't be surprised if their appearance gives rise to suspicions about their gender or mental state. Please don't let your prejudices influence your actions.' They all laughed at the potential trouble that might arise if Mancini gave vent to his natural feelings and inclinations.

'Once I get them out they will be taken to a safe house in Fort Lauderdale. You can organise the pick-up and transfer to the training camp in the Everglades. They will be away from prying eyes – the camp is fully protected with electrified fences and attack dogs. From this point everything is down to you except transportation to Jamaica. I've got that organised' commented Mancini keen to show his clients he was on top of the task.

'Joaquin will take over the training and operational details' replied Roberto.

'Sounds nice and easy for once - I'll need my usual 50% up front and the rest when they are safely off my back – whenever that might be. ' Mancini slowly got to his feet and again extended his fat sweaty hands. And with that final comment the repulsive looking Mafia boss departed.

'I take it we can now leave it to you Joaquin. It is good to be fully active again - hitting Castro where it hurts and swelling our bank balance. If we pull this off we will have achieved all we set out to do' concluded Roberto 'and we will have a party to end all parties.'

CHAPTER 28

Kingston was in the middle of a tropical downpour. Flash gulleys were struggling to contain excess water. The road directly in front of the Pegasus was submerged under two feet of filthy black water and closed to light vehicles. Wynton took one look outside, snatched an umbrella from the rack by the hotel entrance and sprinted through the back streets to rendezvous with Mitch parked 300 yards south on Half Way Tree Road. The streets were deserted – the rain having driven everyone inside. The Jamaican womenfolk not risking a single rain drop on expensively straightened hairstyles.

'Are we going to get through to the north coast?' asked Wynton cursing this latest setback.

'These storms seldom last more than an hour and flash gulleys drain surface water in minutes. Let's get moving, we can't risk the engine getting flooded' replied Mitch keen to get out of Kingston.

'Do you know where these holiday homes are in Oracabessa?' queried Wynton.

'No – no idea. There may be a hundred reasons why Carlton isn't answering his phone but it did seem to be ringing out OK' Mitch referring to the fact they were hoping Carlton could have provided directions. 'They should be easy to find. I just hope Carlton hasn't moved on.'

'We have to check it out – we have to be sure one way or another. There can't be many holiday lets on the banks of Jacks River' replied Wynton.

The rain continued for about another 45 minutes and many parts of the A1 were axle deep in mud brown flood water. Some cars had pulled over but wagons continued oblivious to the consequences of their tidal wave causing Mitch to cut his speed.

They stopped briefly at Ewarton to buy fruit from a deserted vendor's stall – leaving money in an honesty jar. It seemed everyone had found better things to do.

Three and half hours after setting off they arrived in Ocho Rios, turned east along the busy coast road and after crossing Jacks River immediately swung right onto a narrow and deserted dirt track. The track was no wider than the pick-up but eventually opened up to a clearing surrounded by dense tropical forest.

The rain had stopped, narrow wisps of steam were rising from the perimeter vegetation creating an almost mystical backdrop to the five small green painted wooden bungalows perched on a ten foot tall embankment overlooking the river. All with narrow road facing verandas' just big enough to squeeze in two square bamboo chairs. All looked deserted or even abandoned - Muriel's holiday home description was more realtors' than reality.

Wynton turned to Mitch and instructed him 'drive into Oracabessa and find a public phone, ring Carlton's number – I will listen out for it but give me at least ten minutes to move between the bungalows.'

'That's if I can find one' replied Mitch recognising the need to resolve the Carlton mystery as fast as possible.

Fifteen minutes later Wynton started to tread a path in front of the bungalows listening out for Carlton's phone. On his third pass he heard a phone ringing in the one closest to the main road. He knocked on the door – no answer. He shouted Carlton's name – no answer. He looked around to see if anyone was watching and was just about to put his shoulder to the door when he heard the key being turned.

'Good to see you Wynton – are you alone?' whispered Carlton as he opened the door trying his best to make it sound like a response to a routine courtesy call.

'No, I've Mitch with me – answer the damned phone. It will be Mitch ringing from somewhere in Oracabessa. Can I come in?' asked Wynton not knowing what to expect. He still had his suspicions – Muriel had not completely dispelled them with her performance in the coffee bar.

'You've got Mitch with you?' exclaimed Carlton incredulously. 'There are things happening here you need to know about. I need to speak with you alone.' The phone stopped ringing causing Carlton to momentarily clam up. 'We need to have a conversation. I don't answer the phone because it may be bugged or might raise questions why someone is living here. I need to get off this bloody island.' Carlton was clearly a worried man and his worries had just got worse. He hadn't shaved for days, body odour starting to overpower every other unpleasant smell and he made no attempt to hide the gun lodged in his waist band. Empty Red Stripe bottles were neatly stacked on the small dining table.

His appearance worried Wynton. Wynton wasn't too concerned about Carlton's welfare but very worried by what caused this big change in his appearance.

The noise of the Toyota made Carlton grab Wynton's sleeve 'we need to talk and I don't need an audience. You have four weeks before the election and four weeks to stop this place going the same way as Grenada.'

'I need to talk to you as well – there are a stack of unanswered questions not least of which is why you disappeared?' replied Wynton. 'The first question is how do you think I got this phone number?'

'There's only person who knows this number. Muriel Sharma – Business Editor at the Gleaner' answered Carlton somewhat puzzled by Carlton's aggressive questioning.

'Well that stacks up. I had an explosive conversation with your friend Muriel in more ways than one – I still feel the after effects. Judging by the tone of the article published in the Gleaner last Sunday the two of you did a great job of destroying the credibility of the PNP to run the country.' Wynton had started to feel some sympathy for Carlton – it was not difficult to connect his appearance with someone in deep trouble and genuinely in need of help.

At this moment Mitch entered the bungalow 'well guess who – why didn't you answer the bloody phone?'

'We've been through all that' said Wynton.

Carlton was very surprised to see Mitch and struggled to make the connection with what he had witnessed the other night. Wynton hadn't briefed him about Mitch having any role to play in Red Snapper. Their paths had crossed briefly on previous missions but his appearance here in the bungalow was totally unexpected and unsettling. It raised the question in Carlton's mind were these two working together on some scam? Sometimes this CIA mania for secrecy within the organisation, Dexter's so called overlapping circle strategy, had its drawbacks – coordination was impossible and suspicions an ever present consequence. Wynton sensed Carlton's demeanour had changed coinciding with Mitch's return.

'Please tell me you had nothing to do with the murder of your friend Toffy?' asked Wynton desperate to clear up this nagging worry.

'For Christ's sake Wynton, why the bloody hell would I risk killing a low level spook like Toffy? I don't need this from you as well.' Carlton's reaction was a combination of anger and indignation that his boss should connect him with a cold blooded murder. 'You obviously have reason to think I'm involved so perhaps you could enlighten me. The bloody police obviously think so. The question going round and round in my head is why?'

Carlton's outburst was not entirely unexpected but it did force Wynton to question the origins of his suspicions and what or who had planted the idea that Toffy's death was anything other than a brutal robbery. The name of Manuel Franqui sprung to mind.

Carlton continued 'Toffy was a decent, genuine guy – all he did was give me some bloody excruciatingly boring conference papers written by self-righteous bigots and a personal take on the mood of the conference. Not exactly life threatening intelligence or a political game changer. I was more at risk because of all the bloody lies and false promises I made him. The police clearly think I'm involved – stuck here for days has got me thinking someone has set me up. Am I being fingered to hide the real villain?' replied Carlton still angry his boss also had him fingered for the murder.

'Let's get you out of here' said Wynton not prepared to enter into any further argument.

'And where to exactly? You seem to be forgetting I am a murder suspect and I also committed a felony on Waterloo Road – I can't just walk into the Holiday Inn or Intercontinental looking like this and without my passport. My passport is at the Mayfair – no, sorry I am staying here until you come up with a way to get me off the island. A friend – and let's leave it that - is bringing me some food and beers so I won't starve. What are your plans?' replied Carlton.

'Plan A was to find you and Plan B was to check out a worrying development at May Pen.' Wynton was keen to speak with Carlton without Mitch present.

'Mitch, go and get Carlton some food, beers and things to freshen him up a bit – the stench in here is overpowering. Don't get them all in one shop – you never know' said Wynton thinking this is the only way he is going to get the chance of a private conversation.

If Mitch suspected Wynton's motives he didn't let on and set off on his errand.

'Who owns a cabin cruiser with the name 'Lucy Jane'? Carlton fired this question at Wynton as soon as the Toyota set off down the track towards the main road.

'Why?' asked Wynton.

'Do you know – yes or no?' replied an anxious Carlton not prepared to reveal his suspicions about Mitch at this stage of the conversation.

'Yes – it belongs to a tourist operation in Fort Lauderdale. The business is part owned by a Mafia boss by the name of Marcello Mancini. The CIA use it as a 'safe house' for meetings or when they want a front for something best hidden from do-gooders or politicians. Now tell me what the hell is going on?' responded a desperately concerned Wynton.

'Because I have seen it off loading what I think are guns and I know it has been taking on drugs – I don't know whose on the receiving end – could be criminals, JLP or PNP but more alarming your friend Mitch was doing the off loading. No one told me Mitch was involved in Red Snapper. Put the shits up me just now seeing you two together?'

'Just what are you insinuating here – Mitch is supposed to be destroying guns not importing them.' Wynton sat down on a wooden stool – his mind struggling to remember the precise words used by Dexter at their last meeting. Was this another possible twist to Red Snapper? 'How the hell did you manage to be in the place where they just happened to be swapping the merchandise?' Both men were close to losing it, tempers fraying and voices raised.

'Because the friend who is helping me is a JLP activist – a friend of Muriel – and they have been actively involved with at least two trips to my knowledge. There may have been more. The reason they are involved is because of the drugs – amphetamines, marijuana and heroin. The stuff is coming over in plane loads from Columbia and Venezuala – Jamaica is the staging post for supplies to the US. This friend of Muriel's is paid to hide the drugs and deliver them when instructed. They get paid when it is delivered to the pick-up point. They drop the drugs off and hightail it as fast as they can. Someone else is handling the weapons. I went along for the ride but was told to keep out of sight at the landing stage. Your friend Mitch is up to his neck in the operation.' Carlton was nervous as to how Wynton might react to this disclosure and involuntarily put his hand on his gun.

Wynton noted the move. He found himself in the intolerable position of not knowing who he could trust. Everyone connected with Red Snapper could conceivably be playing a double game – using Red Snapper as a cover to achieve objectives closer to home. He expected it of the Cuban contingent but not Dexter, Mitch or Carlton. With less than four weeks before the election it was time for him to up his game. Instead of reacting to events and second guessing personal motives it was time to play them at their own game – expose the double dealing bastards. The big issue was where would he start?

By this time Mitch had returned with bread, canned tuna and the inevitable Red Stripe 'best I could do. Nothing I could see to smarten up Carlton except this bar of carbolic.'

'Mitch, I need to borrow the pick-up. I take it you still have your link with Christian – I will drop you there. I need to get Carlton out of here but I'll have the pick-up back this time tomorrow latest.' It was no longer a question of negotiation but one of firm unquestionable demands. Wynton was determined to take back full control of Red Snapper and make his intentions very clear to all concerned. He was on heightened alert and by way of demonstrating this change checked the gun he carried in his shoulder holster - a small but potent sign of the change.

'Without the pick-up I'm stymied – I can't do my work on the back of a two-stroke motorbike' retorted Mitch.

'All I need is twenty four hours and then when I get back I want you to destroy the arms stores and then get your ass out of Jamaica.' Wynton was determined to set the timetable for future actions – limit the degree of freedom for actions unconnected to Red Snapper.

'Why do I have to be in such a hurry to leave?' replied Mitch taken aback by the noticeable change in Wynton.

Wynton noted the pleading and inwardly questioned why the reluctance to leave Jamaica. 'I thought you would be glad to get out of the place.'

'It's beginning to grow on me but if it's an operational necessity then I'll do as you say' Mitch deciding now was not a good time to renegotiate his contract. '24 hours it is and we'll move on the arms dumps. I'll book an open ticket and aim to fly out 48 hours after we're done. I'll clean up Devon Place – leave no incriminating evidence as they say.'

Wynton dropped Mitch off in Moneague – conversation was strained with Wynton reaffirming his promise to have the pick-up back within 24 hours.

Wynton and Carlton stayed in the bungalow overnight setting off very early the next day. Wynton was beyond caring he had no official documents showing he was legally entitled to drive the vehicle – events were again spiralling beyond control and driving a pick-up without insurance didn't even register.

'Where are we going? You are taking a risk aiding a suspected murderer avoid capture?' enquired Carlton still preoccupied with making his escape from Jamaica and still unsettled by any lack of explanation from Wynton.

'This JLP friend of yours – how far can you trust him?' asked Wynton ignoring Carlton's barbed comment.

'I hardly know him – given what I've been through I don't trust many people' replied Carlton.

'Would he do you a favour if we paid him?' asked Wynton.

'Probably but come on Wynton let me into your little plan' replied an increasingly irritated Carlton.

'I want someone who will travel with us to May Pen and ask a few questions about what is going on. Neither you nor I can do it – wrong colour. I have intelligence that suggests a contingent of soldiers will be billeted there just prior to the election - ready to make a move to help the PNP seize control if the election result doesn't come out right' replied Wynton determined to press ahead with his plan irrespective of any opposition from Carlton. He needed to distinguish truth from fiction and he wasn't going to do it by relying on the word of others.

'We can ask – I don't know how he will respond' replied Carlton.

Carlton directed Wynton to a small hamlet of about six houses called Mango Valley. It could be accessed by following the dirt track further inland – no need to return to the main coastal road and take unnecessary risks. Horatio 'Ratty' Jones was tinkering with some mechanical contraption when Carlton called him over and put the proposition to him. 50 US$ was more than enough to secure his cooperation.

It took Wynton two hours to drive the 50 odd miles to the outskirts of May Pen. May Pen was in Clarendon District and normally a sleepy backwater where little of significance ever happened. Politically it had traditionally voted PNP but according to Ratty was beginning to waver in its support.

Ratty was given the task of enquiring about any new building works going on in and around May Pen. His cover was he was looking for work. After a couple of hours he returned with the answer Wynton was half expecting. There was nothing going on in May Pen – absolutely nothing - no new work had been started for months and no comings and goings suggesting things were about to change soon. Ratty seemed to have done a thorough job in his quest for work – enquired at the police station, the rum bar and spoke to JLP supporters. To make absolutely sure they drove one mile down each of the five roads radiating from the centre of May Pen – nothing remotely like an army camp was visible. It was beginning to look as if the construction of a new army camp was the figment of a very creative and devious mind. The name of Manuel Franqui sprung to mind.

CHAPTER 29

Mitch was left puzzled by Wynton's sudden change of mind. The original plan was for him to ride shotgun and not Carlton. Mitch was used to plans being changed at the last minute and certainly this minor change was not going to trouble him. It gave him more time to focus on the task ahead - the reason he had been sent to Jamaica.

His first job was to find Christian.

The day was hot, sticky, unpleasant and energy sapping. Not the ideal day for heavy lifting. Christian was asleep on the veranda of the wooden bungalow.

'Wake up old chap' said Mitch as he gently rocked him out of his sleep. Mitch was aware that Christian had killed and didn't want to startle him into a murderous reaction.

A grunt was all he got – Christian was either spaced out from the ganja or recovering from a night partying with the local women. 'Come on for Christ's sake we've got work to do.' Mitch brought a mug from the kitchen table, filled it at the outside communal tap and threw it over him making sure he was ten feet away by the time Christian collected his wits.

'OK man OK' drawled Christian struggling to regain composure. 'I'm ready man – been waiting for hours for you to turn up.'

'Let's get the gear. Strap the rollers to the roof rack and anchor them with other heavy gear. Have you got your gun and silencer – just in case things turn unexpectedly?' Mitch had been through the plan with Christian many times and the aim was to eliminate the ships containers without wakening half of Kingston.

They set off late afternoon, aiming to join the tea time rush hour in Kingston and slip unnoticed onto the quay just off Marcus Garvey drive and about 400 yards from the Cuban Cultural Centre.

They arrived at their planned destination point at 19:00 hours – three hours before the start of the curfew and one hour before traffic started to tail off. Christian had monitored security by assuming the identity of a scruffy beggar not too concerned with the amount of ass and genitalia on display. People, including security, gave him a wide berth. Security around the docks at that time of night was minimal – nothing serious just an underpaid casual security guard who could be relied upon to disappear at the first sign of trouble. His pay didn't stretch to him actually safeguarding anything. Work on the docks continued throughout the night and the odd vehicle was not unusual.

'Park there' pointed out Christian 'between those two wooden shacks.'

Mitch parked as instructed. They sat in the growing darkness and waited. The adrenalin was kicking in and both were on full alert. Their first task was to loosen the ties of the 10 foot long 4 inch diameter hollow steel rollers and carry them close to the two shipping containers parked eight feet from the dockside and to the rear of the Cultural Centre. The rollers had been stolen from outside of a linoleum warehouse located on the First City industrial park two weeks before.

'Right, let's go' said Mitch. They lifted the first roller down and each taking an end of the 150 pound roller walked as briskly as possible to within 20 yards of the containers and stacked them beside a pile of discarded nautical junk – ropes, hoists, outboard motors, old fishing nets and other bits of waste.

On their sixth and final run disaster struck. Christian bringing up the rear, and probably as a result of the previous night's recreational activities, wasn't quite as alert as normal. He didn't see the metal hoop concreted into the ground and banged into it with his right toe –his cheap trainers provided no protection and he fell heavily dropping the roller in the process. The sudden drag on the ground caused it to slip out of Mitch's grasp and roll noisily towards and over the dockside. Straight onto the top of a moored and thankfully deserted police launch. Rooftop lights were first to be smashed, followed by the sound of splintering glass and finally a loud thud as it bounced onto the deck of the eighteen foot cabin cruiser.

The sound reverberated around the dock area and seemed to go on forever.

'You OK?' whispered Mitch - a touch unnecessary given the racket they had engineered.

'Of all the fucking stupid things to leave lying around in a dockyard' retorted Christian, obviously sore but not incapacitated and displaying his dry sense of humour.

'Let's get the fuck out of here' the language helping to diffuse the tension as Mitch helped Christian limp back into the shadows of the two wooden shacks.

Just as they reached darkness the security guard put in an appearance. He was a bit more diligent than anticipated and tried to piece together the cause of the noise. A hefty blow to the base of the skull with a Smith and Wesson put a temporary end to his investigation. He crumpled noiselessly into an untidy heap.

'Pull him into the shack and tie him up and stick this rag in his mouth. We don't want any further problems from him.' Mitch was quick to size up the situation – he saw no alternative but to eliminate this uninvited intrusion.

'The pole is out of reach so we are going to have to make do with five, four on the first, one on the second and trust to luck our calculations are right. Take a breather – how's your foot' enquired Mitch knowing the two of them were necessary for the second stage of the operation.

'I'll manage – it's not broken thank God' replied Christian having removed his shoe to assess the damage.

They could see the outline of the Cultural Centre from the window of the wooden shack and there was no visible evidence anyone else had been alerted by the commotion.

'Time for stage two – let's go' Mitch whispered and helped Christian up and they went to the back of the Toyota pick-up. They grabbed a two-handled thick canvas sports bag – one used to carrying all the paraphernalia required by a cricket eleven. It was heavy – about 200 pounds and they struggled, resting every twenty yards or so.

Eventually they got to the rear of the first of the two standard twenty foot long shipping containers. These things were about eight feet wide, weighed 4,000 pounds empty and up to 40,000 pounds when full. Mitch hoped they weren't filled to capacity.

They dug out the heavy duty lifting jack – the ones used by commercial vehicle maintenance crews – and positioned it centrally harbour side end of the first container. It was critical for it to be positioned central to the load distribution in the container. Get it wrong and they could be faced with a mission aborting type problem. They accurately measured the central point, stuck the jack under and slowly pumped up the lifting screw – they could feel it leaning left and quickly let it down. They experimented like this for twenty minutes before they were happy they had located the point of equilibrium. Christian quickly shoring up the growing gap with old building bricks and broken concrete slabs conveniently stacked close by for reasons unknown. At a pre-marked point they stopped pumping. Mitch recovered the first of the metal poles and slid it to a point twelve feet from the raised end of the container. He did this four times and each time gently lowering the container until it was resting off the ground and on rollers spaced roughly three feet apart.

'Stay still' whispered Mitch through clenched teeth. He pointed to the Cultural Centre rear entrance – light flooded the area between the building and the shipping containers. Raised voices could be heard and Mitch observed three figures emerging from a rear door.

'Get ready for some action if they come close' mouthed Mitch and indicated to Christian to get his gun ready.

Mitch sneaked his way to where Christian was kneeling 'if they get to the rear of the containers open fire – don't hesitate because we can't make a run for it because of your foot. If they walk between the boxes I'll follow them in but for Christ's sake watch who you are shooting. There are three of them.'

Judging by the sound, and taking into account the Latin temperament, there was little doubt all three were male and arguing. They walked straight to the door of the first container, unlocked it, opened both doors wide and disappeared inside.

Mitch decided to join Christian at the rear 'they have gone into the box – I hope the bloody thing is stable and doesn't start moving. How come they haven't noticed it is four inches off the ground?'

The two of them were seated with their backs resting up against the container – it was Christian who broke the silence 'you take that corner and I'll take this one – lie flat and if anyone attempts to approach our position let them have it. Make sure you put your silencer on we don't want to attract the attention of the bloody Cuban army.'

They both got to their positions and sweated it out. The night was still, not a breath of air, sounds travelled far and it was clear the trio were doing some serious reorganisation inside the container. It was thirty minutes later before a huge shout went up followed by laughter. Two minutes later the two doors could be heard and felt being slammed shut. Bottles could be heard being clanked together and Mitch followed the three silhouettes as they returned to their headquarters. The door was closed and darkness restored to the quayside.

'Christ that was close. Come on let's finish the job.' Mitch was up disconnecting the jack and quickly moved on to the second container. They went through the same motions of finding the central point of equilibrium, lifting the container ten inches off the ground and sliding the one remaining steel pole just two feet from the end. They lowered the container on to the single pole, extracted the jack and pushed it over the side of the quay hoping and praying no one would hear the splash. They sat for ten minutes watching the rear of the Cultural Centre – so intent in fact they failed to notice the coastguard cutter returning to port and heading to a berth directly behind them.

The first they knew about it was when a mooring rope was thrown on to the quay followed by the sound of a crew member clambering up the metal rungs of the dockside ladder ready to secure it.

Quick as lightening Christian was on his feet, hobbled over to where the rope landed and shouted down 'I've got it man, I'll tie it up.'

'Thanks' came the reply and the steps receded back down the ladder.

Christian signalled to Mitch to hide while he waited on the quayside for the crew of the coastguard cutter to come ashore. Ten minutes later the three man crew appeared, thanked Christian and departed without the slightest concern about the identity of the mystery helper.

'Well done, a bit of tension has certainly cleared your mind' commented a relieved Mitch. 'Get the rope.'

Christian limped over to the bag and extracted a forty foot length of one inch rope and passed one end to Mitch. Mitch went to the front end of the first container, threaded the rope through two of the four vertical support bars and knotted it while Christian did the same to the rear doors of the second container with the other end.

'Get back to the car while I get the bag' Mitch whispered. He picked up the sports bag and followed Christian back to the Toyota.

Both were now sweating excessively – the heat, fear and exertion having its effect. They wound their windows down and listened. Not all activity had come to a stop on the docks – stevedores operated throughout the night and a variety of vehicles still operated transferring personnel, equipment and cargo to where needed.

Mitch put the Toyota into reverse and slowly edged his way back from between the wooden shacks. He paused, still no lights and continued slowly in reverse towards the first of the two containers. He backed up until he felt the rear end bump into the back of the container.

'Get your gun ready' he instructed Christian. 'After three' he paused for one final check – one, two, three.' He hit the accelerator hard, tyres began to spin and screech and the ships container began to move. If their calculations were right the rollers would help move the container to a point overhanging the quayside where gravity would kick in and the container topple into the dock. The momentum of the drop would pull the second container on top and into the murky waters of the dock and beyond the reach of the Cubans.

The plan worked perfectly – the first container landing and crushing the small coastguard cutter before sinking twenty feet below the surface and pulling the second container on top. The noise of the steel rollers grinding their way along the uneven quay side was deafening in the still night and the rear door of the Cultural Centre was flung open – light again flooding the now empty quay side and three men with semi automatics stood traumatised by the emptiness before them. It was difficult for them to comprehend – the rear end of the second container slowly disappearing from view.

The grating of gears as Mitch struggled to find first brought them down to earth and made the connection. Three simultaneous bursts of gunfire hit the Toyota – bullets smashed through the rear window before taking out the windscreen. Christian returned fire through the rear window causing a temporary stop to their attack and enough time for Mitch to put some distance between them.

Mitch raced the Toyota west along Marcus Garvey Drive, straight across Three Mile roundabout and down Hagley Park Road. His aim was to lose anyone in pursuit in the maze of roads in Cockburn Gardens. A stray goat blocked his path between two parked cars causing him to break suddenly. The loss of forward momentum flung Christian forward and half out of the shattered windscreen. Mitch immediately sensed Christian was in trouble – his suspicion confirmed as he instinctively tried to grab him. His hand failed to hold on to his blood soaked shirt. Christian was dead.

CHAPTER 30

Marcello Mancini was not going to put himself or any of his boats at risk for this Mariel run. There were too many unknowns in this assignment but he knew a man desperate for work.

Captain Caesar Caine, ex World War Two marine engineer, had sailed the dangerous North Atlantic route, from eastern seaboard ports to Liverpool and back on many a life saving convoy. His tales of German U-boat attacks and exaggerated sea faring yarns made him a legend amongst the weekend leisure sailing fraternity operating from marinas on Florida's east coast. In his late 50's, bulging forearms, pipe resting on protruding chin gave him the appearance of the human manifestation of a well known cartoon character.

A seaman of exceptional calibre but Caesar Caine was no entrepreneur. Immediately the Mariel boatlift got underway he invested a large chunk of his lifesavings in resurrecting a mothballed sub-chaser left over from the war. His first mistake was to believe there were riches to be had ferrying desperate Cubans to a new life in the US. The only income this generated was some measly expenses from Miami based charities. Few Marielitos had anything other than the clothes they stood up in. His second mistake was to overestimate the time the boat run would continue. There were clear and growing signs both Castro and Carter were seriously embarrassed by events, albeit for very different reasons, and keen to halt the exodus. It was becoming very clear the Mariel escape route had just weeks left to run.

So Captain Caesar Caine was delighted to accept an assignment that promised a financial reward many times higher than his daily average. He ignored the very unusual conditions attached to the job like hiding three mentally deranged passengers with indeterminate sexuality from the Miami immigration officials and delivering them to an address in Fort Lauderdale. But deliver them he did to receive his second profitable instalment for his troubles.

Twenty four hours later the three Cuban mercenaries were picked up by Joaquin Roselli from an address which was very close to Las Olas Boulevard. This was typical Mancini black humour – hiding the most dangerous dregs of society amongst the well to do. The hideaway just yards away from the boardwalk sporting upmarket fashion boutiques and jewellery shops and the fabulously rich aged widows with their designer rat like dogs peeking out of designer handbags strutting in search of company.

 Joaquin drove the three mysterious mercenaries south and then west along the 41 until they came to a sign pointing the way to the Miccosukee Indian Reservation bang in the middle of the Everglades. Two miles off the main highway the road forked – one to the Indian Reservation and one to Marcello Mancini's hidden dirty tricks training camp. There were no signs advertising the fact but the twin ten foot electrified perimeter fence with vicious looking attack dogs roaming freely between them projected a clear warning to the uninvited. The training camp had been built and equipped with money laundered from CIA drugs seizures. Mancini was the drugs conduit to the open market creaming off a fat margin in the process.

The camp had been used by a number of US backed guerrilla campaigns against left leaning Moscow backed governments in Central and South America. The CIA had been frequent users in their clandestine war against Castro and many a CIA agent had passed through the Mancini evil tricks academy. Bomb making, tactics for the extraction of information [torture], sabotage, poisons as an alternative murder weapon were just some of the modules on offer.

Mancini was out of his chair in the main wooden hut serving as his headquarters as soon as he heard the Jeep approaching. 'Welcome my friend. Your friends will bunk down in the dormitory over there – beers, food and a microwave should keep them happy for a while – come and have a drink.'

The three mercenaries trooped off ready for a shower and a beer – a sorry looking bunch of deadbeats and still dressed to convey the impression to the Cuban authorities, emigration should be encouraged.

'Who else is here?' questioned Joaquin wasting no time on pleasantries. Joaquin accepted Mancini for what he was and maintained a distant but workmanlike relationship with him. They would never be friends but was quite content to share a drink with the man. They sat facing each other across Mancini's wooden desk surrounded by glass cabinets containing the most effective murder and assassination weaponry in the world.

'You are on your own. You have got the place to yourselves for the next 72 hours when a driver of a white transit Ford van will take you to your next rendezvous - the boat trip to Jamaica. Caesar Caine is an experienced mariner – he's the guy who brought your team over from Mariel. He knows nothing about the real purpose of the trip – he has the appropriate documents to legitimise his visit and for a 48 hour stay over. Your men need to accomplish what they need to do and get back on board unseen before the balloon goes up.' Mancini was stating the limits of his agreement with Roberto and the fact he would accept no responsibility should the time limit expire.

'I take it you have the weapons we asked for?' asked Joaquin ignoring the latter remarks.

'Here are the keys to the weapons store. In addition to those you requested, and the plastic, there is a selection of knives, pistols, grenades – take what you need. There is also plenty of ammunition if you want to use the indoor or outdoor firing ranges – it's all been paid for' replied Mancini. No one could ever accuse Mancini of under delivering on his contracts. He understood the criminal mind better than most – very often ahead of the curve. He sourced his weapons world-wide and it didn't bother him if his import strategy was legal or not – Russian, Czechoslovakian, Israeli companies were regular suppliers. To him it just made good business sense – it made for regular profitable work and put him streets ahead of the competition.

Mancini wished his client good luck and set off back to Miami where no doubt gluttony would be in fierce competition with criminality for his undivided attention.

--------oooooo--------

At 17:00 hours a white Ford van with a double wheeled back axle van pulled up at the gate to Mancini's evil tricks academy, blew its horn and sat with its engine revving. One of the mercenaries, a heavy set man, large ugly features, grey greasy hair held in place with a black Guevara style beret ran to the gate to admit the visitor. The van pulled up outside the wooden HQ, clear evidence he had been before and sat and waited for his passengers.

Joaquin and his team emerged carrying black canvas bags and each with a small rucksack slung casually over the shoulder. All got in the rear of the van with the exception of the man in the black beret who remained behind locking first the HQ and then the security gate – using powerful six digit combination locks.

The team's embarkation point was Key West where Captain Caesar Caine was waiting with his over-priced refurbished sub-chaser. His instructions were to land Joaquin and his team at a small port close to Kingston where they would be met by someone known to his passengers. The only other instruction Caesar Caine was given was to be ready to make a hasty departure between 19:00 and 20:00 hours precisely 48 hours after his arrival. If no one had shown themselves by then his instruction was to leave Jamaica.

After landing the group would split into two – the plan being for Joaquin to be left alone to pursue his personal vendetta against Raphael Gallegos and 'Almeria', together with the mercenaries, taking out the dual leadership of the cultural delegation.

The 72 hours spent at Mancini's training camp had been 72 hours of intense planning, rehearsing and evaluating their assassination plans. This was a once only chance – bungle it and the odds were they would never see Cuba or the US again. Repercussions and reprisals against family members would be brutal and swift. The CIA would deny all knowledge and express suitable outrage such misdeeds were being conducted against a sovereign state!

Joaquin did his own planning. He didn't share his plans with anyone. He was a loner – preferred it that way. Asked detailed questions and insisted on comprehensive answers with relevant photographic images but never shared the outcome with anyone. Getaway options were considered and prioritised. His latest assassination target added a new dimension – the satisfaction of personal revenge.

Key West to Kingston Jamaica is a serious boat ride. Joaquin and the mercenaries retired to the old chart room which had been combined with the galley to create open space. All unnecessary equipment and furniture had been jettisoned by Caesar to accommodate lots of Castro fleeing Marielitos. Just the bare minimum seating remained. They stretched out where they could find comfort and settled down to the sixteen hour boat trip.

Caesar couldn't handle the sub-chaser on his own and for all those things that could go wrong he brought along his two sons. One a trained marine engineer who could be relied upon to keep the powerful inboard motors running at a steady 33 knots and the other a personal fitness trainer armed to the teeth to protect his brother and father should events not work out as planned. Joaquin was happy with the arrangement – father and sons combination left little room for betrayal or double dealing.

Conditions were reasonably benign – a two foot swell and light rain. Visibility was about 800 yards which gave some cover but Caesar was not too worried – he had professionally produced fraudulent documents allowing him to enter Port Henderson and berth his boat in Dawkins Lagoon for 48 hours. His cover was a prospective fresh fruit supply service to Guantanamo.

'Forty minutes to arrival' the personal fitness trainer informed Joaquin. 'It's time for you and your team to disappear until we see if there is a reception committee.'

Joaquin nodded his agreement and together with his three accomplices disappeared down into the engine room and into a small cramped locker – just enough protection against a casual inspection.

The boat cut its engines to one third and glided past the harbour entrance. So far so good – Caesar manoeuvred his boat close to a wooden pier and his son jumped ashore to secure the mooring rope. When he was satisfied he took the passports of his official crew and documents and followed the sign to the harbour master's office, knocked and entered.

He was met by a smartly dressed official – smartly pressed white shirt, black tie, black shorts and knee length socks. 'That's an impressive looking craft you are sailing – I trust you are not about to declare war?' said the harbour master's assistant confirming he had closely monitored his arrival.

'Not soon I hope' responded Caesar laughing and extending his hand. 'The name is Caesar Caine and I'm here with my two sons to see if it's worth us setting up a weekly supply run to Guantanamo – bananas, rum, limes, breadfruit – that type of merchandise. We plan to be here for no more than 48 hours to meet with export agents and to look at loading facilities. They will also be making a visit to inspect storage facilities on board. We have an import licence from the US Government.' Caesar handed all his documents over for inspection.

'Take a seat – my name is Augustas Roberts and I'm acting Harbour Master – my boss was shot and injured at some political rally in Gordon Town.' The acting Harbour Master took out his ledger and recorded details of his visitors before handing back the documents. 'We would normally inspect your boat on arrival but on this occasion we'll forego the opportunity – just keep us informed if you need to delay your departure.'

Caesar breathed a little easier, thanked the friendly official and left. As he walked back to his boat he tried to follow the line of sight from the Harbour Masters office to see what visual protection was afforded by warehouses and other buildings. Not much was the conclusion.

Later that evening as the light was fading a dark saloon pulled up close to the moored sub-chaser. Two men walked to the car from the boat carrying small bags – two men returned to the boat and this continued until Joaquin and his three accomplices were seated in the car. To the neutral observer this was just a procession of two men walking to and from the car but on each journey the personnel changed. Caesar and his two sons remained on board.

'Welcome to Jamaica' 'Almeria' recognised Joaquin as the leader of the quartet. 'Are you ready to make your move? '

'We are as ready as we can be so let's get on with it' responded Joaquin as usual keeping conversation to a minimum. He introduced his three companions but gave little away about the man with the car. There was always the chance they would be captured or plans had to be aborted and identities protected.

After two miles 'Almeria' pulled up and handed Joaquin the keys to a black VW Golf. 'It has a full tank – more than enough to get you there and back. You know the schedule – everything is the same as the original plan. Good luck and let's hope the next time we meet we can enjoy a coffee together in Coral Gables.' Handshakes all round and he was off – on his own to deal with Raphael Gallegos.

The leader of the remaining mercenaries, the heavy set one, joined 'Almeria' in the front seat. They wasted no time and before Joaquin had familiarised himself with the Golf were on their way back into Kingston.

'There have been a number of incidents and these traitorous Cubans are on full alert. Everyone is nervous so no mistakes' so started 'Almeria'. 'We will have just 60 minutes to get back to the boat after our mission is completed.'

'Will you be with us' asked the heavy set man – the man the others called Sevy.

'Yes but I will be travelling with Fernandez and Garcia. They are suspicious of me and fear an assassination attempt so where they go they insist I go with them. They suspect everyone of leaking information but I am the most senior ranked member outside of the leadership and I probably know more than most' replied 'Almeria''.

'Tonight you will stay in a house in the suburbs of Kingston. Food and drinks are available. You must remain out of sight and at 16:00 hours take the black Toyota parked on the drive, join the evening exodus and head back towards the docks and the Cultural Centre. I will be leaving the Cultural Centre and driving Fernandez and Garcia to a big political rally in Montego Bay. I expect to be driving either a Land Rover with a canvas covered back or a white Honda Accord saloon. They interchange them for security but always travel in the rear one. Everyone will be armed with semi-automatics including myself. The plan is to leave the Cultural Centre at 17:30 hours precisely – both have a mania for punctuality. From then on it's over to you and God be with you.' The enormity and unpredictability of the task was hitting home hard and 'Almeria' was feeling no relief even though final responsibility had been taken out of his hands. His life was still very much on the line.

CHAPTER 31

Sevy and his two companions had had enough sleeping rough and each quickly disappeared into their own sparsely furnished bedroom. The house, located in Constant Spring Gardens, was fully protected with steel grills across all windows and doorways – there was also one protecting the open car port. No one was renting or buying these properties any more – too many armed robbers looking for easy pickings. As soon as they became empty they tended to remain so and it was possible to judge the time the property had been vacant by the extent of visible neglect. Overgrown gardens, flaking paintwork, discarded rubbish, broken fences were the more obvious signs.

Next day was spent pouring over maps and the recently taken photographs left by 'Almeria' on kitchen worktops, checking their weapons and other equipment, rehearsing their roles in the planned ambush and working out different escape options.

At 16:00 hours precisely they loaded the Toyota, locked the house and drove into downtown Kingston. Traffic was heavy but most was leaving the city. With no major hold-ups they were in position at 16:45 hours at the intersection where the single tracked railway line crossed Marcus Garvey Drive. To the outside world they were now a team of railway engineers dressed in mud splattered dark blue overalls with the initials JRC [Jamaica Railway Corporation] emblazoned on the back, dark blue hard hats that had seen better days and carrying black canvas bags.

At 17:10 hours an official looking JRC road sign was erected diverting traffic from entering Marcus Garvey Drive from Three Mile Roundabout on Spanish Town Road. The sign had lain hidden behind some overgrown bushes and put there some days before by 'Almeria'. Traffic coming the other way along Marcus Garvey Drive, the planned route for the two car convoy, was left unimpeded. Traffic from this direction, which was mainly factory and dock workers, was gradually easing. Factories normally closed at 16:00 hours and the bulk of dock workers were well on their way home between 16:00 and 17:00 hours but there was always going to be the stragglers, the conscientious and other vehicles using this route.

At 17:26 hours Sevy triggered the red warning lights signalling the arrival of a train. Passenger and dock bound goods traffic both used this railway line and car drivers were used to stopping. Train times were random. One of the team, equipped with red and green flags was waving vehicles through the crossing – anyone querying what was going on was informed that a car had damaged the automatic signal and engineers were working to repair it.

At 17:32 hours Sevy spotted a Land Rover with canvas back approaching followed by a white saloon car – which he assumed was the Honda Accord. All slow moving traffic at the crossing was urged to move quickly before a series of three yellow bollards were placed across the track. The Land Rover was now the lead car about 400 yards from the crossing but was unexpectedly overtaken by an old two-seater sports car. There was nothing that could be done about it – the trap had been set – it was now or never.

The three mercenaries took up their planned positions – two on one side of the crossing and one the other. Their Toyota was parked on rough ground facing the North Causeway crossing Hunts Bay in readiness for their escape.

The old two-seater open topped sports car slowed to a stop ten yards from the bollards. This was the last thing they needed – the target vehicle was now going to have to stop at least 30 yards from the bollards. It meant they would have to break from their planned positions and make a move towards the Honda Accord. Weapons would be exposed and any half alert bodyguard in the Land Rover would be given precious seconds in which to assess and react to the threat.

Still wondering how to deal with this unexpected development a steam locomotive pulling six freight wagons was approaching the crossing and the driver of the old two-seater sports car, an elderly well dressed gent, got out of his car to observe the train and engage Sevy in conversation about his technical problems.

Sevy spotted the opportunity. He ignored the old man's questions and started to remove the bollards. By activating the warning lights to stop road traffic he had automatically switched the railroad signal to green allowing the freight train to proceed. This added a touch of normality to the scene and a potential visual diversion for the occupants of the Land Rover and Honda saloon.

The Land Rover slowed to a stop about three yards off the old sports car with the Honda Accord a further three yards behind. Other cars could be seen approaching in the distance and this was the opportunity before things got complicated.

The three mercenaries, hands wrapped round their semi-automatic pistols, shook off the camouflage of the canvas bags and opened fire. One mercenary had been positioned to take out the occupants of the lead car and Sevy and the other mercenary positioned to target Fernandez and Garcia in the rear.

The lead mercenary quickly used up his first clip and to give himself time for reloading lobbed a hand grenade into the back of the Land Rover. The advantage of surprise was fast diminishing and the driver and one passenger had already exited the vehicle unharmed but the third passenger sitting central on the bench seat took the full blast of the grenade. The Land Rover was now a mangled burning wreck. It was further rocked as the petrol tank exploded

The lead mercenary was now sandwiched between the two Cuban bodyguards who had dropped to the ground and before he could ram his second ammunition clip into place was hit by two bursts – one across the face and one across the chest. He was dead before he hit the ground.

Sevy had run across the front of the Honda Accord in order to give him a clear line of sight and to avoid catching 'Almeria' in the cross fire. But 'Almeria' was already hanging half out the car giving Sevy the clear shot he needed to eliminate Fernandez and Garcia. Bullets were ricocheting off car and road but Sevy was totally focused and emptied his magazine precisely at the point he thought would do maximum damage. Both Fernandez and Garcia were rocked backwards by the force of the bullets impacting on their upper bodies.

The two Cuban bodyguards had reloaded their semi-automatics and had taken up a position in front of the burning Land Rover. Black smoke was belching from the burning wreck but not sufficient to hide the silhouette of the second mercenary. Two coordinated bursts were enough to eliminate him.

'Almeria' had weighed up the situation still lying flat on the ground beside the Honda. He could see the feet of the two bodyguards below the burning Land Rover and let fly with a burst. Bits of cloth, blood and bone burst from between ankle and knee with both left writhing and screaming on the ground. A second grenade through the shattered window of the Honda put to rest any chance Fernandez and Garcia had survived the first attack.

Sevy had been caught in the left shoulder by a ricochet but was still standing and alert. He and 'Almeria' set off towards their parked Toyota, gunned the engine into life and set off at speed across North Causeway. A quick glance through the rear mirror suggested no one was prepared to take up the chase. They raced across the roundabout on South Causeway and onto Augusta Drive before swinging right into Edgewater Docks and the moored sub-chaser.

The explosions and dense black smoke were clearly audible and visible across the three miles of Hunts Bay and a few curious bystanders were watching and trying, no doubt, to connect the incident with the speeding Toyota. Harbour Police were even more vigilant and were fast converging on the Toyota.

Caesar Caine was equally vigilant. He suspected wrongdoing but he also knew he would be implicated. Mooring ropes had been freed, the boat being held in place by the expert hands of the captain and his fitness trainer son ready to jettison the walkway immediately his passengers were on board. The Toyota screeched to a halt just 50 yards ahead of the Harbour Police and 'Almeria' and Sevy sprinted the remaining few yards ignoring the walkway and jumped. Within seconds the sub-chasers powerful engines had them heading towards the narrow harbour entrance and out into Kingston Harbour past Port Royal and into the Caribbean and home. Mission accomplished.

CHAPTER 32

Dexter Broadbent, George T Rosenberg and Wynton McKenna were seated around the highly polished mahogany table in the same secure room at CIA headquarters, Langley, that launched Red Snapper fifteen months ago. The dirty tricks campaign designed to restore Jamaica to a pro-western, US friendly democracy was seven days away from being tested. Seven days before the people of this picturesque Caribbean island exercised their democratic right to choose, of their own free will, without fear, threat or coercion, their next government or so the story goes.

'What's your feeling Wynton, how are people going to vote?' asked a subdued Dexter. No audience to impress, no subordinates to bully and no need of lies, Dexter was in reflective mood. The die had been cast - the outcome now beyond influence.

'Too close to call. Township violence is out of control – the police are powerless to stop it. All they can do is clean up the mess afterwards. I certainly wouldn't want to be casting a JLP vote in Spanish Town or Olympic Gardens' replied a somewhat downcast Wynton. He didn't know what else to say – here he was seven days off an event with consequences for his career. Covert action, dirty tricks and murder, no matter how brilliantly and silently executed, could not be evaluated for its potential impact. No metric had yet been invented capable of monitoring the progress of a destabilising campaign. They just had to sit it out until Thursday 30th October 1980.

For Wynton there was no feeling of euphoria. Instead there was a vacuum where normally some stirring of emotion could be felt. Trust had been the casualty of Red Snapper and several unanswered questions remained. One of the biggest and most intriguing was sitting directly opposite him. Dexter had been playing games with Red Snapper as the sideshow. The cover story, possibly, for one of his much bigger operational 'circles'.

'OK what else is troubling you – you are sitting there with a face like the proverbial smacked ass? It's over – you've done what we asked of you – time to move on' replied Dexter his tone moving one notch beyond the reflective. 'If you are expecting a parade forget it. You know the score for Christ's sake – that's the whole bloody point of covert operations, nobody is supposed to find out. Take the article in the Gleaner – the one showing this big drop in export earnings – stroke of genius. Had the desired effect, World Bank and IMF put an immediate stop to dollar loans until after the election. Now who is going to find out or admit to what went on? The PNP will look bloody stupid if they now admit the statistics were wrong, though they probably suspect it, and no one would believe them anyway and the World Bank wouldn't thank you for pointing the fact out either. They've made their decision.'

'Of course I know that – it's not that what troubles me' Wynton responded angrily.' It's all the double dealing – people you expect to be able to trust turn out to be anything but. Playing their own game – putting lives at risk. Let's start with these three bastards from Cuba. It was your idea to use them. One of them set Carlton up for the murder of the Thai.'

Dexter's colour was beginning to change – a warning sign that worried George but ignored by Wynton 'and how sure are you Carlton didn't murder the guy to protect his own little game?'

'See what I mean, why are you defending the bloody Cuban Franqui. He's the one behind the set up and of all those involved in Red Snapper, Carlton is the one I trust most' responded Wynton no longer worried or frightened by Dexter. If the PNP was going to get back in, and his career down the pan, he was determined to go down fighting. 'If Carlton had been caught and charged he could now be looking at a life sentence – not what you would call a vacation being banged up in a Jamaican prison.'

'You were the one that went running to Manuel Franqui behind our backs giving him advance warning of what we were up to – didn't occur to you then did it? Never occurred to you to let George or me in on your little secret?' fired back Dexter. Spit speckles now soiling the polished mahogany table – a bad sign.

'You said yourself Franqui was a greasy double dealing bastard but now you want to believe him over a guy who has given loyal service to the country for years. What are you going to do about this ghost Brigadista scam they dreamt up? This wasn't just Franqui, your very good friend Roberto Santos was in it up to his neck. Cleverly inter-twined their stories to try and defraud you out of thousands while putting the bloody shits up me. It was Carlton and me who exposed this lie and yet, for some unfathomable reason you want to go on protecting them. Just what is your bloody game Dexter?' Wynton had now lost any pretence of self control – he was determined to get everything off his mind.

George thought otherwise 'this isn't helping – we need to cool it.'

'Cool it my ass – get it off your chest Wynton' Dexter replied now matching Wynton in volume.

'You knew Mancini was up to his usual tricks – selling guns to someone in Jamaica and bringing drugs out. You said so and you made it very clear you were determined to get him off the FBI charge. You were playing games with us at Daisy's B & B – trying to flush out what we knew. Well let me tell you what I discovered since that meeting' and turning to George said 'I'm sorry I haven't told you about this, but Mitch Randall is part of it. He was spotted unloading 'Lucy Jane' on the north coast. So there is a lot more you could tell us Dexter. You owe me that.' Wynton had said more than he planned and the way he did it very much out of character – not his usual style to completely lose it but lose it he did.

The effect was unexpected. Dexter calmed down – a little. 'There are, as you say, games being played out and, like you, I'm not always sure who is pulling what strings. I'll give you another surprise. Joaquin Roselli's assassination of Raphael Gallegos was not what you thought – he was not part of the cultural delegation. He used Red Snapper as cover for a personal vendetta. Gallegos was very close to Castro and for reasons I honestly don't know Joaquin decided the opportunity was too good to miss. Santos put out a press release immediately the deed was done – sent it down the wires to all the press agencies in Jamaica, Cuba, Florida and beyond claiming members of the Jamaican Constabulary Force had foiled an assassination attempt on the deputy leader of the JLP. A paid Cuban assassin had been shot as he lay in wait for the deputy leader to address a political rally in Montego Bay. The press release carried with it the usual delaying tactic 'wait for more' but this only encouraged journalists to go to print without checking its validity. Huge confusion reigns over the incident but Santos did a brilliant job - those looking for a reason to vote JLP just found one. I think we all suspected other agendas were being played out and we end up paying. But when something like this happens I look the other way. I only found this out by accident.'

'How did you find out? Roberto and Manuel put together this very convincing cover story about how the three leaders of this cultural delegation were poised to take control of different parts of government.' Wynton mused inwardly even now he was still being surprised on the downside.

'His name rang a bell – bit of digging and up pops this long standing friend of Castro. Too important to be tied down on risky overseas ventures like this cultural delegation. He was Castro's nominated deputy to liaise with the PNP leadership. He was on a visit to Jamaica to a meeting with them when Joaquin took his chance.' Dexter's mood and tone were stabilising. Maybe he felt he owed Wynton something. It was years since he had been on any covert mission and maybe he was beginning to forget the way danger and isolation impacted on the mind. He helped himself to a generous glass of his favourite whisky.

Dexter continued in similar vein 'Mancini and his kind are a fact of life. Fast opportunists up to new tricks before the Fed have even caught up with the last lot. Businesses could learn a lot from him but then Mancini doesn't let little matters like regulation and legislation cramp his style. But he has his uses.'

'Are you saying you set him up for this Jamaican guns and drugs run?' queried Wynton determined to get to the bottom of things troubling him.

'No I most definitely did not. His arrest by the Fed was the first I knew about it. Mancini could do a lot of damage if he was put on the witness stand – he could blow the lid on a can of worms the size of a gasoline storage tank. I had to move fast and convinced the Fed he was part of a government backed covert operation designed to undermine the PNP. The price for getting him off the charge was for him to give Mitch a job. Red Snapper is probably Mitch's last operational job and he is looking for work. We also need someone who can keep us informed on Mancini' Dexter took another gulp of whisky hoping he had said enough to satisfy Wynton.

'But you are not explaining what Mancini was up to in the first place and why all the bloody secrecy? Mitch was part of my operational team' continued Wynton far from happy with Dexter's explanation.

'I've already given you the explanation at Daisy's – he moves fast and was building the groundwork for his casinos and cementing his supply chain for moving Columbian drugs into Miami. There is nothing more to say. He is expecting a JLP victory and I would bet a year's salary he has got some of these prospective MP's in his pocket. As I said he moves fast. I would also bet another year's salary he is behind some of the upsurge in JLP violence against the PNP.' Dexter had a way of using his massive frame to say that's it – that's the end of the conversation. Take it or leave it.

George sensed it and was determined to change track. He accepted Dexter's explanation about the fat Mafia boss – everything he said about him had a solid ring of truth about it. 'Let's get back to our Cuban friends. A Cuban was behind the murder of the Thai in Kingston and Manuel Franqui, for whatever reason, tried to shift the blame onto Carlton. Secondly they invented this Brigadista detachment and tried to take us for thousands for eliminating the non-existent leadership and finally used the cover of the cultural delegation to assassinate a high ranking official. What are you going to do about them Dexter – this is in your court now?'

-------000000-------

George and Wynton decided to take a walk in the park – a walk to clear the mind and rediscover their sense of perspective. They both felt the need to get away from the crisis driven atmosphere pervading every nook and cranny of the world's biggest intelligence factory.

'Do you remember the time when you were waiting for your examination results to be posted on the faculty notice board? That nauseous feeling in the pit of your stomach – well that's how I feel right now only ten times worse' reflected Wynton managing a weak smile at the thought of what he went through many years before. Even a weak smile had a mildly relaxing impact on the tensions pervading his mind and body.

'I didn't go to university but I guess it was a similar feeling before graduating as a fighter pilot – it was the only thing I ever wanted to do with my life' replied George fully understanding the trauma Wynton was under and his inner torment. He was taking this too seriously – so what if the Jamaicans decided to run with Manley for a second term. But George also knew Wynton was ambitious and Red Snapper would haunt him to the day he died.

'I know this is totally irrational but I feel totally responsible for the outcome of this election. It's as if one million Jamaicans have no influence over the outcome – just me. They have to live with this Marxist bullshit; broken promises, empty shelves, no medicines, petrol shortages – surely they can't want another four years of Manley? They have more intelligence and common sense to fall for it a second time round – don't they?' asked Wynton seeking out any crumb of comfort Thursday's election result will be the right result.

'It depends how deep the fear and intimidation goes. Try and put it out of your mind - we only have three days to go' said George trying his best to calm things. 'I do want you to be prepared if the result goes against us – you realise the blame game will start – and will start big time. Shit will be heading our way faster than a guided missile. Bonesman or not, nothing will stop it hitting us hard and it will stick. The smell will linger. Expect your applications for promotion to stay in the in-tray for a while' said George trying to prepare the ground should the worst happen.

'Thanks George but I guessed that. I'm half expecting the worst because nothing went the way I planned it. Everything I touched had a downside to it. I reckon that's the reason I lost it with Dexter but I don't regret one word. I still think Dexter is holding back. What you see is about all you get from Dexter' reflecting on his confrontation hours earlier.

'You did right to go for him the way you did – spontaneous – from the heart. You left him in doubt there was a line beyond which you wouldn't travel. He has difficulty in recognising a principle – years of lying, twisting words but what surprised me was the way he backed off. He respects you – for the moment' said George. 'He has an odd way of showing things – normally anyone accusing him like you did would feel his hands round their throat so to speak.'

'I would like to be the proverbial flea on the wall when he meets up with Roberto. Surely that has to be the end of the Cuban connection – you could never trust them again' reflected Wynton.

'I am going to tell you something that I only found out very recently' said George altering his tone to match the gravity of his new disclosure. 'Not all Dexter's operational 'circles' are as watertight as he thinks. I stumbled across this totally by accident and he doesn't know I know. The military and the higher echelons of the CIA have had enough of Carter. Jamaica is a much bigger fish now compared to when you first alerted us to Castro's plans. Whatever happens in three days you will at least be credited with the intelligence. Grenada was the catalyst and I'd like to wager a princely sum the outcome of their election might be reversed under a new administration' reported George.

George guided Wynton by the elbow to a wooden bench located beneath a large spreading oak tree overlooking a small ornamental lake.

'If you are trying to comfort me you are not succeeding. I was hoping you were going to say the opposite, Jamaica is of little concern.' retorted Wynton.

'Let me finish. Dexter is part of a dirty tricks campaign being funded by the Reagan/Bush ticket to get rid of Carter. Dexter and other 'old hands' have been waiting their opportunity to get back at Carter for sacking hundreds of Miami based Cuban CIA contract spooks a few years ago. Dexter is funding Roberto Santos to use the Mariel boat lift to discredit Carter. This huge influx of immigrants including the dregs of Cuban society has led to a huge wave of anger amongst the electorate across the whole country. This anger is being partly stoked by Dexter through exaggerated and distorted press releases being put out through local Cuban press agencies. The Marielitos have already led to some very high profile political casualties – Bill Clinton for one. So the stakes are a lot higher than you could possibly have imagined!' concluded George.

'Which probably means, come what may, Santos and Dexter will continue to feed off each other' replied a dispirited Wynton.

'Very probably – but I don't know what will protect Manuel Franqui' George replied suggesting there will be a casualty.

CHAPTER 33

Dexter Broadbent was not prepared to take the risk of driving alone to the Miramar Medical Centre. What he had to say and do would have consequences – potentially unpredictable consequences. His chauffeur for the day was a borrowed hit man from a different directorate. He had his safety and reputation to consider.

Luciano recognised the visitor but didn't relax the protocols. Accompaniment to reception, validation of I.D. and other credentials and handover to centre staff were ingrained procedures. There was no way Luciano would expose his boss and benefactor to risk. The hit man stayed in reception under casual surveillance.

'Welcome to the Miramar Medical Centre' Santos was out in double quick time to greet his visitor. Santos had no idea what the agenda was but he had a lot to hide – he was nervous but trying anxiously not to show it. Dexter Broadbent didn't often grace the Miramar Medical Centre with his substantial presence.

'Good to see you Roberto – nice operation you have here' replied Dexter making his point what had been given could easily be taken away.

The point registered with Santos and with it his growing nervousness. This was not going to be a courtesy call. 'Yes, you are right, a nice operation. Come this way please – into my office.'

They sat facing each other across the cheap round plastic table – the scene played out weeks before with Wynton McKenna. 'Roberto, I want your take on Red Snapper. The election is three days away and I need to put contingency plans in place – just in case Red Snapper is a waste of everyone's time and the CIA's money. Questions are being asked' lied Dexter. Here he was again playing games, applying pressure, unsettling his host and determined to make life as difficult as possible for Roberto.

'Where do you want me start?' enquired Roberto. No need to volunteer anything, stay calm and just answer the man's questions was his thinking.

'No pressure – just tell it how it happened' replied Dexter. He was handing Roberto the rope with which to hang himself.

'OK, let's start with the NAM conference. I think we confirmed what you already knew but hopefully the transcripts of the break out meetings gave you some new insights. It seems a lot of suspicion fell on your mole Toffy – wasn't quite as discreet as perhaps he should have been. Sorry to hear what happened to him in Kingston' started Roberto trying to give Dexter the answers he hoped he wanted to hear.

'And what precisely did you hear because what happened to him and why is still a mystery to us?' shot back Dexter quick as lightening hoping to catch Roberto out.

Roberto was ready 'what we told McKenna – he was poking an unwanted nose into a far eastern drugs syndicate and someone didn't like it.'

'Bit of an overreaction don't you think? Sniffing around, as you put it, is not usually a motive for murder and why wait until he is back in Kingston. It would have been easier to cover up his death in Cuba.' Dexter quickly moved on leaving no opportunity for Roberto to respond. He knew Roberto was not going to speculate further but denying him the opportunity left the outcome unresolved. Unresolved issues strengthened Dexter's hand for what was to come.

Dexter continued 'let's move on to this Brigadista operation. What evidence we have is they have yet to put in an appearance on the island and probably too late now to have any impact. I am very interested to hear how you pulled this off.' Dexter leaned forward, head resting on upturned hands looking Roberto straight in the eye waiting to see what pack of lies he was going to conjure up - looking for any sign that would betray him.

Without hesitation Roberto responded confidently 'It went exactly as we planned it. Joaquin and our mercenary friends took care of them. Magnetic bomb attached to their car travelling back from the camp in the mountains and timed to detonate as they passed through the most deserted passes in the mountains. Joaquin and two of the mercenaries were following to make sure. All three had been killed outright and what remained of the vehicle pushed down a steep ravine. It could take weeks before any one finds them.'

'How did they know when to attach the bomb?' asked Dexter thinking this story was just too convenient – too smooth.

'They engineered a minor traffic accident soon after their car left the camp and during the inevitable argument the bomb was slipped under the driver's side front wing. A very neat operation I believe – no witnesses, no visible evidence and no casualties on our side. They had been monitoring their movements for weeks. No regular schedule when cars left the camp so the decision was taken the bomb had to be planted after they had left the camp and, at the same time, confirm all three were onboard.' Roberto felt he was on secure ground because nothing he said could be verified or contradicted.

So confident was Roberto's response it almost undermined Dexter's expectations – he had either told the truth or anticipated the question and rehearsed an answer. There was no way he could have made up such a convincing response on the spot. 'A very neat operation as you say' replied Dexter thoughtfully. 'You clearly stopped that operation dead in its' tracks. And all three killed outright – are you sure about that?

'No doubt about it – Joaquin was there and saw it all' replied Roberto.

The game continued for another forty minutes. Roberto's confidence grew as he gave a detailed description of the attack on the leaders of the cultural delegation in Kingston.

Dexter had heard enough. He had the noose around Santos's neck but the question was whether to snap the lying bastard's neck or choke off the air supply for a while. Santos still had his uses.

'How long have we worked together Roberto?' asked Dexter and continuing without pause 'ten years off and on and for nine of those years you have been submitting your Medicare invoices which have been paid on time and without question. Now what I would like to know is why you would want to put all that at risk? Why would you want to get so greedy the Internal Revenue Service just can't ignore what is going on?'

Roberto immediately sensed he was in serious trouble – the game was up but which game. 'You've always been straight to the point so what precisely is troubling you? We did everything we agreed with McKenna. If the PNP win the election it will not be our fault.'

'Are you sure you wouldn't like to revise any of your previous stories?' asked Dexter. His style now was more like a criminal investigator knowing he would soon have his signed confession. 'You realise you are putting not only our relationship at risk but the Miramar Medical Centre, which has done good deeds for your community as well as your home in Coral Gables and your continued tolerance here in Florida. Think very carefully Roberto. Think of Naty and the grandchildren.'

'Stop playing games Dexter this is not like you – get to the point' replied Santos. He could feel himself sweating, small rivulets were running down his back, his palms were moist and his toes curled hard against the soles of his leather sandles. He knew he was in trouble.

'Have it your way. Raphael Gallegos was assassinated by Joaquin but Gallegos was not on our hit list. You lied so we would fund this operation and if it went wrong you either had a convenient cover story or relied on us to bail you out. Am I right? Dexter could sense the change in Santos – excessive fidgeting, hand through his hair, chair pushed back to give his legs room. All the classic signs of a conspirator exposed with no place to hide.

'Joaquin had a score to settle. Gallegos was responsible for the death of his parents so we agreed to the plan. Now tell me what harm has been done?' fired back Santos convinced he could talk his way out of this one.

'On its own things worked out great – your press release has got them running around like headless chickens. The harm is the trust we have built up. You misled us. You overcharged us. The question is do we have a future? Something has happened Roberto – this is not like you' replied Dexter. 'I have to ask are you still in control?'

'Of course I am in control. Who else is there?' Roberto was rattled. Not the response he was expecting. He didn't expect Dexter to know he was responsible for the press release.

'The name Manuel Franqui seems to be on everybody's lips. He has a reputation – not one we trust – there are files on Manuel Franqui. Files that spell trouble – others are investigating his activities - allegations including murder, extortion, blackmail, drugs and possible links with pro-Castro factions here in Miami.' Dexter had lit the fuse, time to turn the tables to see what he could force out of Roberto.

Roberto didn't respond. The colour slowly drained from his face. His fidgeting ceased forthwith as he struggled to connect his deep understanding of Manuel with Dexter's accusations.

'I guess it was Franqui behind this Brigadista ruse. You couldn't have dreamt up such a bloody stupid idea. A two hour trip to May Pen, a quick chat with the police, bar owners and JLP activists had them thinking their visitors were from Mars. May Pen hasn't seen movement, let alone construction works, in the last two years.' Dexter was now giving Roberto the opportunity to shift blame, warranted or not, onto Franqui. Dexter wanted rid of Franqui.

Roberto remained silent – as if struck dumb. Better to let Dexter think him a fool than to open his mouth and confirm it.

'You see Roberto Red Snapper is too big an operation for us to let go completely. There are bigger fish to fry if you'll excuse the pun. Now I am going to ask you a question and I want a straight answer. This could have serious consequences for our future business deals.' Dexter took a moment out to ensure Roberto appreciated the significance of the question. 'Who set my agent up to take the rap for Toffy's murder and why?' It was Dexter's turn to slide his chair back, cross his bulging arms – his body language signalling he was not going to leave before he was satisfied with the answer.

Roberto stared back at Dexter – their eyes locked on each other. He was struggling with the question. He was at a total loss as to what to say. He neither knew the name of the CIA agent or the fact the authorities in Kingston had been tipped off about anything. His doubts about Manuel Franqui were beginning to take shape.

Still staring at Dexter, Roberto carefully chose his response. 'I am telling you the truth – I cannot answer your question. I don't know what you are talking about.'

'Only one person knew the name and whereabouts of our agent and that was Wynton McKenna. That is until someone followed Toffy from his arrival back in Kingston to the Mayfair Hotel and his debriefing with our agent. From that moment on our agent was a marked man – someone wanted our man out of the way' responded an uncharacteristically calm Dexter.

'At risk of repeating myself my version ends with the murder of Toffy – there was no further twist in the tail' replied Roberto genuinely puzzled by Dexter's line of inquiry.

'We have two suspects. The first is your slippery friend Manuel Franqui and the second' Dexter paused as he prepared himself for a reaction,' is you.'

The cheap plastic round table was sent flying as Roberto jumped to his feet. At the same time his own chair was pushed back with such force it shattered the glass drugs cabinets. The noise alerted both Luciano and the hit man both colliding heavily as they rushed to enter the room to protect their respective masters. Guns had been drawn but the sight of Dexter sitting unmoved with forearms crossed caused the bodyguards to stop.

'Easy guys – back off. Nothing to worry about' said Dexter trying to calm the situation.

Luciano ignored Dexter's plea and made his move to support his boss.

'It's alright Luciano – nothing is going to happen – just a bit of a shock that's all. Please leave us' said Roberto anxiously straining to regain his composure.

Dexter's hit man put up his gun nodded in his direction and left the room. Luciano hung around a little longer until he was guided out by Roberto.

'What possible motive could I have for alerting the police and whoever about your agent? My understanding of what went on is based solely on Manuel's report.' Roberto was speaking as he righted the table and chair and kicked broken glass fragments into a rough pile behind the door. He sat down again to struggle with Dexter's revelation. Was this Dexter up to his tricks or was Manuel the one to be suspicious of.

Roberto's reaction was either that of a totally innocent man or a very clever actor. He swayed towards the former but was not prepared to let go without seeing his reaction to his reasoning.

'How is your daughter and her children coping these days?' fired Dexter skewering Roberto with his glare.

'For Christ's sake Dexter what has Naty to do with this – why this sudden interest in her welfare?' replied a confused Roberto.

'Do you approve of her latest boyfriend?' asked Dexter.

'What the bloody hell has this got to do with you – keep out of her life?' responded Roberto angrily. Dexter had crossed a line and Roberto's fatherly instincts were blocking all other considerations. The Miramar Medical Centre was not the be all and end all of his life. He would willingly trade that against his daughter's safety and well being.

'I know Carlton Davies well' Dexter paused to see what effect his name would have. He noted Roberto's reaction – clearly recognised the name.

'So?' responded Roberto still on heightened alert to what was coming.

'Well we could hypothesise for a moment that you didn't care too much for Carlton Davies. Perhaps not the ideal suitor for your beautiful daughter and when an opportunity presented itself to have him removed from the scene for a very long while you couldn't resist.'

Roberto studied Dexter for thirty very long seconds before bursting out into laughter – uncontrollable, relieving bellows of laughter. 'Is Carlton Davies and your agent one and the same guy?'

'Sure is – the very same guy who was responsible for the Red Snapper operation and one very angry agent anxious to meet whoever it was who set him up. I wouldn't like to be there when the two of you meet up at a family gathering. That's if he wants to belong to the family that tried to have him incarcerated in a Jamaican jail. And how might Naty react to the news?' Dexter was now piling on the pressure seeing just where it would lead.

'Dexter, we have known each other for nine profitable years – we've done your dirty work, we've protected your ass on some pretty evil missions but I swear by everything I hold dear that I did not inform on Carlton. Yes, Carlton would not be my first choice but he seemed a genuine reliable guy but more importantly Naty was happier than I've seen her for a very long time. The fact he works for you means I'll probably like him a lot less but for Naty's sake I'll put up with that.' Roberto was speaking from the heart.

Dexter had been pretty certain Franqui was the villain but he was now convinced. He still needed Roberto Santos on the books but he also needed to demonstrate unequivocal support for Wynton McKenna and Carlton Davies. His credibility within the organisation would be in tatters if he didn't take steps to eliminate Manuel Franqui – someone who had had the audacity to try and double cross the CIA. 'I want you to listen very carefully Roberto. I want there to be no misunderstanding between us. As you say we have worked closely and profitably together for nine years. But the time has come to reassess our relationship. Manuel Franqui is now persona non grata, he is no longer viable, he is no longer welcome here in Miami, he cannot be trusted and as from this time next week he no longer exists. Do I make myself clear?' And with that final statement Dexter unfolded his arms, slowly got up from the table, laid his heavy podgy hand momentarily on Roberto's shoulder and departed.

THE EPILOGUE

THE DAILY GLEANER – Friday 31st October 1980

Massive 80% turnout of voters in General Election – JLP wins in landslide – Could win 50 seats – 10 PNP Ministers defeated. Edward Seaga described the Jamaican Labour Party's victory in the General Election as 'an overwhelming mandate by the people of Jamaica' and his government to 'give the people the policies and programmes to restore the economy.'

FACT

The police reported that approximately 889 persons were murdered in Jamaica prior to the 1980 general election.

THE DAILY GLEANER – Saturday 1st November 1980

JLP wins 51 seats, PNP 9 – Seaga sworn today as Prime Minister. The massive victory at the polls by the Jamaican Labour Party sparked off a spate of celebrations throughout the island from Thursday evening up to yesterday evening.

US welcomes Seaga victory – Administration officials today welcomed Edward Seaga's election victory in Jamaica, discounted rumours of possible Cuban intervention and predicted increased US financial aid for the new pro US Government. State Department spokesman said 'we warmly welcome this further demonstration of democracy in this hemisphere.'

THE DAILY GLEANER – Monday 3rd November 1980

Castro asked to recall Estrada – The Ministry of Foreign Affairs is instructed to say that it is the belief of the Government of Jamaica that the hoped for development in our relations will not be served by the continued presence in Jamaica of His Excellency Ulisses Estrada Lascalles because intercourse between him and the Government of Jamaica will be extremely difficult.

THE DAILY GLEANER – Thursday 6th November 1980

Special US help likely for Jamaica – both Carter administration officials and special advisers to Ronald Reagan have hailed the victory of Edward Seaga, a pro-Western moderate in Jamaica's parliamentary election as a revolutionary defeat of socialism in the Caribbean.

WASHINGTON Thursday 6th November 1980

Ronald Reagan's overwhelming election victory triggers Wall Street buying spree and fundamental change in US Foreign Policy.

WASHINGTON POST

Thursday 13th November 1980 [Ben F Mayer]

The defeat of Jamaica's pro-Cuban prime minister might become a very significant development in the future of this hemisphere. The US lost a critic and gained a friend. It is hard to avoid giving too much importance to what might have happened in Jamaica and elsewhere in the hemisphere had Manley been re-elected.

THE DAILY GLEANER –Wednesday 19th November 1980

Seaga reports on start of recovery with $40m bank loan for food and raw materials – IMF talks begin – Jamaica qualifies for $600 million of quota arrangements at attractive and concessionary rates of interest.

THE DAILY GLEANER – Thursday 20th November 1980

Malpractices in government departments to be probed - files on Brigadistas missing.

THE SUNDAY GLEANER – Sunday 30th November 1980

Prime Minister Edward Seaga is to hold top-level talks in Washington this week with International Financial Institutions, private investors and members of President elect Ronald Reagan's transitional team.

THE DAILY GLEANER – Saturday 31st October 1981

All eleven staff of the Cuban Embassy and their families as well as Cuban doctors stationed at the Savanna La Mar hospital left the island of Jamaica last night.

www.ingramcontent.com/pod-product-compliance
Lightning Source LLC
Chambersburg PA
CBHW071247170626
46809CB00001B/100